THE COST OF FIRE

RUNNING IN PARALLEL
BOOK 3

THE COST OF FIRE

WRITE
ON GIRL

KARA O'TOOLE TREECE

THE COST OF FIRE

Write on Girl books are available from your favorite bookseller or from www.KaraOTooleTreece.com

Hardcover ISBN: 978-1-7371380-8-2
Paperback ISBN: 978-1-7371380-7-5
Ebook ISBN: 978-1-7371380-6-8

Library of Congress Control Number: 2022906769
Cataloging in Publication data on file with the publisher.

Layout Design: Rachel Thomaier

Printed in the USA

10 9 8 7 6 5 4 3 2 1

For my Dad. I miss you.

BLU

Midwest Territory, Present Day

I didn't know how long Jyston and I had been sitting in this abandoned building, but I knew it had been longer than either of us intended. I needed to get back to the Compound, probably as quickly as he needed to go wherever it was that he went when he left me. More than likely Jurisdiction headquarters. That thought didn't make me happy, but where he went was low on my shit-to-worry-about list. At least, for now.

I pulled back from him slightly so that I could study his face. He was still kneeling in front me, his hands entangled in my hair. After what he'd just revealed, I wasn't quite ready to release him, and he was just as reluctant to leave. If only our enemies could see us now—two of the deadliest people in the world holding each other. And the reality of that statement struck me.

Our *common* enemies.

Because we weren't enemies. We were allies. Possibly more, although I wasn't going to think about that just yet. Jyston and I were going to take Jurisdiction apart, piece by piece. Together. I couldn't fucking wait.

"What is it?" Jyston rubbed his thumb gently over my cheekbone. His gaze was disconcerting, not so much because it was deadly, but because it wasn't.

"I was just thinking that I'm looking forward to tearing down Jurisdiction with you."

"I appreciate a woman who is as bloodthirsty as I am."

"I'm glad. I have no plans to change on your account, or anyone's, really. So, what are you going to do now?"

He brought his lips right under my ear, gently brushing a kiss on the spot. "For one thing, we need to carve out some time to do more of . . . this . . ."

I snorted and stood up, telling my naughty bits to get it together. "If this whole act of asking for my help is just a giant ruse to get into my pants, you are going to be sorely disappointed."

He chuckled and stood with a grace that belied his size. "Blu, while getting in your pants has crossed my mind more than once, my story was not simply conjured for that purpose."

"Good to know."

"Anyway, now that I know that you will help me, I need to buy myself more time. I think it will benefit both of us if I can keep my deception going as long as possible."

I didn't like the idea of Jyston having to go back to Jurisdiction. It was risky. He could be found out at any moment and killed, especially if Dagna was on to him. But I also had to trust that he had been playing this game for close to twenty years and was fully capable of taking care of himself. Even if I didn't like it.

"You know that I need to tell the Team what we discussed today?"

"I hoped you would. As lethal as you are, it might be beneficial to have some more help. If at all possible, I would like to meet with the Captain soon so that we can start coordinating our efforts." I gave him a look. He sighed. "Blu, this is not a ploy to kill her."

"Fine. I'll ask."

Even after everything he'd told me—that he was from a parallel universe and hell-bent on killing Barrington Park for slaughtering his parents—it would take me a little time to adjust to being on the same side. Old habits and all.

As we got ready to leave, I watched as he put on his Second Counselor persona piece by piece. The look of boredom alighting on his face. The predatory stillness that settled around him. All of it. It was as much a weapon as my daggers.

"As soon as I get to a secure location, I will contact you through the comm." He bent down and kissed me. "While I would never presume to tell you what to do, beautiful Blu, if you would be so kind as to not bring a lot of attention to yourself before the PITs, I would appreciate it."

"Like, avoid burning down Jurisdiction headquarters?"

"That wouldn't be the worst thing I'd ever heard of. More like avoid getting caught or killed at Dagna's building. It will be hard to gather information covertly if I am trying to save your life."

"You know that I don't need you to save me, Jyston."

His lips turned up into an almost-smile. "I would never question your ability to rain down destruction on your enemies."

I kissed him quickly, then cupped his face. "Jyston? I'll kill you if you die on me now. So stay alive, all right?"

2 FARA

Midwest Territory, Present Day

"Blu's running late."

Styx had settled in the chair next to me at the Captain's table. I sipped my coffee, letting the second breakfast Ink and I had just consumed digest. At some point I'd need to stop eating like I would never eat again, but today was not that day.

"Where is she?" I asked.

"She was meeting with Jyston. She said, and I quote, that 'things got interesting' and it had taken longer than she had anticipated." Styx raised one perfect eyebrow, and I couldn't help but laugh. She looked just like Adora when she did that.

"That sounds promising."

Even with Styx's happy banter, the panic I had been feeling earlier at Barrington Park's threat had tangled itself into a knot in my stomach. I hoped that when I opened the portal to Calum's place, I wouldn't find another business card from him. Or worse, that Jay and Calum were in some sort of danger. All I had to do was wait a few more minutes and I'd know. But waiting sucked. I took another sip of coffee and sent a prayer out into the universe that everything was going well in my world.

Eventually, the Captain's office door opened. With her armor and weapons and her purple windblown hair, Blu was like a punk rock star who could kill you. I couldn't help but compare us. Would I ever look that badass?

"Nice of you to join us," Ink drawled. Blu shot him a glare as she took her seat.

4

"Sorry I'm late," she directed to the Captain. "What'd I miss?"

"Nothing, yet. I'm assuming you need to talk to me?"

"Yes. After this?"

Styx was smirking. "What? And leave us guessing at all of the fun details?"

Blu ignored her—which was unusual—and kept her eyes steadily on the Captain. She looked worried, which was also unusual. What had happened with Jyston? I had a feeling it wasn't what Styx was insinuating.

"After this," the Captain said. "All right, Fara, if you could open a portal so that we can see . . . Well, let's just see what we see, shall we?"

Beyond the portal was Calum's apartment. There was no sign of either Jay or Calum, but a plain white envelope lay on the coffee table with "open" scrawled across the front. I reached through and grabbed it. The handwriting on the envelope wasn't Calum's or, thank god, Barrington's, so I figured it was from Jay. He was alive, or at least he had been when he wrote this. There were two pieces of paper inside, one addressed to the Captain and one addressed to me.

Fara,

Calum's place is being watched by both my department and Barrington's goons. I'm not sure how much longer Calum can stay here, or if it is safe to use his apartment as our place to exchange information. We need to come up with an alternative. Calum might have to move there until all of this blows over.

Blu mentioned that someone at the compound might be able to rig a device to open a portal to another location. I've asked the Captain to move up our face-to-face meeting to tomorrow or the next day at the latest to discuss this.

I'll see you soon. Please be safe.

Jay

The room was quiet as the Captain and I read and re-read the notes. She passed around her note, and eventually it came to me. The content was the same as mine, more or less, except for two things. The first: they planned on bringing Willow to Jay's doctor tomorrow, which was welcome news. Getting partially disemboweled on a mission at Dagna's building with Jack had caused her more injuries than this world's medicine could heal, so under Sage's orders and Jay's care, she'd gone to mine. She'd been nothing but sweet to us since we landed here, even spending time with Jay while he recuperated in the infirmary to ward off the boredom. I hoped our world treated her the same way. Or at least was able to heal her effectively.

I'd have to worry about it later, though, because the second thing actually bothered me. A lot. It was a plea from Jay—no, a directive—to keep me from going on missions. He wanted the Captain to restrict me to the Compound until I could safely return to my own world. My anger rose so much, I had to shut down a portal.

Hadn't we gotten past this?

I understood that he'd made the request because he was worried, and he cared about me. His desire to protect me came from a good place. He wasn't trying to be a controlling jerk; he was trying to keep me safe in the only way he knew how. But it still didn't change the fact that he'd gone over my head to the Captain. Like he believed that he knew what I needed more than I did. That he knew better than me.

I stifled a sigh, pushing down my disappointment and anger and hurt as far as it would go. I didn't have time to worry about that now, and it wasn't like I could have a conversation with him about it anyway. I'd talk to him when I saw him in person. I'd deal with it then.

Styx broke my reverie. "Just to get this out in the open, I'm nowhere near figuring out how to configure a palmbox to open portals."

"Fara, have you been able to open portals to anywhere else?" the Captain asked.

"Unfortunately, no." I had tried and failed multiple times to direct where my portals opened.

"Then I guess we need to keep using Calum's apartment," Jack said.

"I hate to be the bearer of bad news, but it will take some time to rig the palmbox. A lot of time, actually," Styx said. "Even though I have Fara's mom's calculations, she still had the benefit of possessing Barrington's original tricked-out palmbox. She wasn't starting from scratch; she was just figuring out how it worked. I'm trying to figure out how opening portals works *and* how to put it into another palmbox. It might take months."

"It might be a bit more complicated to replicate than you think."

"Fara, what do you mean?" the Captain asked.

"I mean that according to my mom's notes, Barrington's OG palmbox could do a bunch of stuff with the portals that I can't do. The ability might not be easily transferred to a regular palmbox. I just don't know enough to tell you."

"Like what?" Styx asked.

"My mom's notes say that the OG palmbox is supposed to be able to target *where* in the world you want to go and open a portal to that exact spot. I can't do that."

"What's 'OG'?" Jack asked.

"It's a phrase that my world uses when something is the first thing . . ." How to explain this? "Never mind. Sorry." The corner of Jack's mouth curved up. Sometimes I missed people understanding my pop culture references.

"So, theoretically," Blu said, "that palmbox could open a portal from your room to Jurisdiction headquarters? Or the PITs?"

"I guess?"

"No offense, Styx, but it sounds like we need that . . . OG palmbox."

"None taken, my purple-haired friend. But I hate to break it to you; it's in a different universe with some people who probably won't let us borrow it."

There was a shadow of a smile on Blu's face. "I'm not suggesting that we ask."

"Steal it?" Jack said. "I'm not opposed to the idea, but how do you propose we do that?"

"We could use me as bait."

I couldn't believe I'd just said that! But now that I had said it, I knew it made sense. Blu was right. I read my mom's notes over and over. Without the OG palmbox, my mom hadn't been able to control the location of her portals. And I had tried and failed to control mine. If I wanted to take Calum out of the middle, we needed the OG palmbox. And I could help.

"What are you proposing, Fara?" the Captain asked.

"Jay told me that my mom's old assistant has the OG palmbox. From what I understand, she's been the driving force behind trying to get me in for questioning since this whole thing started. Couldn't that be our way in? I go in for questioning, but don't really answer questions. Then we steal it and, I don't know . . . I portal us out of there?"

"That's not a bad idea." Ink was grinning at me.

"Not to state the obvious, chica, but if you go into your world, Barrington will be after you too."

Blu smiled at Styx over her coffee cup. "I think I have an idea of how to handle that."

3 FARA

After the meeting, I had time to kill before having to open another portal. It was a weird experience, having nowhere to be for a couple of hours, and nothing that absolutely had to be done. I wasn't sure what to do with myself. I caught the smell of cologne in the air. Ink. I wondered what he was doing, but before I got too far with the thought, I saw Sage heading up the path to the mess. Third breakfast didn't sound like a bad idea.

Sage led me to a quiet table in the back of the mess where the stares of the other diners were less pronounced. Just looking like Blu meant I was famous at the Compound, and that meant a lot of attention. It also meant there were a fair number of people who were afraid of me.

Sage watched as I took my plates off my tray and arranged them on the table in front of me. "You are uncomfortable with people staring."

"I'm just not used to it, is all."

"You don't have the same sort of notoriety where you're from?"

I snorted. "Not even a little."

"Well, I'm happy to ignore everyone else as well. I have something I need to ask you."

"What?"

"I'm afraid it's a bit awkward." He smiled sheepishly.

"No more awkward than the fact I've been actively trying to hide in my coffee cup since we walked in here. But then again, things here are weird, so I'm getting used to it."

"Well, then I don't feel bad potentially adding to the weirdness." Sage set down his fork. "Have you met the other me in your world?"

I didn't know what I thought he was going to ask, but that wasn't it. "No, sorry. I wish I had. I think we'd be friends."

"I do too." Sage was quiet for a moment, picking up his fork again, then setting it back down. Something was on his mind.

"What is it?"

"Do you believe in fate?"

"I don't think so. I don't know. Maybe? I've never really thought about it."

"I would assume that you have."

I picked up my bacon. "What do you mean?"

"I mean, you can't deny that there are a stunning number of parallels between your world and this one."

"I haven't really thought about it much. I've been trying not to die."

"Fair point. But hear me out for a minute." I gestured for him to continue. "Thank you. From what I understand, there are infinite universes, but you just *happened* to be able to open a portal here, where every person that you are close to in your world has an equally important role to you . . . Blu . . . in this world?"

"It could be coincidence—"

"Or it could be fate telling you that no matter where you go, Styx, Ink, Jack . . . Fate wants you all to be together."

"Why would fate want us together?"

"I don't know."

"Nope!" I waggled my half-eaten bacon at him. "You don't get out of it that easy. I think you have a theory, or you wouldn't have brought it up."

He smiled, which was rare. I couldn't help but smile back. "It's just something I've been pondering since you told me about how your portals work." He pushed his plate to the side, then leaned closer to me so he could speak quietly. "You have these amazing powers, but little experience with rebellions."

"I have *no* experience with rebellions, Sage."

"That's my point. Don't you find it strange that you just *happen* to see our world through Blu's eyes, who also just *happens* to be one of the most accomplished rebels in the short history of the Compound? And she has the experience, but not your powers."

"Where are you going with this?"

"I can't help but wonder if you . . . Blu . . . the Team . . . are universally meant for something, and having you together prepares you for . . . whatever it is. Maybe it wasn't an accident that it's you that has these abilities."

"I got these abilities by accident. Literally."

"But what if it was destiny? What if the universe knew you needed to have these abilities to save your world? Or ours? Or maybe your abilities are needed in every world; to make sure that the Counselor or Barrington, or their equivalents, don't destroy their worlds like they destroyed this one? I don't know what it is, but it feels like there's something more going on."

"Are you saying that the universe has chosen me to save it?"

"Could be."

"Sage, if the fate of all universes rests with me—then we're royally hosed."

He picked up his apple. "I'm serious, Fara. What if someone is dreaming through your eyes right now? Or they were when you were in your own world? What if we're all connected, and you're the fulcrum?"

"I'm serious too! We might be all right if most of the Faras out there are like Blu. But if they're like me, or if the world is depending on me—just me—then I have to question the universe's sense of humor."

"Don't be so hard on yourself. You're doing pretty amazing right now."

I snorted. I didn't feel like I was doing amazing, but then again, what would that feel like?

"Just . . . think about it, OK?" he continued. "And do me a favor and pay attention to more of the coincidences? I'm curious."

Iris was making her way across the mess toward us. Her hair lay in shiny raven waves to her shoulder blades. She wore a version of what every other person at the Compound wore, a black shirt and pants, but she made it look like haute couture. She walked like a runway model, but I didn't think it was on purpose.

"Fara! So good to see you again."

"Hey, Iris," I replied. "Do you know Sage?"

Sage answered, "We've met once or twice."

"Yes! Nice to see you again. So, Fara, I've heard such good things about you!"

"You have?"

"Yes! The whole Compound is talking about you. It's pretty crazy."

"That is pretty crazy."

"It is! I'd love to hear how it's going with the Team and everything. We should get lunch or dinner sometime! It's got to be hard being new here."

"It's a bit weird, but I don't mind."

She giggled. "That's a good perspective. You know what we should do? Go shopping! I know that Blu doesn't really do . . . girlie things . . . so I could take you to the market, maybe? We could just hang out and get to know each other. Wouldn't that be fun?"

Why did she want to get to know me better? I wasn't that interesting. Was she hoping that I could convince Ink to take her back? If she thought that, then she didn't know Ink at all.

I didn't know him that well, but I still knew that trying to use someone else to get to him wouldn't work.

"I'd need to talk to the Captain. My schedule really isn't my own right now. Maybe once things calm down?"

"Sure! I do have to ask, what's it like being on the Team? It sounds exciting!"

"It's busy? That's about it for now."

She giggled again, placated. "Well, let me know when you have a free moment, and we'll catch up."

"OK. Great. Thanks."

As she walked away, Sage watched me watch her.

"What?"

"You don't like her."

"Why do you say that?"

"Because you don't, and anyone who has spent more than fifteen minutes with you could tell."

"Oh no! Now I feel bad—"

"Fara, don't. She couldn't tell because you were very nice to her. I know it's none of my business, but why don't you particularly care for her?"

I sighed, picking up a piece of toast, then thinking better of it and putting it down. Third breakfast might be too much after all. "I really don't know why. I'm afraid it's some sort of weird girl jealousy thing."

"You don't seem the type to get jealous."

"Of course I get jealous! I mean, look at Iris . . ."

"She's not really my type . . ."

I snorted. "Seriously, though. She's gorgeous and talented. So maybe I don't like her because of that."

"I haven't known you long, but I've never sensed any sort of jealousy from you."

"Is that so? I'm super jealous of your purple headband right now."

He chuckled. "All I'm saying is that destiny is putting her in your life for a reason, and you don't like her. Listen to that."

"I still don't think I believe in destiny."

"Pay attention to it, just in case."

"For you. Just in case."

4 BLU

The Captain sat quietly as I finished telling her about what Jyston had said.

"And you believe him?"

Of course I had considered that Jyston was lying about working against Jurisdiction in order to get me to trust him, or some other convoluted scheme. But taking all of the information I had—and my gut feeling—I knew deep in my bones that he was telling me the truth. I'd seen the pain in his eyes as he described Barrington slaughtering his parents. I'd seen his rage in describing what he saw and endured at the hands of Jurisdiction.

"Yes."

"Well, then that answers some questions."

I snorted. Understatement of the century. "Yeah."

"What do you think we should do about this new information?"

"Other than the obvious answer, which is *help him*, I think we need to keep this to ourselves until we know more. He took a huge risk in telling me everything, even knowing that we have a spy here. You know as well as I do that if Dagna or the Counselor find out that they've been played for almost twenty years, they'll flay him alive. Do you think it's safe for the principal Team to know about Jyston?"

"I do, but I'll leave that up to you. At least for now."

"I'll tell them before the PITs."

The Captain tapped her pen, the only indication that she was mildly irritated. I couldn't blame her. "Blu, I like your tenacity in repeatedly asserting that you will be entering the PITs, but I'm still not convinced that it's our only option for getting into Dagna's building. Entering the PITs, even knowing that Jyston is on our side, is so dangerous, it borders on reckless. What do you hope to get from it?"

"At best? I'm hoping that I'll be able to get one of Jurisdiction's driving jobs—the ones that bring the people to Dagna's building. That would be our way in. At worst? We get information from the drivers."

"That's not a worst-case scenario. Worst is that you are captured, tortured, and killed. Or you manage to get yourself killed in the PITs themselves, which isn't that far outside of the realm of possibility. You've never seen the PITs in action, Blu. It's horrific, even by Jurisdiction's standards."

"Well then, we'll burn it down as we leave."

The Captain held up her hands in surrender. "All right, all right. Let's focus on getting Barrington's . . . OG . . . palmbox away from Fara's government, and then we'll plan for the PITs."

5 FARA

The next morning came earlier than I thought possible. Even Ink's donut and coffee didn't help with my exhaustion, although his usual banter did bring a reluctant smile to my face.

Yesterday had been a long day. Saying goodbye to Jay and Calum was hard. Add the worry of waiting to see what happened to them when they went back home. Barrington's threat. Training with Ink in the rain and short-circuiting myself (water and my balls of electricity don't mix). Trying desperately not to be hurt by Jay's directive to the Captain. I was tired.

But that was too bad for me. Did the Captain ever give the Team a day off? If she did, it wasn't today. I found myself going with Blu and Styx to visit the head armorer, Drake. The Captain thought that I needed updated gear, but it was also an excuse for Blu to subtly question Drake about Iris. She had approached the Captain and asked to join the Team as a trainee, and Blu was adamantly opposed to the idea, considering she thought (and I agreed) Iris's motivation for wanting to join had more to do with getting Ink back than taking down Jurisdiction. Drake was Iris's boss. The Captain had told us to ask some general questions, to get a sense if something else was going on. I planned on keeping my mouth shut—I had no idea how to question anyone about anything.

I had to admit, I was sort of intrigued by the idea of Drake. Not only was he the head armorer, which apparently was a thing, but Ink seemed to be a bit jealous of him too. And that was completely out of character.

"He writes poetry, cooks dinner, makes jewelry . . ." Blu said as she led us down the broken brick path. The cool wind sent shivers down my arms.

"Or in your case, a dagger," Styx said.

"Or a dagger. If you keep from getting swept up in his romance bullshit, then he's a good time. He's actually my go-to for a good time."

"Before your new boyfriend," Styx added. Blu snorted. "I've also been there, and it was everything Blu said. Although he's not really my type, even if he looks good enough to eat. He can keep his poetry. I want someone who can program a palmbox to open portals."

"Anyway," Blu said, "I'm not sure how much information we'll get from him. He's not the world's most . . . observant . . . person." Styx snorted. "Plus, you really need some better daggers and a sword, Fara. I also need my dagger replaced. I left the one he made me in the eye of that goon at Barrington's estate."

Styx went on her way to the tech building with a wave. Blu led me down the path to a one-story crumbling structure. It had a low retaining wall running the entire perimeter. Smoke was coming out of the chimney, and the sound of hammering drifted on the air. It certainly had a castle ramparts vibe to it.

When we entered the warm, dimly lit room, it felt like I was stepping back in time. Like I'd walked into a renaissance fair or a castle or something else medieval. Some light came through the small windows that were scattered around the open room, but most of the space was illuminated by real-life torches mounted in sconces on the wall. The two open fireplaces in the back of the room were blazing, providing a backlight for the person working in front of them.

Standing at an anvil, carefully hammering a glowing piece of metal, was a man who looked like he'd be right at home in a book on Arthurian legend. His close-cut beard accentuated his stupidly good-looking face. His light brown hair hung to his shoulders. Even his clothes were rustic, with a leather apron tied around his waist. I placed his age as older than me by about ten years or so, but it made him all the more attractive. Just looking at him conjured thoughts of riding horses over lush green hills and having slow sex on a wool blanket to the sound of bleating sheep.

He looked up. His eyes landed on me, gold in this light.

"Blu, I was wondering when you were bringing your cousin in here," he said, his voice gravelly and low. I was relieved that he didn't have an accent. I think if he had, I'd wonder if he'd really escaped to this world via the Lady of the Lake. "Give me a moment to finish this."

He took the glowing metal thing and dipped it in water, causing it to hiss. I'd never seen a blacksmith, so I had no idea what was happening, but it was sort of cool. Once he got the metal . . . whatever . . . situated, he walked over to us and grabbed Blu in an affectionate hug. She extricated herself from his embrace, which allowed him to grab my hand and bring it to his lips, his eyes never leaving mine. That look promised me that he could give me everything that I could ever want, which I knew was a big fat lie. I also knew why women fell for it.

"Nice to meet you. I'm Fara."

"Drake. The pleasure is mine. Your family resemblance is remarkable, I must say. Although as stunning as Blu is, I count myself lucky that there are now two as lovely."

Blu rolled her eyes. "We're here on business."

"A pity, but any opportunity I get to spend with you is a good one."

Blu and Drake talked about what gear I would need. They settled on a set of upgraded daggers, armor, and short sword, at least until I'd had more training. He could make different types of weapons based upon my fighting style. But considering my fighting style currently consisted of frying a goon, opening a portal, and then running away, I wasn't sure what I needed. Once I got better at fighting, he could make me whatever I wanted.

As Blu and Drake continued to discuss the details, I had to stifle an inappropriate giggle, my brain in overload. Never in a million years did I ever think I'd be in a place like this, having a conversation like this with a guy like that; like it was the most normal thing in the world.

He promised us that Iris would start working on my gear as soon as today.

"How long has Iris been here?" Blu asked.

"Fifteen years, more or less."

"How'd she come here?"

Drake wiped his hands on a towel and took off his apron. "The same way most of us did, I imagine. She approached the old armorer begging for coin when he was in the city center. Her mother had abandoned her." He hung his apron on a peg behind him. His shirt was unreasonably unbuttoned. "You remember the armorer? He was a kindhearted soul—he couldn't leave the little girl to fend for herself, so he brought her back here knowing the Captain would never turn a child away. He trained her up with me."

"What do you think of her?"

"Why so interested in Iris all of a sudden?" He stopped poking the fire and turned to Blu. "Is it because she's dating your friend?"

"I think they broke it off. Not that it's any of my business."

Drake shrugged, and they continued their conversation—Blu asking subtle questions about Iris, and Drake flirting as he did this and that with iron and the fire. I wasn't sure if Blu was getting information, but I did notice Drake was doing a lot of deflecting. I kept my mouth shut and tried not to openly stare at the Lancelot lookalike.

Eventually the conversation wound down, and Blu made a move to leave. Drake turned his attention to me.

"Fara, not that I have anything against the Team, but they are not known for having fun. If you ever find yourself without something to do, stop by. I'd love to cook dinner for you or show you around the Compound."

"Thanks. I'll keep that in mind."

He dipped his head. "Please do."

He took my hand and gently kissed my knuckles, his lips soft. They lingered on my skin just a heartbeat longer than necessary. Heat rose in my face, and my mind went to blanket sex again. I needed to get that under control.

Blu sighed. "You can let my cousin go now. And just so you know, because she's too nice to tell you, she's already in a relationship."

He released my hand and winked. "We'll see about that."

BLU

I wasn't sure I'd ever get used to seeing Fara open portals. Ripping the membrane between two worlds didn't seem to faze her as she and Styx left to retrieve Calum and Agent Hanlon for our meeting. I also knew that I'd never get used to seeing people appear out of thin air. The Captain didn't so much as flinch.

"Agent Hanlon, you asked for this meeting to be pushed up to today."

"Mind if I get started? I don't have much time."

"Please do."

The agent's face was unreadable as he looked around the table. Fara looked away when his eyes landed on her. She was pissed at him, and considering what he'd written in his note to her, I would be too. Then again, it wasn't my business. I just knew that if someone went over my head and tried to tell me how I should spend my time, it wouldn't end well for them.

"Thank you. First, Barrington's goons followed Calum to work this morning."

"What happened?"

Calum shrugged. "The guys who've been staking out my apartment came into the restaurant and tried to talk to me."

"Not just talk," the agent added. "They grabbed you and tried to take you with them."

"Yeah. Luckily Douche, The Grill's manager, told them that if they weren't paying customers then they had to leave."

"For once, Douche's . . . douchery . . . actually worked out in our favor," Fara said.

"It seems so," the Captain said, the corners of her mouth turning up. "And Agent Hanlon's department has been contacting you as well?"

Calum nodded.

"Then it appears that you are not safe in your home world, Calum. Would you be willing to move here, at least for a while?"

Calum agreed that he wouldn't mind moving to our world (making Silver and Fara both smile), and since it was a longer-term situation, the Captain offered him his own apartment. Jack would have to get him a backstory. Looking like Ink would turn multiple heads, especially given that Fara was already here. But, considering everything else we had to worry about, that was pretty low on the list.

"Unfortunately," the agent said, "moving Calum still doesn't solve the problem with using his place to exchange information. Are you any closer to getting a device to open portals to other places?"

"Not yet, but we might have a different solution," the Captain answered. "I'm not going to beat around the bush, Agent Hanlon. We plan on stealing the palmbox that is currently in your government's custody."

"Steal it? How do you plan on doing that?"

"We need you to take Fara in for questioning."

"No."

"Agent Hanlon, we know that you would never willingly put Fara in danger, but we have a plan," the Captain said.

"That would be playing right into their hands!"

Fara met his stare. "I need to do this."

FARA 7

Jay was staring directly at me, wary and confused in equal measures. "What are you talking about?"

I steadied myself. "Well, we know that we can't keep using Calum's apartment to pass information. It's not safe. You just said that. And I can't open a portal to anywhere else—believe me, I've tried. So, our only two options are for Styx to fix one of the palmboxes here, which could take weeks or months—"

"Or years," Styx added.

"Or, we steal the OG palmbox from the assistant. So that's what we'll do."

"OG palmbox? And you're going to force me to use you as bait to do it?"

"I can walk right in with you. Then, once I'm there, I'll grab the OG palmbox and portal out of there. I mean, not exactly like that. It'll take some planning, but that's the general idea."

Jay had gone very still, and his face had become unreadable. "Whose idea was this?"

"Mine."

A pause. "OK. Captain, I would like to be part of the planning."

"We hoped you would. You know the layout, security . . . You have the information we need. We can begin now, if you want."

Jay shook his head. "I have to get back before they miss me."

As the Captain and Jay made plans for us to meet again, it hit me that it was already time for them to leave; but I didn't want them to. I didn't want Jay to. I wanted the opportunity to talk to him; to ask him why he wrote what he did to the Captain. I wanted to tell him about my day. I wanted . . . more time. I knew that this was going to be hard, living in two separate worlds. I was the one who chose it.

But it still hurt.

I reluctantly opened the portal when they finished. Jay caught my eye as I made my way through, and I motioned for him to follow me to Calum's room.

"This sucks," I said. I didn't know how else to start.

"It does."

"I want to be mad at you for asking the Captain to keep me from going on missions, but we don't even have time to have a proper fight."

He slid his arms around my waist, bending so that he could rest his chin on my head. "Fara . . ."

"Don't, Jay. Just don't. I don't want to spend the few minutes we have together fighting. We'll deal with it later."

"OK."

"Do you think maybe tomorrow after our meeting you could stay with me? Just for the night?"

"As much as I want to, I can't. Things are too crazy here, and I need to get my shit together."

"Then maybe I could stay . . ."

He shook his head. "It's not safe for you to do that yet."

When I didn't say anything, he pulled away and looked in my face. "I don't like it either, but now that I'm back and am starting to see what we're dealing with, I agree that you can't stay in this world. But I'll see you tomorrow. OK?"

He was doing what he thought was best for us. But I didn't have to like it.

FARA

Ink managed to pack his backpack and drive to our special training area, all the while eating a giant ice cream cone that we had picked up in my world. When I mentioned how it was pretty impressive, he smirked and made a lewd comment about the dexterity of his tongue. I blushed a thousand different shades of red, then smacked his arm for good measure. The ice cream still didn't move.

In what was a rather fun end to dropping Jay and Calum off in my world, Ink and I had ended up at an ice cream shop before portaling back to the Compound. I couldn't portal out of Calum's apartment for fear of bringing all of the assholes back that way, but being on foot, our options were limited. Luckily, the ice cream shop was in walking distance, and had an alley behind it that was perfect for portaling. It didn't hurt that it also had ice cream.

When we got back to our apartments at the Compound, I couldn't bring myself to go inside. I told myself it was because it was a beautiful day, not because I was still upset about having to leave Jay. I almost believed it. Ink had suggested that we go train. I hadn't argued with him.

And now we were at our normal spot in the clearing, Ink continuing to eat his ice cream without dripping on himself. Sunlight flitted between the clouds, and the flowers were becoming a blanket of riotous colors that danced in the light, cool breeze. I took a deep breath, appreciating it all.

"It's not raining today, so electric balls?"

He dropped the backpack on the ground. "Sure, although I think I want to change up how we do this."

I was immediately wary. "Change how?"

"I want to make a bet with you." He chuckled. "Don't look so scared! I won't hurt you."

"I'm not scared. But that doesn't mean I'll enjoy whatever you've cooked up. Betting against you seems like a bad idea."

"It probably is. So, this is what I was thinking: if you can make three sets of electric balls hit the same tree without passing out, then you win."

"I have to hit the tree?"

"The same tree."

"All three times?"

"Yup."

"What do I win if I do that?"

"Anything from me you want."

"Anything?"

Ink's eyebrows shot up to his hair and he grinned.

"Ugh—no! That's not what I was thinking. I'm just trying to figure out the parameters of this bet."

"Sure you are. I can think of a thing or two . . ."

"You're incorrigible!"

"Yes, yes I am. But as long as it is in my power to give it to you, I will. That's the truth." He popped the last bite of ice cream cone into his mouth.

"Why the bet?"

"I'm just testing a theory."

"What theory?"

"That you and Blu are more similar than either of you think . . . and I know that betting always makes her focus better. I really want you to start training with fire, so I'm using all of my tricks. Fair?"

"OK, fine. But what if I lose? What if I don't hit the trees?"

"Then I win."

"And what do you win?"

"Anything I want."

I rolled my eyes. "Fat chance."

He smirked. "Get your mind out of the gutter . . . or maybe keep it there? Whatever is best for me . . ."

I couldn't help but laugh. "Do you have something non-naughty in mind?"

"In fact, I do. I was thinking something very specific. I want you to take me to your world again, but this time to do something fun. You can choose whatever it is."

He had to be out of his mind. "Ink, we can't go back to my world, especially for fun! It's not safe."

"At some point it will be. Isn't that the whole point of"—he gestured at me, at the backpack, at the tree that I was supposed to hit with my electric balls—"all of this? To make it safe for you to go back home, and for us to visit?"

"True . . . but we aren't there yet."

"I know, but we will be. Plus, after stealing the OG palmbox, it'll be safer. Those assholes won't be able to track you. We'll be smart and talk to the Captain, but that's what I want."

He had lost his smirk, and although his posture was still relaxed, something was bothering him.

"Ink, what is it?"

"It's nothing."

"It's not nothing."

"If you win, then maybe I'll tell you."

"Fine! When I thoroughly whup your ass, then I want you to tell me what was bothering you. And I want to start training with fire."

He held out his hand, and we shook on it. "Deal. Ready?"

I pictured the old-school program wheel in my head so I could access my abilities. At first nothing happened; I was still pushing down my emotions. I reluctantly let them out, and my hands tingled. I quickly changed my focus to the "lightning" program; *program* being the word my brain was using to interpret what was happening inside of me. I didn't know how else to describe it. The electricity drained out of my hands and hovered about two inches above my outstretched palms in spheres about the size of softballs.

Ink was smiling at me and motioned toward the trees at the edge of the clearing, about twenty feet away.

"Hit the middle one," he said.

I switched to the "shoot lightning" program. As I did so, I threw my hands out dramatically toward the tree. I felt sort of ridiculous, throwing electric balls. I was sure that there was a way to move the balls mentally without the dramatic arm waving, but I wasn't a Jedi yet and needed the throwing motion for it to work. And work it did, because they both hit their mark—one after the other.

"Nice! One down, two to go."

I couldn't help my grin as I grabbed a water bottle from Ink's backpack and took a sip, handing it over to him when I was done. He took a long swig, eyebrow raised in challenge. Fine.

I went through the process again and, amazingly, hit the same tree. Again. I was going to win this bet, and then I'd make Ink tell me what he was thinking about as he stared into the distance drinking my water.

"Do you think you could do it all in one motion?" he asked.

"What do you mean?"

"Right now, there's a pause between when you pull up the electricity and when you throw it. In a fight, it would be helpful if you could do it at the same time. It would give you the element of surprise."

"I don't know, but I can try."

This time when I pulled up my emotions, I concentrated on visualizing something that would be able to both create and shoot lightning at the same time—an "all-in-one" program of sorts. My brain must have liked that idea, because an "all-in-one" option appeared on the program wheel. The electricity drained from my hands, but before I could focus on where I wanted it to go, it shot out. Ink dove for the ground as lightning crashed into a tree at least ten feet from where I wanted it to go. Shit.

"Oh my god! Are you all right? I am so sorry!"

He got up and brushed himself off. "No need to apologize. I'm fine. Really! Stop looking at me like that. It just took me by surprise, that's all."

"I almost flambéed you!"

"What are you talking about? That was amazing! Can you imagine? Once you get that under control, think how beneficial that will be in protecting yourself! That's so cool!"

Right now, it didn't feel cool. It felt like I'd almost killed my friend.

"Stop beating yourself up, Fara."

How did he know?

"I know, because I know you," he answered like he was reading my mind. "But if it makes you feel better to feel bad . . . you lost our bet."

I went from feeling bad to irate. "That's not fair! You changed the rules of the game."

"Doesn't matter."

"That's cheating! I could have hit the right tree a third time if you hadn't asked me to do an 'all-in-one.'"

He was grinning. "But you didn't."

"But I could have!"

"Doesn't matter. You didn't."

Bastard! I threw up my hands in exasperation. Now we had to wait until I tossed my electric balls however many more times he deemed necessary before we worked on fire. That was totally unfair!

But he wasn't the boss of me.

I grabbed onto that feeling—of irritation and righteous indignation—and focused on the program wheel in my head, creating a "fire" option. I'd need to refine the naming of the program once I got the hang of it, but right now all I wanted to do was prove a point. So "fire" it was. I felt it click.

"Whoa, Fara. What the hell?"

A tiny flicker of flame was in the palm of my hand. It was no bigger than a birthday candle, but it was there. I cupped my hand so that it didn't blow out. Ink reached for my hand.

"Careful! I don't want to burn you!"

He stared at the tiny flame in my palm. "Does it hurt?"

"Not really. I can tell it's there because my hand is warm . . . although now that I'm thinking about it, I'm starting to get really hot."

Ink's face went from smiling to concerned. He reached out and touched my forehead, then pulled his hand back with a hiss.

"Shit! Fara, you're burning up. You need to turn off your flame."

Not knowing what else to do, I blew at the flame—like I would a candle—and it went out. Why did I feel so hot?

"Fara, are you all right?" Ink reached for me and cursed as he touched my skin. "Can you walk to the stream?"

I nodded and lurched in the general direction of the running water. Ink ripped off his shirt and wrapped it around his hand. Burn holes were appearing in my pants, and the bottom half of my shirt was slowly smoldering into nonexistence. What the hell was right.

Using his shirt like a hot pad, he eased me into the stream, which was deeper than it looked. He started to strip off the remainder of my shirt. I batted at his hands.

"What are you doing?"

"Your shirt is smoking. I think you're making it catch fire."

He said it so calmly—like it was a totally normal thing that I was setting my clothes on fire with internal combustion—I couldn't help but giggle. I lay all of the way into the stream, my skin and clothes making a hissing sound as they hit the water. I giggled some more.

"Are you all right?"

Was I all right? Weirdly, I felt fine. I looked down and assessed myself. Other than my clothes barely hanging on, my body had no outward sign of any damage. But I was the only one unscathed. Ink was dunking his hand in the water, grimacing.

"Did I burn you?"

"It's from when I touched you."

"I am so sor—"

"Do not finish that apology. I'm serious, Fara. Do not feel bad for one second. We knew that testing out your abilities came with risks, and a few blisters are a small price to pay."

"But I was just irritated that you cheated! I was trying to prove a point. You told me that I wasn't ready, and I ignored you, and you got hurt because of it!"

"Fara, you have every right to test out any ability you want to, when you want to, and to tell me to fuck off in the process." He sat on the bank of the stream to face me. "Neither of us knows anything about any of this—not really—so my 'training' is just best guesses, all right? We're winging it. And what you did right there? Fucking amazing! You created fire!"

"But not without hurting you in the process!"

He stopped tearing strips off his shirt and wrapping them around his hand and looked at me. "Can you please, *please*, for once just celebrate what you did instead of beating yourself up?"

"Says the guy who expects perfection from himself."

He shrugged. "Yeah—but that's me. We're talking about you."

"Fine. We'll celebrate at some point. But first I need to figure out how to not hurt you by being smoking hot, or ending up looking like an extra from *Mad Max* in the process."

"Mad what? No worries, we'll be celebrating in no time. Maybe the armory can make some fireproof clothes for you. Although, I really do like the 'less is more' look you have going on right now."

"You're obviously used to it." I stared at his bare torso. He had a stupid amount of ab muscle definition in relation to the amount of ice cream we just ate. It was wholly and utterly unfair.

But as he grinned at me for staring at him, my fear began to subside. Once again, he'd kept me from panicking. Not only that, but he was also taking all of this—all of me—in stride. Again. He was acting like this was a perfectly acceptable thing. Like he was used to dealing with a girl who'd just shot a ball of lightning into a tree, or held a self-made birthday candle in her hand. Like burning his hand while touching me was totally normal. That there was nothing scary or wrong with me.

I nodded to his hand. "You need to get Sage to check that out."

"You need Sage to check you out to make sure you didn't fry your internal organs."

I snorted. "Fine. Back to the Compound?"

His perma-smirk reappeared. "But I still won."

BLU 9

Jyston's comm buzzed as I walked into my apartment, the noise bringing a smile to my face. I hadn't admitted that I had wanted to talk to him, but my heart gave a little flutter anyway.

"I was hoping it was you," I said before I thought better of it.

There was a pause, then Jyston's deep rumble of a chuckle. "I don't know whether to be afraid or flattered."

"Probably both."

"Fair enough." He sighed. He sounded tired. "One of these days, you and I are going to have an entire conversation that doesn't involve business."

"Do you think either of us would even know how to do that?"

"Maybe. Maybe not," he said. "Anyway, I was wondering if you had told anyone at the Compound about my situation."

"Just the Captain for now. Was that all you wanted?"

"Were you hoping for a more drawn-out conversation?"

I moved a pile of clothes so I could sit on my couch. "Not really, although I do have a question for you if you have time."

"Beautiful Blu, for you I will make time."

"Whatever. What are you doing right now?"

"That's your question?"

"No, I'm trying to have a normal conversation."

He laughed. "Oh! Well, I am currently sitting in my car outside of a petty lord's house, trying to convince myself to go talk to him. He's . . . what would you call him? Ah yes . . . an asshat. And, it appears that he's spotted me and is on his way to say hello."

"I'll make it quick, then. I need information about Barrington's original palmbox. Do you know anything about it?" I heard voices in the background, then the slam of a car door.

"I do," Jyston spoke in a low voice, "but I can't talk now. Soon."

"Jyston, be careful," I said. The comm was already dead.

FARA 10

Jay was supposed to leave a note telling us when the meeting with the government would be held, but getting that set up on his end would take a while. It left me with some time to kill before I had to open a portal.

I didn't want to sit in my apartment with my thoughts. They weren't happy ones. This morning's Team meeting hadn't gone well, or at least the part where I had hoped to spend time with Jay hadn't. I hated leaving him. I hated being in a different world.

The pain of it all was bad. But the conversation we'd had after the meeting was worse.

Although I wouldn't have categorized it as a "fight," it still wasn't what I'd hoped. He was worried that I was still insisting on using myself as bait to get the OG palmbox. He was worried that I was training with fire, even if he didn't quite mind that I burned Ink's hand in the process. He didn't want to spend the night here, or me to spend the night there. He didn't like that I was training with electric balls. He was just unhappy with all of it, and I didn't know what to do to fix it. So, after he left, I grabbed my bottle of Jameson whiskey from Calum's apartment to bring back with me. Not the best coping mechanism, but it was better than setting myself, or someone else, on fire.

Now I was at a loss for what to do. I had already visited Calum in his new apartment (which came with a really cool art nook). Blu and I had already started planning her part of the

OG palmbox mission. My apartment was already clean. I had a bath. I considered finding Ink to go train, but the thought of hurting him again made me pause. It also gave me an idea.

The sconces on the wall flickered as I shut the huge wooden door of the armory. I could see Drake in profile, backlit by the fires burning brightly behind him. He looked up; a slow smile spread across his stupidly good-looking face.

"Ah Fara, I was just talking about you. Give me a minute and I'll be right there."

Drake continued to do whatever it was that blacksmiths did, which looked cool and complicated. I was staring at him like some sort of creeper, and by the way his lips were curled up a bit, I knew that he knew I was staring too.

"Feel free to look around, although there's nothing very exciting here."

The armory was one giant room with nooks and crannies, every available space packed with one thing or another. Large wooden tables were filled with material and bits of metal of various sizes. Swords and daggers hung on the wall; the workmanship beautiful even to my untrained eye. Hammers and other work tools that I couldn't identify were laid neatly on another table. Tucked in the corner was a cozy sitting area, complete with a giant leather couch. Plush blankets were haphazardly thrown on the furniture.

"I sometimes sleep out here." I hadn't heard Drake come up behind me, and I tried to calm my skittering heartbeat. He was so close I could smell him. He smelled like a campfire in the wilderness: woodsmoke and pine. If this guy wasn't a medieval knight in another world, I would be sorely disappointed.

I turned to face him, backing up a bit. "I'm sorry to bother you."

He didn't seem to mind being just a hair inside my personal space.

He shook his head. "Not a bother at all. Would you like some coffee? I was just brewing some."

"That would be great."

He quickly tossed the blankets out of the way and indicated that I should sit on the couch. He disappeared from view, but I could hear the rattle of dishes.

"How do you like it?"

My mind immediately went to the naughtiest place it could. I blushed.

"I'm sorry?"

"Your coffee. How do you like it?"

"Oh! Two sugars and milk if you have it."

I needed to get a grip.

A moment later, he emerged with two coffee cups, handing me one as he sat on the giant leather armchair across from me. He studied me while I took a long sip of coffee. It was delicious.

"Fara, I am happy to see you again, although I have a feeling this isn't a social call."

"I was hoping you could help me with some different sort of gear."

"What is it that you're looking for?"

I wasn't sure how to ask for what I needed without creating questions, but I couldn't keep destroying Blu's clothes. Or Ink's hands. Straightforward would have to do. "Do you have, or know how to make, armor that is fire resistant?"

"Fireproof? Or fire resistant?"

"Something that could withstand high temperatures, but not necessarily have to withstand fire. Although that wouldn't hurt either."

"Something like the gloves that I wear while working?"

"I guess? I don't know."

He sat back and studied me some more, his face thoughtful. "Can I ask what it will be used for?"

"It's for me."

"Well, now I'm definitely intrigued. What would Blu's cousin need with armor like that?"

I gave him what I hoped was a noncommittal shrug. I was a terrible liar, so the less I said, the better. "Is it something you could make?"

"I think I could come up with something. It might take a while—I'll need to test it out."

"No rush. Thank you, Drake. I really appreciate it."

He dipped his head. "It is my pleasure, although I noticed you didn't answer my question."

"I noticed that you never told me why you were talking about me."

He chuckled. "You're a lot like your cousin, aren't you? It actually wasn't me, as much as I would like to take credit. Iris was asking about you."

"Why did Iris ask about me?"

"She just wanted to know what I thought of you."

"What did you tell her?"

"That I found you intriguing."

"And why do you find me intriguing?"

He winked. "It's my little secret. I told her that I thought you were lovely."

"That's very kind, but I'm kind of a nobody. I'm not sure why she cares about me."

He peered at me over his coffee mug, his eyes full of mischief. "I would hardly call you a nobody. You've been the talk of the Compound ever since you arrived here. And did I mention that you're lovely?" I blushed. I couldn't help it. Traitorous hormones. "But that's really beside the point. Not that I get into her personal life, but ever since that playboy broke up with her, she's been a little out of sorts. I think she is looking for a way to get back together with him."

"Through me? That's unlikely."

"From what I understand, you and Ink are close."

"We're friends, yes, but not like that."

"So you're unattached?"

The way he said it made me laugh, which I think was his point. "As Blu told you, I'm already in a relationship."

"And as I told Blu, we'll just have to see about that."

 **BLU**

I couldn't put it off any longer; I needed to go to the market to buy hair dye so I could turn myself into Fara for the OG palmbox mission. That sentence even sounded weird in my head, considering we were, in fact, the same person. It was something that I forgot more and more the longer she was here.

I hated going to the market. Truly. Shopping was not something I particularly enjoyed to begin with, and the little issue of having to wear a disguise so I wasn't immediately hauled into Jurisdiction made it all the more annoying. It seemed really stupid to be risking my ass to buy bobbles and trinkets; the Compound provided most of what I needed. I splurged for hair dye and good underwear. I might buy a book when one interested me (although they were a scarcity), but otherwise I didn't need anything. I just didn't care about stuff.

Unfortunately, this trip couldn't be avoided. My purple hair stood out, and for this mission to work, I needed to convince Barrington's goons that I was Fara. I considered sending a trainee to get the dye, but I couldn't risk that either. Having more than the principal Team know what we were attempting was dangerous. We still had a spy wandering around. Another principal Team member could have gone for me, but they would be in as much danger going to market as I was. So, I had to go myself, even if I didn't want to.

I pulled on a brown wig that I found at the bottom of my closet, then searched for some clothes to change into. Even if I wasn't on wanted posters, the clothes that I usually wore made me stick out as someone from the Compound. Not so much the daggers or armor, but because my clothing was in good repair. Most of the people who shopped at the market weren't the elite or Jurisdiction, which meant that they were struggling to survive. Their clothes were worn and patched as best they could, or handmade with scraps of fabric they'd scrounged. But well-made armor without holes or rips? I would stick out.

I eventually found what I was looking for and slipped the drab gray dress over my head. It was worn and frayed, with patches at the elbows. It hit right above my ankles. I put on some old sandals, then as the final touch, donned fake glasses. They were tinted with enough of something that they muted the color of my eyes to an indistinguishable gray. Drake had once told me what his arm-techs used to tint the glass, but I immediately forgot. I just wanted them to work. I looked at myself in the mirror and shrugged. I didn't look like me, and that was the point. I'd fit right in.

◊ ◊ ◊

The market's main entrance was hidden between two buildings. I parked the Compound's truck outside, between a scooter and a giant, rusted-out car. I had to grudgingly respect anyone brave enough to get around on a scooter. I had seen more than one completely eaten by giant potholes.

I was greeted at the market's entrance by a massive wanted poster of myself. This one in particular was a personal favorite. The artist had drawn me with long red hair standing out from my head like snakes. I hadn't even been a redhead in a couple of years, but whatever. What made the poster a favorite was the matching red blood dripping from my dagger, which was pointed toward the viewer in threat. It was fantastic. With the snarl on my face and how they had depicted me at least a foot taller than I really was, I looked like someone who wanted to dine on your kidneys. That was how Jurisdiction wanted the general public to see me—someone who would rather kill you than look at you. While that description was often accurate, it wasn't my normal attitude. I suppressed a grin.

Right inside of the market doors were the wanted posters for the remaining principal Team, some other Team members, and a gang member or two. There were a lot of wanted posters. I walked by them all, checking the bounties on each. While mine was the highest, Ink's was getting up there. He might even catch up to me in a couple of missions. I might not tell him. His ego didn't need any help.

Ink's poster was the funniest by far. Even though the artist had tried to make him seem as if he'd slit your throat, he still managed to look gorgeous. I was fairly surprised to even see his poster. They usually went missing almost as soon as they were put up, and (from what I heard) would mysteriously show up hanging on some teenager's bedroom wall around the territory. A trainee had one hanging from her wall last year, which I gave Ink copious amounts of shit for. This one would probably be gone by the time I left.

I made my way inside, trying to blend in as much as I could as I wound my way through the various tables and wares. There was a lot of area to cover between the door and where I could find hair dye. It hadn't always been that way. The market had started as a handful of tents strung together, but now it was huge, out of necessity. The country's infrastructure was in shambles, and Jurisdiction wasn't going to fix it. People had to start pooling resources and bartering what they could for survival.

Now the market took up two giant, one-story buildings, and a person could barter or buy almost anything—from homemade shampoo and the cologne Ink wore, to fresh deer meat and underwear. There was also the black market business that you wouldn't see on any of the tables: medicines, booze, weapons, and a lot of information. The traders made sure that those items were only known to folks who could keep their mouths shut. I happened to be one of them.

I scanned the area as I trudged through the shoppers. The vendors were restless, eyes darting around like they were waiting for something bad to happen. What was going on? I needed to be discreet.

After buying my hair dye, I made my way to the fruit and vegetable vendor, Rowena. She was a rebel ally; she'd been selling and giving away the Compound's excess food from our greenhouse for as long as I had been there. She also happened to be the vendor who every person in the Compound knew to go to if there was trouble in the market. And unfortunately, my gut was telling me there was about to be some.

She looked up as I approached, her eyes giving only a hint that she recognized me.

"The apricots are particularly lovely today," she said as she absently wrote something on a piece of paper.

"How much are they?"

"Ten coins for a basket."

"I only have seven coins. Will that be enough?"

"I suppose."

I handed her the coins and my backpack so she could put the basket of apricots into it. When she handed it back, she slipped the note into my hand. Just from our brief conversation I knew that there were at least ten minions outside, but I didn't know why they were here.

As I pretended to rearrange the contents of my bag, I opened the note.

"They are looking for you—have description of disguise. Leave through side door."

Well, shit. How in the hell did they know I was here? And how did they know what I was wearing?

As quickly as I could without drawing attention to myself, I circled the other vendors and made my way to the side door. I took a moment to peek out through the glass. At this point, the minions hadn't made it to the side of the building, but it wouldn't be long. I needed an extraction, or a distraction, or a commotion, or any sort of thing that would get me out of here. I reached in my backpack to grab my comm.

Well, shit. Again.

In my haste to get ready, I'd grabbed the wrong one. I had Jyston's comm instead of the Compound's. That wasn't going to do me any good. I was stuck.

I slid through the door, walking as nonchalantly as I could to the corner of the building. Some minions had completely surrounded my truck, while another group was about to invade the market. All told, there were closer to twenty than ten—and I was really screwed. It was only a matter of time before they realized I had left through the side door. These vendors wouldn't necessarily turn me in on their own, but they wouldn't die to protect me. I couldn't blame them.

The comm buzzed. "Now is not a good time, Jyston."

"I thought that perhaps you could use a ride. I'm two blocks east of you. Although if you would prefer to fight your way to your vehicle, I won't stop you."

"I'm not sure I want to know how you know that."

"Probably not. Two blocks east."

BLU 12

I ran, pissed at myself for forgetting my comm. Styx was never going to let me live to see another sunrise if I died from my own stupidity. How could I have been so careless? But worse than that, how did the minions get to the market so fast? Who had sold me out?

I hurdled some debris and landed awkwardly as the dress caught around my legs, the cement biting into my skin when I fell. Fucking dress and sandals. How was I supposed to run for my life in these clothes? I'd be better off barefoot. I kicked off my shoes and took off my dress as I ran, tossing them to the side. Someone would pick them up and use them. I also took the wig and glasses off and put them in my backpack. By the time I saw Jyston in an old car, I was wearing just my underwear and bra, which was not ideal attire for a rescue. At least I was wearing boy shorts and not a thong. That would have been worse. But not by much.

He peered at me with a raised eyebrow as I hopped over the hood of the car and slid into the passenger seat.

"Is there a reason you are in your underwear, or is it just my lucky day?"

"You know I can still kill you, right?"

"You could try, but where's the fun in that? Anyway, I think that if one is forced to run for one's life as often as you are, one should be able to do it comfortably."

I chose to ignore him. "Nice car." The inside was as old as the outside, which surprised me.

He chuckled as he pulled onto the street and started driving. I ducked down low and sat on the floorboard.

"This is my personal vehicle. All of the cars that are manufactured and used by Jurisdiction and the elite have tracking devices that can be monitored at any point. This one doesn't. I thought you might approve of not being followed."

"Does Dagna know you have this?"

"There are many things that you know about me that the Counselor's spymaster doesn't."

After a while, the road became bumpier. We were out of the city center.

"We're clear."

I hoisted myself off the floor, rolling my neck and shoulders to undo the knot that sitting in the footwell had created. We drove in silence for a while. Eventually, he turned in to a clearing in the trees, hidden from the road. He killed the engine.

"Why are we stopping?"

"We need to talk."

"Can't you talk and drive at the same time?"

"Not for this."

The way he said it make me look at him warily. "Please tell me that you don't want to have a heart-to-heart as I'm sitting in my underwear."

His laughter reverberated through my chest and down to my toes. "Heart-to-hearts are an oddly specific fear, brave Blu. Is it hard to believe that I stopped the car so that I could fully appreciate your attire? I was having a hard time concentrating on driving."

"Stop being a creeper, Jyston." I sighed. "Why are we really stopped?"

"All business, all of the time. All right. First, I was hoping to meet with the Captain, sooner rather than later. I have set things in motion that will need the Compound's cooperation."

"What things?"

"Hopefully laying the groundwork for some help when the time comes to take Jurisdiction down."

I gave him a grin that I hoped was as feral as his. "*First* implies a *second*. What else?"

"It seems a bit awkward to ask as you're sitting in your underwear and calling me a creeper."

"Get on with it."

He chuckled. "I have been terribly remiss in my duties as your boyfriend. While going out in public is probably ill-advised, I was hoping that I might have a couple of hours of your time when neither of us is running for our lives."

"You mean, like a date?" He couldn't be serious.

He brushed a whisper of a kiss over my lips. "Yes, Blu. Exactly like a date."

My heart started pounding, decidedly not from fear. "Is that a good idea?"

He nipped my ear. "When has that ever been a prerequisite for us?" He breathed into my neck, his free hand gently rubbing up and down my spine. "I'll even bring you flowers."

All I wanted to do was straddle him and rip his clothes off. This was going to end up a whole lot of bad if we kept it up. It would serve me right for getting caught because my naughty bits couldn't get it together. I pulled away.

"All right."

"Good. Maybe after we meet the Captain. I know just where I'm going to take you."

"Where?"

"Where would the fun be in telling you? And no, it's not some elaborate trap to get you captured. If you remember, I saved you today from having to slaughter a bunch of Jurisdiction thugs. Not that I think you would have minded killing them all."

◊ ◊ ◊

Jyston knew where the Compound was without my giving him directions. He had known for close to fifteen years and had never breathed a word of it. If nothing else, that proved that he was on our side. It wasn't just my hormones that said so.

By the time I made it down the mile-long drive to the Admin building, my bare feet were bleeding from the gravel, and I was shivering in the spring mist. In just my bra and underwear, I was sure I was quite the sight. I was relieved that Sage was the first person I saw. The only indication that he was confused by my appearance was the single eyebrow that shot up.

"Don't even start."

"I wouldn't dream of it," he said.

"Can I borrow your comm?"

"And my shirt?"

"If you have an extra?"

"Remarkably I seem to be wearing two for just such an occasion." He stripped out of his long-sleeve training shirt, revealing a T-shirt underneath. He handed me the shirt, which I gratefully put on.

He eyed my bloody feet and hands as I grabbed his comm. "Do we need to take a trip to the infirmary?"

"I don't think any of them are deep—just annoying. My first aid kit should do the trick."

He eyed me skeptically but didn't argue.

"Hey, it's Blu," I said into the comm. "Could someone patch me through to one of the principal Team?"

Whoever was at the other end of the line was not expecting me, so they stuttered and sputtered until I finally cut them off.

"Any one of them will do, although Fara would be my first request."

"O-OK, Miss Blu, I'll try to reach her."

Sage shook his head. "Starstruck."

"Only because he can't currently see what a mess I am."

A moment later my voice—Fara's voice—came through the comm.

"Blu? Are you all right?"

"Yeah, I'm fine. I need a favor."

13 FARA

"Need something, Ink?"

He was leaning against my doorframe, perma-smirk on his face. I had just walked back into my apartment after taking Blu shoes, pants, and her first aid kit to the Admin building. She was a hot mess when I got there, though she looked more embarrassed than hurt.

"I was looking for you earlier." Ink pushed himself off my doorframe and began prowling around my apartment, opening a bottle of shampoo that I had picked up at the Admin building and smelling it before putting back on the cap. "I looked everywhere and couldn't find you. Where were you?"

"Nunya."

"What?"

"Nunya business."

His eyes widened, then rolled. "Really?"

"It's something my dad used to say when I got nosy."

Out of nowhere, the ache of missing my dad slammed into me, and I had to steady myself. Why did that memory hit me so hard right now?

Ink walked over to me and tucked a piece of hair that had escaped my bun behind my ear. The act was weirdly intimate. I looked up to see him smiling at me.

"What is it?"

"Nunya."

"Asshole."

"Yes, yes I am." He walked away and looked out of my window. "So, really. Where were you?"

"I went to see Drake."

"What were you doing with Drake?"

"Licking his face."

The look on his face was completely worth whatever crap I had just started.

"Fara! What in the—"

"Calm down! I'm kidding. Not that it's any of your business anyway. I went to ask if he could make fire-resistant armor for me."

Ink cocked an eyebrow at me. "Too worn out from face-licking to train, then?"

"Not even close. But first, I need to open a portal."

🔥 🔥 🔥

Jay's note said that he was to take me into his department tomorrow afternoon. Ink and I took the note to the Captain, who told us that with as big of a day as we were going to have tomorrow, we should take the night off. With that, we got into Ink's car and headed to the clearing.

The mist had cleared, and a shaft of sunlight broke through the clouds onto the stream at the edge, sending light dancing off the overhang of trees. We stood at the edge of this woodland paradise, taking it all in.

I sighed. "I really love this place."

"I'm glad. Me too."

"Can I ask you something? It's really none of my business, but why haven't you ever brought any of the others here?"

"I'm not sure how to explain it."

"You don't have to. It really isn't my place—"

"It's not that. It's just . . ." He ran his hand through his hair, making it look even more expertly bedhead and sexy. "Every second of my day is spent doing something for someone else, or with someone else. Training, fighting, planning, missions . . . there's very little that's mine, including my time. This is *my* place. And the time I spend here is just for me. I just didn't want to share it with them."

"But you're OK sharing it with me?"

He shrugged and set his backpack down, digging through it.

"Well, thanks. It might be my favorite place in all of the worlds."

"I thought it might be."

And without waiting for me to say anything else, he stood up with grace (and thigh muscles) that I envied and started walking to our practice spot.

"Six electric balls at the same tree, and you win."

"Six?"

"Three times with two balls?"

I couldn't help the snort that came out. Ink rolled his eyes. "Same bet, same rules."

"Fine, but this time we're not changing them midway. Deal?"

BLU 14

"We owe Rowena, and Jyston as well," the Captain said after I told her what went down at the market.

"We do."

"It also confirms a few things."

"It does."

She carefully placed some papers in a tidy pile on the corner of her desk. "Though he's known of the Compound's location for fifteen years, he hasn't revealed it, yes. And the spy is getting desperate. Who knew what disguise you were wearing?"

"Drake and Iris were talking by the parking lot, but I'm not sure that they saw me. Even if they did, they probably didn't recognize me. I passed half a dozen other people as well."

"Make a list and I'll have Jack look into it. As unpleasant as this situation was for you, it might be the break we needed to discover the spy who has been plaguing us."

"I'm glad some good will come of my humiliation. The thing I can't understand is that unless one of the people who saw me told someone else at the Compound, no one was new."

"What do you mean?"

"I mean, why is the spy acting now? Every single person who saw me has been here for years. They could have turned any of us in eons ago."

The Captain steepled her fingers. "That's a good question, and one I don't know the answer to. Hopefully Jack can find out."

"I hope so too, because being stuck in Jyston's car in my underwear was not one of my favorite things. I would prefer not to repeat it."

"Really? I would have thought just the opposite."

🔥 🔥 🔥

The Captain's statement stuck with me as I made my way back to the apartments. It bothered me, but I wasn't sure why. I wanted to say that I hated sitting in Jyston's car in my underwear. But did I really? How did I feel about him? Though I hated to admit it, I was struggling with having feelings for a guy I'd actively wanted to kill for the majority of my life. I had too many emotions running through me, and I wasn't used to it. I didn't like it. I needed to talk to someone, which was also a new feeling for me. Normally I ignored my emotions and focused on the task at hand, but that wasn't going to work for this large of a life shift. I sighed, resigned. I needed a friend.

As if summoned by the universe, Styx walked out of our apartment building onto the path. She waited for me to catch up.

"Where are you headed?"

"I need food," she said. "You?" She looked me up and down. "OK, spill it."

"Not here."

She slid her arm through mine, an act that was both natural and caught me by surprise. I'd seen her do it with Fara, but never me.

"Whatever is happening in that pretty head of yours is very unlike you, my friend."

"I know. I'm weirding myself out."

"Well, we can't have that. Let's get food and go curl up in my apartment."

"Not mine?"

She shrugged. "We don't have to move mountains of clothes in mine."

Her place had the same basic setup as the other apartments, except where mine was barely a place to put my shit, hers was awash in colors and fabric. The smell of vanilla hung in the air from candles she had purchased from the market. Handwoven rugs covered her hardwood floors, and a colorful quilt lay across her bed. Although her furniture was the same hand-me-downs the rest of us inherited—functional, worn, and, for the most part, comfortable—she had managed to find colorful pillows and blankets that she had thrown casually around the area, making the entire space inviting. When I'd teased her once about her shopping habit, she replied seriously that even though our lives were rough, our living arrangements didn't need to be. I looked at my apartment as a place to sleep; she looked at hers as home. I couldn't fault her for that.

"Is that a new blanket?" I asked.

"Isn't it cool? The tailors patched together scraps of leftover fabric to make it. This one was their first attempt, which is why I have it. Otherwise, they're handing them out to the homeless in the city center."

"It's cozy."

Styx snorted. "Don't even think about pilfering it, Blu."

As Styx got situated, I took the time to really appreciate the focal point of the room: The far wall was covered entirely by a painting Ink had created at Styx's request. It was vibrant and huge and beautiful. The most prominent feature of the painting was a tree fully bloomed in the white buds of spring. It was sitting in the middle of a small green space, with pots of colorful flowers off to the side. Rooftops were drawn in the distance, along with the suggestion of tall buildings. Ink had created the illusion of sunlight dancing off the grass and tree and buildings. The blue of the sky was beautiful.

"Did Ink change the painting?"

Styx nodded. "He finally found red and orange paint, so he was able to add the fire to the buildings in the background."

She once told me what the painting was of: it was her memory of the view from her bedroom window, before Jurisdiction destroyed everything she loved. When I asked why she wanted the painting, she told me she wanted to remember what she was fighting for. We left it at that.

We finally got settled on the floor, using the reclaimed coffee table as our dinner table.

"OK, chica, spill it. It's not like you to get all moody, so something must be bothering you." I didn't even know where to start. I picked at my food. Styx sighed. "Blu, you are the baddest bitch I have ever met. You are strong and funny and loyal. You fight with a speed that is inhuman and will put your life on the line for each and every one of us. But you are shit for talking about your feelings. I get it—this place, this life isn't really easy for that sort of thing. But it looks like you need to talk. If not to me, then someone."

"I know. But you're right. I suck at it."

"Well, lucky for you it's one of the few things you suck at. You are pretty fucking amazing with everything else." I snorted. "Why don't you start at the beginning? Sometimes that's the easiest."

And so I did, telling her everything that had transpired with Jyston, including his deepest secret. I had to trust someone other than the Captain and was taking a gamble that Styx was not the spy.

Styx had stopped eating altogether by the time I was done.

"Holy shit" was all she said.

"I know."

"That is a lot to unpack, my friend."

"I know."

"So, what are you going to wear on your date?"

The look on my face must have been priceless because she started to laugh uncontrollably.

"I was kidding! Looking good for your date is important, but it is not *the* most important thing."

"Honestly, Styx, it's crazy. I'm not sure what to do."

She reached over and squeezed my arm. "Blu, can I be honest with you?"

"Only if you're not going to yell at me."

"There's really not much to do. Once you decide—really decide—that you have feelings for him and consider him your boyfriend—partner, mate, whatever—then be his girlfriend. You two will decide what that looks like. But the feelings about it, about him? Those aren't complicated. As scary as it is, especially with as much baggage as we all have—including him—it's still pretty simple. You either trust him, or you don't. You either love him, or you don't. The rest is just a distraction."

I put my hand on top of hers, and she turned her megawatt smile to me. "However," she continued, "your situation is a little more fucked up than most. He's really from a different world? Does anyone else know?"

"The Captain does, but I haven't told anyone else."

"I can understand why. Not only is it crazy, crazy shit, but there's the little fact we still don't know who sold you out at the market. And don't think I forgot that you left without a comm. Again."

"I had one, just not the one I needed."

"And your mistake did leave you making out with Jyston in his car in your underwear. Which is hot, by the way."

"It kinda was."

"Life can be more than slitting throats and planning missions, Blu. Surviving is fine, but don't forget to live too."

15 FARA

"Even though you cheated, I still won," I said as we got back into Ink's car.

"That wasn't cheating, sweetness. You need to learn how to use your abilities under distracting circumstances. I was just helping."

"I'm pretty sure that a minion won't be breathing in my ear during a fight."

"Probably not, but it proved my point."

I had managed to throw the electric balls and hit the tree all three times in spite of the fact that Ink had insisted on standing so close that my back was up against his chest. He hadn't said anything crude or naughty, but just his breath tickling my neck and his body pressed up against mine had been enough to drive me to distraction. I reminded myself over and over that he didn't mean anything by it—that he was just training me the best way he knew how.

"You didn't seem to mind," he said with a smirk.

"You are absolutely incorrigible!"

"I am."

We pulled into the Compound, and he got out with grace I didn't think I would ever be able to replicate, no matter how much training I had. He moved with such an effortlessness that it was hard not to stare, and once again, I wasn't the only one. A dozen young kids, no older than six or seven, were gathered on the Quad. They had stopped whatever they had been doing and gaped at him. The looks on their faces were almost like they were staring at Superman—the level of awe and adoration was that apparent. A genuine smile spread across his face.

"C'mon. I want you to meet some of my favorites."

He took off his daggers and swords as he approached them, laying the weapons on the grass. The kids were nervous, excited balls of energy.

"OK, OK, kids. Calm down," the harried Team member who'd been training them was saying. The kids ignored him, clamoring for Ink's attention.

"Lines, now!" Ink snapped, and the kids immediately broke into two lines, standing ramrod straight and as still as little kids can be. He walked up and down the lines, fixing the posture and stances of some kids, but mostly telling them that they were doing great. He was looking at them seriously, but his eyes were twinkling.

"Everyone, this is my friend Fara. She wants to see what you've been working on."

Their eager little faces turned up to me in anticipation, and my heart melted. Then I got pissed. Because of Jurisdiction, they were out here combat training, instead of coloring or playing tag. I smiled at them, and they beamed at me.

"She's pretty. She looks like Blu!" one of the little girls whisper-yelled to her friend.

"Yes, she does. And they are both very pretty," Ink replied, with a wink to me. "But she's also smart and funny like Blu, which is why she's my friend."

I couldn't help but blush at Ink's response. I didn't think I was nearly as smart or funny or pretty as Blu was.

The Team member led them through simpler versions of the drills Ink had taught me. When they were done, they stood in quivering anticipation of whatever was coming next—they obviously knew, even if I didn't.

"You guys did great!" Ink said. Their smiles got even wider. "You know what comes next, because you worked so hard?" The kids almost burst with excitement. Ink turned to me, and the pure joy that radiated off him was almost palpable.

He threw his head back and yelled, "I'm king of the mountain!" then started a slow, backward jog away from the kids. That was all it took for the tenuous grasp of order to devolve. The kids squealed in delight as they took off after him, racing as fast as their little legs would carry them. He led them on a merry chase around the Quad, dodging as they tried to tag him, and when that failed, tackle him.

The Team member came to stand next to me.

"What's the goal of this game?" I asked.

"Technically? Whoever tackles him becomes the next king or queen of the mountain. But really, it's just to play with him for a little while. He does this every couple of weeks. Sometimes more. He also personally trains them when he has time. The kids love him."

"I can see why." Watching him play with these little kids . . . They were so tiny next to him that the sight of their collective effort to take him down was the loveliest kind of chaos. He played into it, every so often picking a kid up over his shoulder and running away, the squeals of glee infectious. It was a side I'd never seen before of him. It was sweet.

"It's good to see them have fun," the Team member said. "After Blu rescued them from Dagna's summer cottage, most of them were in bad shape."

"Is that why Blu burned it down?"

"That's the rumor. I heard that she took out all of the minions stationed there in order to get to the kids, single-handed. She was pretty beat up when she got back, but she refused medical treatment until each of the kids were treated."

Eventually Ink fell dramatically to the ground. The kids dog-piled on top of him with exuberant whoops of victory. Amid the joyous pandemonium, Ink found my eyes, and the look he gave me was so unguarded, so happy.

For as horrible as this world could be, and as scared as I was, I was starting to collect moments like these. Moments where I felt like I was not just surviving, but really living.

16 FARA

"I still won. Why are we arguing about this again?"

Ink held the door to the apartment building for me. "Because it's fun. Anyway, I agree that you did. You'll just need to think about what it is that you want me to do for you. Or to you . . ."

"Ugh!"

He laughed. "I didn't realize that the thought of being with me seemed so terrible to you. That's not usually the reaction I get from women."

I snorted. I knew all too well the reaction he got from most women. The death stares I'd received a few minutes ago in the mess just for eating with him were prime examples.

"I know one thing that I want."

He cocked an eyebrow. "I'm waiting with bated breath."

"I want you to tell me what bothered you earlier today."

"You still remember that?"

"I have a very, very good memory."

"Apparently. What if I told you that it was nothing?"

"I'd call you a liar, liar, pants on fire."

"What if I said nunya?"

"I'd call you an asshole and tell you that you weren't holding up your end of the bargain."

He let out a dramatic sigh as he stopped in front of my apartment. "Fine, but can we at least talk about it from the comfort of your place?"

"Fine."

He made his way across my apartment, taking off his swords and daggers and putting them on the floor before sinking into one of the giant armchairs near the big window. "Your apartment is so clean. It still weirds me out."

"Because you're used to Blu's?"

"Yeah, I guess."

I looked around my apartment. It was clean. I made the bed because I liked the feeling of it when I went to sleep. My dirty clothes—at least the ones that hadn't been burned to a crisp—were in the hamper. "Well, I don't have enough stuff to make a mess yet. Want a drink?"

"Of what?"

"Whiskey."

"If you're having one."

"The Captain said we had the night off, so why not?"

I poured us a drink, then flopped down in the other chair, tucking my feet under me. This chair was twice the size of a normal chair. I grinned, reveling in the fact that it was mine.

Ink took a long drink of the whiskey, making a face as he did. "What about your apartment back in your world?"

"What about it?"

"Was it as weirdly clean as here?"

I had kept it clean. I also spent a lot of my time picking up after Beck. Ugh. Beck.

"What was that look for?"

I hadn't realized that I had made a face. "I was just thinking how pissed I am at myself for wasting as much time on my asshat ex as I did. My apartment was a shithole because it was all I could afford, but I was proud of it, not because it was a shithole but because it was mine. Beck didn't care about it, but then again, he didn't care for much other than himself."

"He sounds like a treat."

"Or something."

Ink was already done with his drink, so I poured him another.

"Why did you stay with him?"

"You're like the zillionth person to ask me that question. Adora asked me almost daily. Anyway, stop trying to change the subject."

He laughed. "You got me."

"What bothered you earlier today? And by the way, this is only part one of my prize. We're still going to train with fire."

He paused, his glass almost to his lips. He was already over halfway done with the second glass of whiskey. I hadn't even finished the first.

"I'll tell you, but I'd like to know why you want to know."

"Can't I just be curious?"

"No."

"I guess it's because other than, well, the time you found out about Jack spying, you never talk about yourself. Ever. And you're always forcing *me* to talk about myself. I mean, I understand why. We're trying to figure out my abilities, and because they are attached to my emotions, I can't avoid it." I studied the drink in my hands. "But even though I feel like I know you because of Calum, it's almost an illusion. I don't know anything about you, really. So when I see something bothers you, which is rare, I want to know what it is so that I can start to figure you out better. So I can be a better friend."

Ink was quiet for a moment, studying his now empty glass. He put it on the table.

"You are already a great friend, Fara. Better than I deserve."

"Naw. I'm the one that's lucky."

"No—"

"I am, Ink. I'm lucky that you're my friend. But we aren't talking about me; we're talking about you. What bothered you?"

He rubbed his hands over his face. "Honestly, it wasn't that big of a deal, so it's weird that it's hard to talk about."

"Don't you talk to the Team? To Blu?"

He shrugged. "We tend to cope more by giving each other shit."

"Oh. Well, I'm not trying to start some sort of therapy session. If it's that big of a deal . . ."

"I'm just not used to it, is all. Actually, I'm not used to someone asking about it. Blu's theory is that I'll go to her if it's bad enough." He chuckled. "But if you really want to know, it's about why I want to go to your world."

"That upset you?"

"Not exactly. I was just thinking how I want to do something fun and maybe a bit stupid. And in this fucking world—and everything that I have to do, and everything that has been done to us—that option has been taken away from me. I don't have the luxury of time. So, for just a night, I want to know what it's like to be young and carefree."

Oh.

He ran his finger around the rim of his glass, not really looking at it.

"And then," he continued, "I saw that when you mentioned your father after the *nunya* thing, you got sad. And it made me think about my father, and how I don't remember him anymore. I don't remember his face or his laugh or anything about him. And it's so shitty, you know? To not remember my parents or know a life where I can get three different flavors of ice cream and not be constantly looking over my shoulder."

"How did they die?" I blurted. "I'm sorry, I didn't mean—"

"No, it's OK. Dagna tortured and killed my parents. I was forced to watch."

"I'm so sorry, Ink."

"Yeah." A single tear slid down his cheek. "After she killed them, Jurisdiction was going to ship me off to be a minion, but I escaped and made it to the market. Someone called the Captain, and I ended up here." He wiped the tear away with the back of his hand. "I don't know why I'm blubbering on about this."

"It's a sad story Ink. For god's sake, I almost cried because Barrington gave me a business card. I think you're entitled to freak out over what happened to you."

"But it was so long ago. I don't know what's gotten into me."

"Whiskey can do that to you. I'm sorry I brought it up. If I'd known . . ."

Another tear slid down his cheek. "No, Fara. I'm glad you did. Really."

No way. He couldn't mean that. "I'm so sorry, Ink. Seriously. I just wanted to get to know you better, not force you to relive your most horrible experiences."

I felt awful. What had started out partially as a joke had ended up with one of the fiercest people I knew silently crying in my apartment. I shouldn't have pushed him to tell me. This was my fault. I'd caused him pain and I couldn't take it. My eyes filled with tears for my friend.

Ink stood up, steadying himself on the table before walking around it and kneeling in front of me. He reached up and cupped my face, wiping a tear away with his thumb. His eyes were still lined with silver, which made my tears fall harder.

"Don't cry for me, sweetness. It might not look like it, but I'm glad you asked me. Seriously. It's been so long since someone has."

"They care about you."

"I know they do, but you care . . . differently. We've told ourselves that dealing with our feelings isn't important.

That the mission is important, taking down Jurisdiction is important, but not this. But it is. And you're helping."

He stared at me like he was trying to get me to understand something else, something he wasn't saying, but just as soon as it started, his eyes lost focus and he swayed . . . grabbing my leg to steady himself.

Ink was drunk.

He put his other hand on my face and leaned in, the smell of whiskey overpowering his cologne. He paused, searching my face for something.

He was waiting for permission to kiss me.

He held my gaze, questions in his eyes. For a split second, the desire to kiss him was almost overpowering. I felt like the most horrible human in all of the universes. Not only did I have a boyfriend who did not deserve that, but Ink was drunk and not fully thinking about what he was doing.

"Ink. You don't want to do that."

"I really do."

"The whiskey really does." I took his hands off my face and held them in my lap. "I think it's time for you to sleep it off."

◊ ◊ ◊

We walked out of my apartment and into the hall, his arm heavy over my shoulders, and my arm clamped around his waist in an effort to steady him. He leaned precariously, and it took all of my strength to turn him toward his apartment. How did he get so drunk? Calum didn't get hammered off two whiskeys, but then again, we'd both been drinking since well before we were twenty-one, a supposed benefit of being on our own from a young age.

A young woman—Team? Trainee?—sat with her back to Ink's door. She had been waiting for him. But tonight wasn't going to be her lucky night. Not in his condition.

She got to her feet and looked between the two of us, confused.

"Ink, I was hoping—" she started.

"Not tonight, I'm afraid," I said.

"Ink?"

He shook his head at the young lady. "Not t'night."

When she didn't move, I decided to ignore her. "Ink, where are your keys?"

"Don't remember."

I sighed. I guess I was going to practice one of my abilities. But not in front of his fan club.

"Hey, I know you're hoping that he'll change his mind, but I'm going into his apartment with him and probably won't be leaving for a while." I winked at her for effect. Let her think whatever she wanted; I needed her to go away so I could unlock his door. She finally got the hint.

"Thank you for that," he mumbled.

"Thank me once I get you into your apartment."

I pulled up my emotions, which was easy. I felt so terrible at the moment. Not only for unintentionally getting Ink drunk and forcing him to tell me painful stories, but also because I really cared for Jay, and I should not have wanted Ink to kiss me. Even for a moment. I was not that person.

With my self-flagellation raging, I put my hand on the lock and concentrated on the "unlock" program. After a moment, the mechanism started making noise, and I heard it click.

"Deadbolt isn't locked," he muttered.

I opened the door and half dragged him to his bed, where he sat down with a thunk. He didn't make a move to do anything else. He still looked broody. I couldn't take the sullen silence, or the way he'd looked hurt when I rebuffed his advances. I couldn't take the tears streaming down his face when he'd told me about his family. But mostly I couldn't take whatever weirdness had blossomed between the two of us in the last few minutes.

"Ink, you need to sleep this off. Can you get yourself ready for bed?"

"Why are there two of you? I mean . . . there's three of you because of Blu . . . but . . ."

"Because you drank too much whiskey."

"Oh. Is that why I feel weird?"

"Yep."

"And people like feeling this way?"

"Some. Although I don't like getting drunk like that."

"I don't think I do either."

"Well, next time don't drink so fast. Do you need help?"

"I can't feel my teeth."

I sighed and started the process of taking off his boots. He watched me with curiosity.

"Why are you helping me? Blu would just make me sleep in my boots."

"I should too, but it's my fault that you're drunk and sad. So I need to do whatever I can to help."

"You really think that?"

"I do."

"I don't deserve you."

"You mean you don't deserve having someone make you relive your horrible past and getting you drunk? On that we can agree."

"No, I—"

"Shhh. I can't take whatever you do or say tonight seriously. Just help me help you." I got his boots and socks off. "Shirt on or off?"

"Off."

He held up his arms as I stepped between his legs and grabbed the hem of his insanely tight shirt. I might need a can opener to remove it. With a yank I finally managed to pull it over his head, getting a good view of his tattoos. The one that had looked red earlier was healing, although it still looked a bit raw. I reached my hand to touch it, then pulled away. I needed to stop doing that.

"Pants on or off?"

"I'm not wearing underwear."

"On, then. I'll be right back. Please don't fall off the bed in the meantime."

"You're coming back?"

"Yes."

"Promise?"

I sighed. "Yes."

"OK, I'll stay right here."

I ran back to my apartment and grabbed a couple of ibuprofen. He'd need them in the morning. When I got back, he was still sitting in the same position, staring off into space. I put the pills on his bedside table, then gently lowered him onto the bed, having done this routine more than once with Beck, although I wasn't as irritated as when I had to do this with that asshat. Maybe because I felt like this was my fault, and with Beck I knew it wasn't? Anyway, I didn't want to think about Beck right now.

I lifted Ink's feet onto the bed and pulled the covers over him. His eyelids were starting to droop. I went to his kitchen, grabbed some water, and put it by the pills.

"Ink, in the morning your head is going to hurt. Take these pills and drink the water. It will help."

"Mmmkay. Thanks."

"Will you remember?"

"Uh huh. Hey, I noticed you were looking at my tattoo."

I made my way to the door, anxious to get out of there. "Yeah, it's pretty cool. What is it?"

"It's a design. It's all of the names of everyone that I care about. I put it over my heart so I'll remember them. My parents, Robin . . . Blu, Jack, Styx, the Captain . . . there aren't that many, really."

"That's really awesome, Ink."

"I'm not done. I just added one more."

"Do you want to tell me who?"

I waited. He didn't say anything. His eyes closed, and his chest fell up and down in the rhythm of sleep. I turned off the light, hopeful that he would sleep off this melancholy and we could go back to our usual banter tomorrow. I took one last look at him as I opened the door, then heard his voice. Just one word.

"You."

17 BLU

Today was mission day, and we had work to do. Jay would be bringing Fara in this afternoon, so we had only a few hours to get ready. Calum was already in Fara's apartment when I showed up to dye my hair. He would be with me, but I didn't want to have to rely too heavily on him. Hopefully pretending to be myself wouldn't be hard.

"I was thinking," Fara said as we got settled, "I should probably shave the side of my head just to be safe."

"Are you sure you want to do that? I mean, I didn't want to do it, and it's on *my* head."

She handed Calum some clippers, which earned her a raised eyebrow. "I think it looks pretty badass. Anyway, it'll grow back if I hate it, right? But we need to make sure that we are as identical as possible. We don't want Barrington's goons to be able to tell us apart."

"As long as you're all right with it."

"I don't want to take any chances."

When we were both done with the hair, makeup, and wardrobe, we stood side by side in the mirror. The change was remarkable. We looked identical, which shouldn't have seemed as weird as it did. We were the same person, after all.

Calum stared at us as we walked out of the bathroom. "Honestly I'm not sure I could tell you apart right now."

Fara grinned. "Should we try it out on Ink?"

"I don't see why not."

Ink opened the door before we even knocked, opened his mouth to say something, then closed it with a snap.

"Can you tell us apart?" Fara asked. She was smiling.

"Now I can," he said, returning her smile with one of his own. "Blu rarely smiles."

I flipped him the bird, but knew he was right. The way she smiled at him was special to him. She didn't smile at anyone else that way. And I didn't smile as much as I probably could.

"But close enough?"

"Close enough. You know that the mole is going to wonder why—"

I held up my hand. "Fara is portaling us out of her room, so no one will see us."

"I figured you guys had a plan. Don't go burning down the whole world, Blu. And be careful, you two."

"She's not the only one you should worry about doing that, you know," Fara said.

18 FARA

I had always assumed that the Department of Weapons Technology was housed downtown. When Jay parked next to an ugly building in the parking lot of a suburban strip mall, I was surprised.

"The 1950s called. They want their building back," I quipped. Even the sunlight did nothing to help its sad facade.

"The inside isn't much better."

"Awesome."

I tried to calm my nerves. Although I had technically been on a mission before, this was the first one I was attempting without the Team's help. And while it had sounded easy when we planned it, I knew there was a huge likelihood that it'd all go to shit.

I was going to try to steal something from the government. Something that they guarded very carefully. This was like an *Ocean's Eleven* level of theft. What could possibly go wrong? I didn't want to answer that, and I wasn't going to focus on that. I had my mission, and I was going to see it through. I rubbed the shaved side of my head, enjoying the new sensation. It weirdly made me feel better; it made me feel more like Blu.

Jay was watching me. He looked concerned.

"What?" I asked.

"Fara, are you sure you want to go through with this? I am still not comfortable—"

We weren't having this conversation now. "Jay, we've been over this a zillion times. We have a plan, and if that goes to shit, I'll get out of there. But we need that palmbox."

"There's only so much I can do to protect you in there without blowing our cover."

"I know. It'll be fine. I'll just try not to stare at your butt, and they'll never know we're together."

"You stare at my butt?"

I suppressed a smile. "More than is probably healthy. An obnoxious amount, really."

"One last shot to back out."

"Not happening. Let's go."

Time to get to work.

The doors of the sad building led to a foyer of sorts. Low ceilings, beige carpet, and brass fixtures did nothing to improve its overall aesthetic. It looked more like a holding area for forgotten luggage than the lobby of a major government division. It also felt familiar—then I figured out why: it was the government version of my crappy old apartment.

The guard behind the desk stood as we entered the room. He was fit and young, not some hired mall cop, but a true agent of some sort. He had a gun on his belt, along with a baton. His eyes lit in recognition of Jay.

"Agent Hanlon, they are expecting you." He motioned to the door on the side of the desk, and I heard the buzz of locks clicking to allow us through.

The next room had the same sad decor and sad lighting. Another security agent guy stood to intercept us. He had the same young, eager look of the first. He also had a gun.

He nodded to Jay. "Agent Hanlon. Miss Bayne—if you would?"

He held up a metal detector wand and indicated that he needed to make sure I wasn't harboring any weapons. A month ago, I would have found the thought ridiculous, but at this moment I felt naked without my dagger. I didn't really have time to contemplate all the major changes in my life as he searched through my purse at a table a few feet away. I did, however, have time to look around the small room. There wasn't much, just a closet and a lot of cameras. They were serious about security here.

"Your phone needs to be turned off."

The guard continued to go through my purse with an admirable singlemindedness, pulling out my wallet, keys, hair ties, gum, ballpoint pens, a notepad, wet wipes, lipstick, and dental floss, holding a tampon like it was a live grenade, and finally stopping as he pulled out a pair of bright pink Hello Kitty underwear. He hurriedly shoved everything back in the purse, handing it back to me with an embarrassed dip of the head.

"You're free to go through."

The doors buzzed open as the locks disengaged. Jay put his hand on the small of my back, and we made our way down the hall.

"Hello Kitty?" He said it so quietly I could barely make it out.

"A girl's got to be prepared," I replied under my breath. I could feel rather than hear him chuckling.

The windowless hall gave the impression that we were heading down, although it was hard to tell. The only sound was the tread of my Converses on the sad carpet that was the same sad color of the sad walls. And then there were the sad fluorescent light fixtures. The hall ended in another locked door that only opened once Jay had held his hand up to a scanner. That door might be tricky to unlock with my powers. I'd never tried to break into—or out of—a place with biometric door locks. I might need to create a program in my brain just for that. Hopefully, I wouldn't need it.

The next long, sad hall was a tunnel just as empty as the first. This must the part of the building where they took people when they didn't want to be *interrupted*.

It led to another door. This one didn't have a lock on it, but then again why would it? The only way out was through the biometric door, and even if you got past that, there were still the two other locked doors guarded by agents with guns. They were really serious about keeping whoever they brought here from escaping.

It opened onto a room that looked like it was directly co-opted from every police procedural drama I had ever seen on television. A metal table stood in the middle of the room with four plastic chairs—two on one side, two on the other. The fluorescent lights hummed, and I could hear the air conditioner kick on, sending a cold draft of air that gave me goose bumps. We sat down.

It wasn't long before a man walked into the room, giving a curt nod to Jay as he stood. The man stuck his hand out to me, a serpentine smile on his face. I instantly wanted a shower.

"You must be Fara Bayne. I'm Caldwell Wheeler, the director of the Department of Weapons Technology."

I shook his hand and fought the urge to wipe my palm on my jeans. His suit was expensive but didn't quite fit him. His hair was short and otherwise unremarkable. His eyes seemed to be in a state of permanent contempt. I immediately disliked him.

He sat down and placed a file folder right in front of him, tapping it a couple of times with his index finger. Was he waiting for me to start divulging my deepest secrets based on a finger tap? He'd have to do better than that, if he wanted me to start talking. So we sat in silence. I studied my hands and checked the camera out of the corner of my eye. The little red light was blinking. Someone was watching us. My bet was on the assistant.

Jay was also a master of silence. He sat and patiently waited for his boss to do his thing, whatever that was.

Eventually, the director cleared his throat. "Aren't you going to ask me why you're here? Aren't you just a bit curious?"

I needed to play this absolutely perfectly. I cast my eyes down and hugged myself. "Director Wheeler, I came here because I had to. You guys have the wrong person. Whatever it is that you think I have, I don't have it, and I don't know what you're talking about. I've told Agent Hanlon that over and over."

"Yes, you have, but then I have to ask myself: why did you run and hide?"

My shudder wasn't forced. "Because Barrington Park kidnapped me, and I'd prefer not to have that happen again."

He actually tutted at me. "Mr. Park said that you came with him willingly."

"Is that why one of his goons held a gun to my friend's head?" I forced tears into my eyes. "I was scared, Director Wheeler. I'm still scared, and no one will tell me what it is that I'm supposed to have."

"Didn't Agent Hanlon show it to you?"

"I did," Jay answered, "but she just kept repeating that it was a BlackBerry."

The director tutted again. Asshole. "I assure you, Miss Bayne, it is not a BlackBerry."

"But I'm not sure why you think I have this . . . whatever it is."

He continued to pepper me with questions, and I continued to play dumb. I made sure I appeared confused and afraid, which really wasn't a far stretch. Jay did his part as well, pretending to be irritated with my lack of knowledge of the palmbox and my ditzy behavior. On and on it went, as the director tried to trip me up or confuse me. Eventually, he let out a dramatic sigh. I was really starting to hate this guy.

"Miss Bayne, it's a pity that you are unwilling to cooperate."

"I am cooperating! I'm answering all of your dumb questions."

"No, you aren't. And I know you're lying."

"I'm not lying!"

"We shall see about that."

He turned to face the camera and nodded. Less than a minute later, a striking woman walked into the room. She was tall and slender, with white-blonde hair that hung just at her shoulders. Her red pantsuit hugged her frame, and I put her somewhere in her late thirties or early forties. Jay tensed as soon as she walked in. I wasn't about to like whatever was coming.

She smiled at me, and my blood froze. "Fara, you look so much like your mother. Do you remember me? I'm Dr. Dagna Novak, and I was her assistant."

19 BLU

"Where to first?" Calum asked.

I slid into his car, lamenting my choice of pants. How anyone thought that these jeans things were comfortable had never lived in leggings. But Fara was wearing them, so I had to as well. The mission was to fool Barrington's goons into following me so Fara could deal with the government. If these horrible pants helped the cause, then I'd suffer through.

"Whatever makes the most sense logistically for you. Get your car fixed?"

Calum chuckled as he began to drive. "Just the windows. Driving around with bullet holes all over my car is strange, but I can live with it. I couldn't live with the rain soaking me every time I drove. Wet ass is sort of terrible."

I snorted. "The worst."

The city passed by as Calum maneuvered through the traffic. Cars of all shapes and sizes fought for dominance on the street. It was a kind of organized chaos, and I felt my blood pressure rise as people nearly ran into our car and everyone else simultaneously. Someone moved right in front of Calum's car. He honked and the guy gave him a one-fingered salute through his open window. I shook my head in wonder. How did they drive in this mess? And more importantly, how did they drive without killing every single asshole?

I glanced over my shoulder. "Well, they're following us."

"That's good, I guess."

The scenery started to change when we made it out of the worst of the congestion. The houses and buildings became dirtier and more run-down. There were fewer people out walking, and those who were kept their heads down. Even the sunlight had a hard time filtering through the gloom that this area radiated.

We pulled into a parking lot in front of a two-story building that had seen better days. Or maybe it hadn't—it was hard to tell. The goons parked in the back of the parking lot. So far so good.

"Fara's apartment?"

"Yeah."

"It's . . . sad."

"It is, but it's what she could afford. I offered to turn my art nook into a room for her, but she refused. She said she wanted her own place, and as shitty as this place is, she was proud of it because she did it on her own."

I ran into a wall of unpleasant smells and sounds as we reached the second floor. The paint was peeling off the walls, and the lone lightbulb barely illuminated the hall well enough to avoid tripping over the trash lining the floor. No wonder she loved our apartments. They might be held together with willpower and vines, but they weren't nearly this depressing.

"Beck is going to meet us here in a couple of minutes to get his stuff."

"Oh, goody." The look Calum gave me as he opened Fara's apartment door reminded me so much of Ink that I blurted out a laugh. "What?"

He gave me a small smile. "I know that you're supposed to convince Beck that you're Fara, but I wouldn't be sad if you made him cry a little."

"That bad, huh?"

"He never deserved her."

"Then why did she stay with him?"

"She thought she deserved him."

The apartment was tiny and empty, except for a few full plastic bags in the middle of the floor. The space was still dim, even after Calum turned on the light. The sunlight from outside barely crept through the single window.

"Are those her things?"

"I think one bag is Beck's, but yeah—that's her stuff."

"Where's the rest of it?"

"Trashed. She didn't have a lot to begin with."

I opened one of the trash bags to find a book with a picture of food on the cover. There were also some clothes. Calum rummaged through the bags until he found what he was looking for, then set it aside.

The door opened, and Dev—Beck—walked in, giving me a lopsided grin. I could see where Fara thought he was kind of cute, in the same way Dev was kind of cute, or a puppy was cute. However, I was into men who wore armor in the bathtub for fun. He definitely wasn't that.

"Hey, Fara." He shoved his hands into the pockets of his shorts. His brown hair was tousled, and his T-shirt was wrinkled. He gave the impression that he had just gotten out of bed. Knowing what I knew, he probably had.

Calum handed Beck the bag he'd set aside. "Here's your stuff."

He took the bag without so much as looking at Calum. His gaze was still on me. "Hey, man, could you give us a minute?"

Calum raised an eyebrow at me. I shrugged. I wasn't worried about safety . . . for myself at least. I just needed to remember who I was pretending to be—and that person wouldn't punch this asshat in the balls. Yet.

"I'll start bringing your stuff down to my car, Fara."

Calum grabbed most of the bags and walked out, a small smile playing on his lips; the look saying that he didn't think I'd last as Fara for two minutes. I didn't necessarily disagree with him.

Beck walked up to me and reached to touch the shaved side of my head. I dodged him.

"You're different."

I began gathering the rest of the bags. "Having your apartment trashed will do that to a girl."

"Not planning on staying here anymore?"

"Nope."

"Fara, can you stop for a second?"

I dropped the bags and wrapped my arms around myself like Fara would have done. "What?"

"It's just—I miss you."

He tried to reach for me again, and I dodged, just barely keeping my hand at my side. What my hand wanted to do was grab his wrist and break it.

"What's with you? I'm sorry that I haven't talked to you in a while—"

"You broke up with me, Beck. Through *Calum*. That's a little more than not talking to me."

"I know. And I'm sorry! I was just stressed, you know? About my new business and my guitar and life and . . . everything. But I know now that I made a mistake."

"What are you talking about?"

"I think we should work things out, babe." He gave me another lopsided grin that I was sure worked on a lot of women. Unfortunately for him, I wasn't a lot of women. No wonder Fara always said "ugh" when Beck's name came up. This guy really was the worst. The worst part? He didn't realize that he was the worst. He thought he was awesome.

"Name my favorite breakfast food, Beck."

"What?"

"Name my favorite breakfast food. I'll wait."

"What?"

"You can't, can you? It's donuts, by the way. What's my favorite dinner? By the look on your face, you don't know that either. It's cheeseburgers. We were together a year, Beck, and you don't know the simplest things about me. You don't know what I like to eat or drink, or what wakes me up in the middle of the night, or even how I like to be kissed right under my ear. You never took the time because it was always about you."

"I don't know what you're talking about. I know that I miss you! And I think we should work it out and find a place together—"

"Where are you staying now?"

"Mickey's, but his new roommate's moving in soon."

Ah. "He's kicking you out."

"Not exactly—"

Enough. This guy used Fara. Used her kindness against her. Used her work ethic against her. Used her compassion against her. And now he thought she'd take him back so that she'd give him a place to live. I was done. I didn't care if he knew I wasn't Fara. She told me *she* didn't care if she ever talked to him again—so I was going to guarantee it.

"Beck, I'm going to speak slowly so that you can understand me. You are a sponging, lazy asshat who is terrible in bed. I will *never* get back together with you. Ever. Go find someone else to mooch off. I'm done with you."

"What?"

"You keep saying that word like it will make you smarter. It won't. And I'm not sure if I can be any clearer: I am done supporting your dumb ass. Get your shit and get out."

"It's because of Calum? You're fucking him, aren't you?"

I stalked up to him and got right into his personal space, letting the deadly calm that scared the piss out of minions come into my eyes. He blanched and backed up a step. Good. "Don't ever speak to me like that again. Come to think of it, don't speak to me at all. Ever."

"What's gotten into you?"

"Nothing. I just realized that I don't need you. Never did. Now get out."

20 FARA

DAGNA

It seemed fitting that the doppelgänger of Jurisdiction's sadistic spymaster was my mother's traitorous assistant.

"Dr. Novak, what are you doing here?" Jay asked. His leg casually brushed against mine, and I nudged him back. Game time.

She walked around the table and put her hand on Jay's shoulder, a move that was both threatening and possessive. He tensed and I kept my face as blank as I could. I would not let them know that I cared about him. It would be bad for both of us.

"I hadn't seen Fara since she was little, and so I thought I'd come by and say hello."

"And?" Jay stood. She dropped her hand, and the vise clenching my heart relaxed a bit.

"And it appears that Fara needs help remembering what the device looks like."

"I don't know what you're talking about! I don't know what you think I have. I don't even know who you are."

She pulled the OG palmbox out from her suitcoat and placed it in front of me.

"I know you're lying, Fara. You have to remember that your mother and I worked closely for years with this, and some of the time you were with us. You've been in the same room as this device."

"What do you even think I know? Why do you want me?"

"We believe that your mother replicated this device and gave it to you, then taught you how to use it."

"Taught me to do what?"

"We think this device might have had the same capabilities as the one you have, but it doesn't work. We need to compare the two."

"What does this even do? It just looks like a busted BlackBerry."

"It opens portals, but you already know that."

"Portals to where?"

The look on her face was frightening as she bent down, mere inches from me. "Stop playing dumb," she hissed. "We have ways of getting you to talk."

"I've already told you everything."

"Don't lie to me, you little brat! I will force the information out of you if I have to." She grabbed my wrist and squeezed, and it took everything I had not to turn on my internal birthday candle and burn her fucking hand off.

"Don't you dare touch her!" Jay was seething, and it clearly was not an act. He stepped in between Dagna and me, forcing her to drop my wrist. She made a move to get around him, but he stood firm.

"I'm not sure what you believe you are doing, Dr. Novak, but threatening civilians isn't something we do in this department."

Director Wheeler stood. "We need her to talk, Agent Hanlon."

Jay took a step closer to the director, right into his personal space. He towered over him, creating a giant wall between me and them. I could feel the anger seeping out of him. "You're OK with someone outside of our department threatening a civilian over something she clearly knows nothing about?"

"Dr. Novak believes—"

"I don't care what she told you." Jay took another step toward the director, his face mere inches from the rat bastard. "I believe that allowing this woman to hurt a civilian is beneath us. Beneath you."

"Agent Hanlon, stand down."

"Not until you agree that you will allow no harm to come to Miss Bayne! You heard Dr. Novak. She wants to torture her!"

"Agent Hanlon," Dr. Novak purred, "I believe your personal feelings for the girl have clouded your judgment."

Jay spun around. "You stay out of it! And if you knew anything about me, then you'd know that my personal feelings have nothing to do with it. I'm doing my *job*. And what is your job, exactly?"

She opened her mouth to say something, but Director Wheeler stopped her with a raised hand. "Dr. Novak, will you please give us a moment?"

She looked like she was going to argue, but one look from Jay and she walked out of the room.

"Please, Agent Hanlon, have a seat." Director Wheeler went completely still. "Miss Bayne, what are you doing with the device?"

I was dangling the palmbox over the floor. "I was wondering what you would do if I smashed this busted BlackBerry into the floor."

"Put it down."

"Or what? You'll lock me up? You'll let that crazy lady torture me? You'll sell your soul? How far are you willing to go?"

"This all could be over if you just told us where the other device is."

And I knew then, deep down, that I'd never be able to convince them that I wasn't involved. That Dagna-times-two had convinced them that I was the key to all of this, and the director saw me as his ticket to the top. Reasoning with them was never going to work. They were confident that I knew something and were willing to do anything to get it out of me. The only hope I had was to keep Jay out of it and get out of this building alive—OG palmbox or no.

"You know I could drop this on the floor and step on it in less time than it took for you to reach me. And so, right this second, I have the upper hand."

"Miss Bayne, put it down."

"Director Wheeler, I'm not going to sit here and let that woman torture me for information I don't have. I'm tired of being harassed. I'm tired of being followed. So, I'm going to take this thing, and you are going to let me walk out of this building."

"Miss Bayne, we aren't done here."

I held up the palmbox. "I believe we are."

21 BLU

Calum was quietly chuckling as I put Fara's remaining bags in the trunk of the car and closed it.

"Beck certainly left in a hurry."

I briefly told him what happened, not even feeling a smidge bad about it.

"Good riddance."

"My thoughts exactly," I said. "Except that I wish Fara could have had the satisfaction of putting that asshat in his place. *Ugh, Beck* is right. Anyway, Barrington's goons are still following us."

"That's good, right?"

"As long as they're with us, they aren't with Fara. So, to her job next?"

"Yeah. We need to pick up her last paycheck. Adora's working, so you'll get to meet her."

"And Jackrabbit's double. I hear he's a real treat."

"He's . . . something."

We walked into the lobby of the restaurant where Fara worked. A young woman was standing behind some sort of wooden podium. Her eyes scoped Calum with the same sort of greed Ink inspired, then landed on me. Her smile turned to a sneer.

"Look who it is. Douche is maaaad at you, Fara."

"Carrie, we're just here to pick up Fara's paycheck."

The young woman walked around the podium, shaking her ass as she did, then slid her arm around Calum's waist. He sighed and moved out of the way, earning himself a pout from her. She continued to ignore me.

"I was hoping that maybe tonight—"

"Sorry, can't."

"Tomorrow—"

"Can't. Fara, you ready?"

"You know I'm better than her, right? I'm not sure why you even bother—"

I whipped my head around and took a step toward her. She scuttled back. "You know I can hear you, right? It's rude. *You* are rude, and very, very wrong. So, I'd recommend shutting up, right this fucking instant."

Without waiting for a response, I turned on my heel, and Calum led me into the next room. The dining room.

"Who was that?" I asked.

"Someone who needs to take the hint."

"I'd be glad to help her along."

Calum grinned. "Thanks, but no."

The dining room was dimly lit and as large as the mess. Maybe larger. Men and women in black carried plates of food to people sitting at the tables. I stopped to watch for a moment. I had only been to a few restaurants, and only on missions. I'd never actually eaten at one.

I felt someone walk up behind me, into my personal space. I reminded myself that I was Fara and in a very public place, so punching whoever it was would be a bad idea.

"Have you missed me?" a familiar voice breathed into my ear.

"Leave her alone, Hewitt."

"Or what, loser? If you hit me again, you'll lose your job."

"I've already quit, so it won't bother me—"

I spun around so that I was in Hewitt's face, grabbing his hand as I did and pulling it back into a painful position. "Or *I* might hit you."

"Let go of me, bitch."

I felt bad because the guy looked like Jack, but I got over it quickly. "Don't you *ever* touch me again. I won't be this nice next time."

I let go of his hand. He rubbed it and glared at me. "I'll find you later, when we can be alone."

"Let's see how well that works out for you."

He stalked away. How the hell did Fara put up with this nonsense for so long? No wonder Calum spent so much time protecting her. To live with this sort of idiocy took a lot of courage. I'd had a huge desire to smack around almost everyone I met here. With my fist. I hoped that whenever Fara decided to come back here, she'd have the same desire and act on it. I wanted to give her the honor, even though I'd happily take it.

I followed Calum through the room, when the trainee I'd hit in the face, Bullfrog, walked toward us.

"That's Douche."

"Of course it is."

"What?"

"Tell you later."

Douche approached. "Fara, I'm not sure what you're doing here. After not showing up for work without calling, I had to find your replacement."

"She's just here to pick—"

"I wasn't talking to you, Calum. Fara, why are you here?"

No wonder they called this guy Douche. "I'm here to pick up my last paycheck."

"If you're asking for your job back, I won't allow it."

"Good thing I'm not."

He stared at me, his giant mouth slightly agape. That reaction wasn't what he was expecting. He probably thought that I would crumble and cry—and maybe I would have, if I had to rely on this shithead for my next meal. But luckily Fara didn't have to worry about that now. And neither did I.

"I'd like to know where you've been," he said.

"I'm sure you would. My paycheck, please."

"Barrington Park has been looking for you."

"Really? That's interesting. My paycheck, if you would."

"I don't appreciate him pestering me about you."

"You might want to start by telling him that. Paycheck." I was out of patience with this guy.

"I told him I'd find out where you were staying."

I shrugged. "You'll both have to be disappointed. I'm going to give you to the count of three, and if you don't bring me my paycheck, I'm going to make a huge scene in the middle of the restaurant. One."

"Fara, I demand—"

"Two."

"You will never work here again."

"I can live with that." I stared him down. "Paycheck. Now. Or do I need to get to three?"

"What's gotten into you?"

"Interestingly, you aren't the first person to ask me that today. The answer is: you're a douche and I've finally realized I don't need you anymore. Now, do I need to accompany you to your office to get my paycheck, or will you bring it to me?"

He paused, looking for all of the world like he was going to argue again, then finally sighed. "I don't have it."

I stalked directly into his personal space. I seemed to have to do that a lot here. "Excuse me?"

"Barrington Park asked to hold it for you."

Calum shot me a glance. "That's illegal and you know it. You need to cut her a new check."

"It will take me a couple of days."

"Then I'll be back to pick it up then."

"He's not going to be happy."

"That makes two of us."

"If it's not ready when we come back," Calum added, "then you'll receive a visit from law enforcement. We know people. Giving someone else Fara's paycheck is a crime, and you know it."

Douche stalked off, passing a Styx with short hair. She ran up and gave me a hug, and I managed to hug her back. "That was amazing, Fara!" she whispered in my ear.

"Fara might not thank me for that," I said, extricating myself from her hug with an apologetic smile.

"Oh! I get it." Her grin lit up the room, just like Styx's did. "I'm Adora," she whispered. "It's so nice to meet you in person. And that was the best thing I've seen in forever."

"Hopefully Fara was serious when she said she didn't want to come back here. Otherwise, I just made her life awful."

"Oh girl, she would have been cheering you on."

◊ ◊ ◊

My stomach growled so loudly that even Calum heard it. Being hungry was a weird sensation for me. I took it for granted that I could grab food whenever I wanted at the Compound. But not here. I was starting to understand why Fara was thrilled with the mess. I would be too if I was this hungry all of the time.

We had over an hour before we were to meet Fara at the extraction point. We needed to keep the goons off her tail. Calum offered to take me to a restaurant. I couldn't help but be a little excited.

We pulled into the parking lot of a long row of stores, where you could buy just about anything if you had coin.

Clothes, and kitchenware, and all sorts of things that you needed to survive here. Calum explained some of the stranger things to me, but otherwise it looked like the stores where the elite shopped. The rest of us were not so lucky. It was a far cry from the market.

The restaurant was at the end of the row. As soon as I got out of the car, the smells of spices I didn't recognize drifted over the air. My stomach growled again.

"The inside isn't much, but the food is amazing."

Calum had been downplaying the place. The restaurant was small, with brightly colored tables crammed together. The walls were painted alternating vibrant colors, with happy-looking skulls drawn here and there. I would have thought that the look would be macabre, but with how brightly colored the flowers woven through the skulls were, it gave the impression we were walking into a skeleton party. I loved it.

We were seated at our table by a young man who handed us what Calum referred to as a menu. There were pages of options. I hadn't heard of most of them. They all sounded delicious. Ink was going to be so jealous.

"Fara always orders the taco trio."

"Then I'll go with that."

The waitress brought over some food before our actual meals. I couldn't remember having this much fun with food in, well, ever.

"Just wait until you try the tacos. Fara told me once that if she could find someone to make tacos like these, she'd never leave the house."

"If they are as good as the chips and salsa, then I might never leave here."

Calum glanced at me over the rim of his glass of water. "You know, you could choose to live here if you wanted."

The statement surprised me, more so that I had never considered it. If Jurisdiction was defeated, then I would be free. Free to do what, though?

"That might cause a problem for the Fara who actually lives here. I'm assuming having two of us with the same genetic makeup might cause some issues."

He grabbed a chip and dipped it in the salsa. "I'm not sure that Fara will ever move back here."

"Why do you say that?"

"It's a guess, really. But I've never seen her as happy as she is right now. Ever. Even with all of this horrible shit going on."

"Honestly, I'm not sure how she dealt with all of the bullshit in this world day after day. It took everything I had not to bash each and every one of those assholes in the face."

"I tried to protect her." He tucked his hair behind his ears.

"Don't blame yourself, Calum. No one can singlehandedly combat what that would do to her."

It was taking a little bit of getting used to, but I found myself really enjoying spending time with him. Calum was quiet and thoughtful and kind. He was a lot like Fara, actually.

"Anyway," I continued, "her boyfriend is here."

"Right, but—"

But Calum was never able to finish that sentence.

"Miss Bayne, you continue to be a very hard girl to track down."

I was pissed at myself for letting my guard down. Barrington Park was standing next to the table, and under the coat on his arm, he had a gun.

FARA 22

Our plan had gone to shit.

I was running toward a locked door with the director and at least one guard hot on my heels. It wasn't supposed to go like this, but as Blu and the Team continued to remind me, it *always* went to shit.

Our plan had been simple: I would convince the director and the assistant (Dagna!) that I was clueless and scared. We'd get them to bring in the palmbox. I'd grab it and walk out before they knew what was happening. Easy peasy.

Except that I now understood they were never going to let me go. There was no way to convince them I didn't know anything, and they were going to do horrible things to me in order to get me to talk. They were never going to leave me alone. So, getting the palmbox, while originally the plan, was secondary to getting out of here.

"Miss Bayne, wait."

Even hobbled by his medical boot, Jay caught up with the director. I reached the door and tried to open it to no avail. Time to learn if I could open biometric locks with my brain.

The director was holding up his hands in a placating manner, his eyes focused on the palmbox. "Miss Bayne, I can see we've upset you."

I started the process of creating a program in my brain. What should I call it? The *unlocking a door while trying not to die* program?

"Upset doesn't even begin to cover it."

"I think we have a misunderstanding."

How about the *if this door doesn't open, I'm in a world of shit* program?

"I think you misunderstand. I'm not staying here, and I will smash this gadget of yours if you get any closer to me."

Jay held my gaze and subtly dipped his head. He understood what I was doing. "We just want to talk."

"Well, I'm done talking to you."

"You can't leave with the device." Dr. Novak had joined the fray.

"I *don't* want this stupid device! I'm only hanging onto it so that you'll let me leave!"

She smiled at me, the effect scary as fuck. "If you give us back the device, we'll let you leave, Fara. Otherwise, we'll have to take it from you and keep you for more questioning. You'd be charged with stealing government property, among other things."

I was out of options. I had to get out of here. "Promise me that if I toss this to you, you'll let me go."

"You have my word," she said.

I tossed her the palmbox. I didn't have a choice.

"You shouldn't be so trusting, Fara." She nodded to the guard. He took a step toward me. Her smile was vicious and victorious. Too bad for her that my brain had just opened their lock.

I suppressed a triumphant whoop as I opened the door, rushed through, and slammed it behind me. I sprinted down the sad hallway, hoping to put some distance between us. I needed to get the hell out of here, or at least hide until I could open a portal. With cameras everywhere, it was going to be trickier than I thought. And I thought it was a clusterfuck.

I made it to the guard's door. Wasn't there a closet of some sort near him? I remembered looking at it while he went through my purse. That might work, but I'd have to get around him. I didn't want to hurt him, but I really couldn't risk having their cameras pick up my portal ability. And right now I was out of options. I needed to get into that closet. Let them wonder how I escaped.

I unlocked the guard's door to find him sitting with his feet up. He hadn't heard me come in over the director yelling into his intercom, telling him to detain me. He stilled when he felt my hand on his neck.

"Sorry about this," I said. I pulled up the tiniest bit of electricity I could manage and let it go immediately. He slumped onto his desk, his head making a loud thump. That was going to leave a mark. I could see his chest move up and down. He wasn't dead. Good.

The closet door was ajar, so I maneuvered my way into the tiny area filled to the brim with cleaning supplies. I bumped into mops and buckets and coveralls, knocked over a pallet of paper towels, and eventually cleared a space big enough to stand. I took one last look: no cameras. It was now or never. I heard the director cursing from beyond the door. I opened a portal, jumped through, and closed it with a thought. A broom fell through with me.

"Hello, Fara. I didn't expect to see you for a while. I'm assuming the plan went to shit and that's why you're here with a broom?" The Captain's mouth was curved up slightly. I was probably quite a sight.

"A bit. I'm just passing through. Oh, and I brought you a present."

"I like presents."

I reached into my purse and pulled out the OG palmbox, which had finally stopped beeping. "Can you hang onto this for me? I need to go get my friends."

23 BLU

"You're going to come with me. Right now."

The look in Barrington's eyes was batshit crazy. And deadly. There was barely any humanity left in him. He had slaughtered Jyston's parents. And Fara's. And countless others.

I was done being scared of this asshole. He needed to die.

"I don't think so."

He subtly turned so that the gun was pointing at Calum. "I'll kill him."

Calum shrugged, a move that had to be more nonchalant than he was feeling. "I'd rather die than have Fara go with you."

I shifted slightly, grabbing the restaurant's knife as I did. It wasn't a dagger, but it could cause some damage, assuming he didn't shoot me first.

"Mr. Park, it appears that both of us are willing to die. Are you?"

He stared at me with his cold blue eyes, and I felt a chill run down my spine. As Fara would say, this guy was a whackadoodle. I stared back at him, letting the deadly calm come over me. Barrington actually stepped back a pace, then regained his composure.

"You have something that belongs to me," he spat through his clenched teeth. "I want it. It's not yours. It's mine."

"If I told you that I have this thing and gave it to you, then you'd leave me alone? Be quick about answering. Your little scene here is drawing a crowd."

"I want the device."

"More than me?"

"For now. But I'll get you eventually."

I pulled a palmbox out of my handbag and set it on the table, just out of his reach.

A slow smile spread across his face, one that held no warmth or humor. "I knew you had it, treacherous girl."

He reached over in an effort to grab the palmbox, but I slammed the knife into the table, between two of his fingers. The two goons who had been flanking him took a step toward us as people at nearby tables started to whisper.

"I want you and your goons to disappear from my life. Permanently. Do we have an agreement? Or does this need to dissolve into violence?"

He stared at me, the smile slipping, hate seething through his pores. He wanted to kill me right then and there. Well, he'd have to wait in line.

"We have an agreement. Although someday, Fara, you'll change your mind. You'll eventually see the value of working with me."

He put his gun into his pocket as I handed him the palmbox. He studied me.

"You have changed quite a bit since the last time we met, Miss Bayne. I have to wonder if you're even the same person."

24 FARA

"You didn't have any problems switching the palmboxes?" the Captain said.

I had just finished regaling the Team with how the mission went. "It weirdly went according to plan." We actually did it. The OG palmbox was sitting on the Captain's table, along with tacos Calum had brought back. "When Jay got into that slimy director's face, he made sure he was blocking me from sight—both from them and the camera in the room."

"Smart," Jack said.

"He creates a pretty good wall. Anyway, I just traded them out under the table, then made a big deal about wanting to smash the decoy." That had been the plan all along: for Jay to create a distraction so that I could switch the OG palmbox with one from here.

"I can't believe security didn't find the other palmbox in your handbag," Styx said between bites of taco.

"It was in a secret compartment, but still. The guard was too embarrassed by the underwear and other things that I packed in there. But honestly, I can't believe it worked either."

Ink turned his perma-smirk to me. "I can't believe that someone would be that flustered by panties."

Blu snorted. "Well, my bad boy friend, not everyone is as experienced as you are." Ink threw his taco wrapper at her.

The Captain ignored them. "And Dagna is the assistant?"

"Yeah. She's a menace," I said, suppressing a shudder. "She couldn't wait to get her hands on me."

"We'll need to figure out what to do about her when we take out Barrington. OK, Blu. You're next."

Blu, back to her purple locks, had talked to me privately about how she'd put Douche in his place, threatened Hewitt, and told Beck never to contact me again. My initial response was panic. Fear of retribution. My heart started to pound, and I felt the knot in my stomach grow as she described what she said to all three. However, once I got over the shock, I realized it was a learned response. Deep down, I didn't care. I didn't need them anymore. That realization was the best part of my day. I just wish I could have been there to see it. Maybe when I went to get my paycheck in a few days, I could repeat the experience and kick Hewitt in the nutsack.

"Barrington took the bait?" Styx said when Blu was finished.

"Yep. I'm not sure how long it'll be before he realizes the palmbox is not his original, or until he increases his efforts to capture Fara, but hopefully it will give us a little breathing room while we figure out a way to kill him."

"Styx, do both of the palmboxes have your new tracking program on them?" the Captain asked.

That had been a brilliant idea by our resident tech genius.

She nodded as she finished chewing her taco. "Theoretically, we'll know where Barrington and crazy-bitch-Dagna-number-two are when we're in Fara's world. They will have to be powered on for it to work. As long as those bastards have the palmboxes on them, then we should be able to track them. These tacos are amazing, by the way."

"We'll take whatever advantage we can, at this point. All right. Styx—Fara, you have your orders. Let's see what this OG palmbox can do."

"How do you want to go about this?" We were sitting in Styx's apartment, which could possibly be the most cheerful place I had ever been. It wasn't just the colors; the smells and pillows and blankets and everything reflected her vibrant personality. If Adora had her own place, it would look just like this. But she shared an apartment with her brother, so it wasn't quite.

Styx handed me a mug of coffee, and I settled into the comfort of a giant chair. She moved a blanket out of the way and sat on the couch.

"The painting is lovely."

"Ink did that for me. It's where I used to live." The way she said it was more of a sigh than a sentence.

"Sorry. I didn't mean to pry . . ."

"Not at all. I can't expect people not to ask about the giant painting on my wall."

"Want to talk about it?"

She reached over the coffee table and squeezed my hand. "I don't, but thank you. You really are a good person, Fara."

I didn't feel like a good person. I'd fried a goon and a federal agent, left my boyfriend behind with a certifiably crazy bitch to deal with the aftermath of me escaping, and had even thought about kissing Ink for a second. None of that was upstanding behavior. But I didn't say that. Styx released my hand with another squeeze and a smile.

"OK, chica. According to your mom's notes, there's a portal program somewhere on the OG palmbox. We need to access it, then see how to use it."

"I'd love to say it sounds simple, but with how everything else has worked out, I highly doubt it."

"You're starting to sound like Blu."

"I'll take that as a compliment."

She picked up the OG palmbox, pushing buttons and doing other things that looked complicated. I sat and drank my coffee, staring at the painting. Ink had made the light dance off the beautiful tree in the foreground.

"Does Ink paint much anymore?"

"Painting was never really his thing, mostly because paints are hard to come by around here. He usually uses pencil or, well, ink."

I chuckled as I remembered Blu telling me the story of how he got his name.

"He's certainly talented."

"He is. Ah! Here's something promising. See here? If you press this button, it provides a menu of the programs you can access. That's weird."

"What's weird?"

"How the programs are named."

I got up and sat next to her on the couch so that I could get a closer look. Admittedly, I'd never really studied palmboxes before. Technically, I didn't need to. I *was* one. It had a keyboard and a screen. It looked like a tricorder and a smartphone had had a baby.

The list of programs, if you could call it that, didn't seem to have any rhyme or reason at all. Each listing was just a jumble of letters and numbers. It could have been alien script, for all I knew.

"Is this how the menu looks on a normal palmbox?"

She snorted. "Hardly. Here, take a look at mine."

She handed me her palmbox, and when I pressed the button she indicated, a list with real words popped up on the screen. I could actually decipher most of it.

"I guess I should have looked at this before. Do you think that I could do all of these things? What does 'disable' do?"

"Oh man! I never considered that you might be able to do all of this stuff! 'Disable' is what we use to take out cameras and other surveillance devices. I wonder if you could do that?"

"I can always try. That would have been helpful today."

"Right, but you did good anyway. See how the OG palmbox programs are named? Unless we crack Barrington's code, it's going to take forever for us to go through each of the programs and figure out what they do."

"If the naming is different, don't you think he'll figure out that we gave him a decoy as soon as he switches it on?"

"Probably. He might just think that your mom screwed around with it enough to cause the issue. Or at least, that's what I'm hoping. Otherwise, we're hosed."

"So what now?"

"Let me sleep on it. Maybe something brilliant will come to me. I'll also talk to Blu. She has someone on the inside who might provide us some good information."

"Jyston?" She didn't answer and I didn't push. Something about the way she'd said it led me to believe that there was more to the story. They'd tell me when they were ready.

"In the meantime," I said, "I need a favor."

BLU 25

I had woken up this morning nervous, but it wasn't until this moment that I realized why: my date with Jyston.

The Captain and I had met with him earlier, the small butterflies in my stomach making random appearances as they discussed tactical alliances. I dropped the Captain off, took a bath, and changed into clothes that were mostly clean as my pulse increased. But now was the time. I was going to see him. Never in a million years would I have imagined that this is what my life would come to.

Jyston had assured me it would be secluded enough to give us a couple of hours together. Which was probably why I was nervous. I could face down minions. I had completed mission after mission. But sitting alone with him, without someone trying to kill us? I wasn't sure I could handle it. What did people outside of the Compound actually do on dates? It was too late to back out now. I was almost there.

The coordinates he'd provided were out in the middle of nowhere. My car groaned as I drove carefully down a trail. I was supposed to park under that dense cluster of trees, then follow the path through them to our meeting location. But what path? I was about to call it off when, just behind where I'd parked, I found a single red rose lying in the dirt. Deeper in the trees, I could just make out another rose. I picked up the first and went to the second. I saw another farther along. Then another; Jyston had laid red roses leading me to him. I couldn't help the smile that appeared on my face, or the warmth that spread up my cheeks.

Picking up the roses as I walked, I eventually came to a small, secluded clearing. A grassy area with a small pond was surrounded by thick tree cover. In the light of the setting sun, it was beautiful.

Jyston was standing off to the side, a blanket laid out at his feet. He was dressed in Second Counselor attire and holding a single red rose. It looked tiny in his hands. Although I couldn't tell what food he'd brought, from the smell of it, at least part of it was coffee.

"I'm glad you found this place. And the flowers."

"Jyston, you didn't have to—"

"As I have said before, I have been remiss in my obligations as your boyfriend. I need to make it up to you."

"You don't need to do anything."

"But I already have. I have some meats and cheeses and—"

"Coffee."

"Yes. While I have technically stopped spying on you—I believe you would be unhappy with me if I did—I cheated and asked Jackrabbit what your favorite drink was. I made educated guesses on the rest."

I walked over to the blanket and took it all in: him. The rose he was now holding out to me. The platter of exotic cheeses and meats that we didn't have access to at the Compound, but which I was dying to try. The plush blanket. The thermos of coffee. All of it. I took the rose from him, letting his hand linger on mine.

"Well, it is a little disconcerting that you haven't accused me of poisoning the food or tried to kill me yet," he rumbled.

"Do you want me to stab you in the leg, or something? Would that make you more comfortable?"

"Not really, no. But then again, this is new territory for me as well."

Was he nervous too? We sat on the blanket, although as giant as he was, his legs poured over it and into the grass. He handed me a plate.

"This is really amazing. Where did you get all of this?"

"Being Second Counselor, while having its obvious problems, does have some perks."

My eyes rolled into my head in pleasure as I took a bite of a piece of cheese I'd never tried before. I might need to reconsider my favorite food.

"If I knew you'd have that sort of reaction to cheese, I'd have done this sooner. Actually, I would have delivered cheese to you daily until you agreed to meet me."

"Whatever. Anyway, we don't get this good stuff at the Compound."

"Hopefully we can change that in time."

"Hopefully."

We sat in not quite uncomfortable silence as we ate amazing meat and cheeses. He also handed me a flavored cream of some sort to put in my coffee. It was delicious. I needed to figure out what Jurisdiction storehouse I could raid to get myself some.

Eventually, I found myself gradually relaxing into the situation. This might actually be what fun felt like.

"Jyston, thank you."

"It truly is my pleasure. It is very rare that I am able to do nice things for someone."

"Have you done this before?"

"You mean, date?"

I snorted. "No. I'm assuming you've dated, Jyston. I've actually seen you on the arm of various elite ladies in Jurisdiction's tabloids. There was one recently who was particularly lovely."

"Not nearly as lovely as you."

"I highly doubt that."

He sighed. "Blu, I need you to understand something." He had lost the teasing smile. "Everything I have ever done since arriving here has been to further my plan. Every elite woman I have seduced, every dinner I have choked down, every party I've attended, or person I have killed—it has been to further the goal of dismantling Jurisdiction. Except you."

"Please don't play me, Jyston. You need my help."

"I do need your help, but that isn't why I brought you here. That isn't why I had Jackrabbit tell me your whereabouts. That isn't why I kept you talking at the High Governor's party, or why I picked you up from the market. My reasons for doing those things are selfish. I enjoy spending time with you and will do almost anything to do so. It really would be easier if I didn't care about you. But I do. I hope, in time, you'll trust me on that."

"But you barely know me. And I barely know you. I don't believe in *instalove*, Jyston."

He chuckled. "I don't believe in *instalove* either. But you do know me, Blu. Better than anyone in this godforsaken world. And I have a feeling that I know you pretty well too."

He smiled as he tossed me a piece of cheese and grabbed one for himself.

"If it makes you feel better, ask me anything. I'll oblige."

I thought about all of the things I could ask him about Jurisdiction, about his role—any information that I could gather to help our cause.

But that wasn't what tonight was about.

Jyston looked as relaxed as I had ever seen him, leaning back on his elbow, legs stretched out in front of him. His jacket had been casually tossed to the side, and his smile was unguarded. He had decided, for whatever reason, that I was the person who he could be himself around. I could at least do him the courtesy of getting my head out of my ass. So, what did I want to know?

"What's your favorite food?"

He picked up a piece of cheese from the tray. "It's actually this cheese right here. You should try it." He leaned over and put it in my mouth. "But really, any cheese will do."

"Do you have a girlfriend?"

"Yes. You."

I nudged his arm. "You know what I mean. I'm sure that the Counselor has been trying to marry you off to some lady."

"Actually, Dagna has tried to convince him that the best way to shore up Jurisdiction's rule is for the two of us to get married. Luckily he hasn't agreed to that yet."

"Yikes. We'll need to kill her before then."

"Preferably, yes. What else?"

"Do you snore?"

"Not that I've been told. Are you concerned?"

I laughed. "Just wondered."

"I do sleep naked, though."

I managed to choke out something that resembled "Interesting." His eyes were full of mischief, and the corner of his mouth was turned up in an almost-smile. "OK, Jyston. I can tell that you're thinking something. What is it?"

He brushed my hair behind my shoulder. "I'm thinking about how I'd like to feed you another piece of cheese. And maybe sleep with you naked and see if you snore."

"I can feed myself, you know."

He chuckled. "There's not much that you can't do. But in my home world, feeding someone is an act of . . . Well, let's just say it's a big deal."

"What was your home world like?"

"I was wondering when you were going to ask me that." Jyston gently put the piece of cheese he was holding back on the tray. "It is—was—beautiful. So very different from here. Mostly farmers live there. My parents were the . . . Well, they were the king and queen of our kingdom, which is roughly the Midwest territory."

"You're a prince?"

"I haven't been called that in a long time." He actually looked embarrassed. "But technically, yes. I'm the prince of my homeland."

"Do I need to start calling you Prince Jyston?"

"Not if you want me to answer. Anyway, I abdicated when I came here."

"If you're not ruling, then who is?"

"My younger sister should be queen."

"Should be?"

"When I left, she was only eight years old. More than likely one of our uncles or aunts stepped in as caretakers of the crown until she came of age." He fiddled with a piece of cheese. "Other kingdoms might have raided and conquered the kingdom once they heard of my parents' demise. Or, one of my relatives could have married my sister off for an alliance."

My face must have said what my mouth didn't, because Jyston held up his hands in placation. "I know it sounds medieval, and it's something that I was going to remedy once I ascended the throne, but that plan has obviously been waylaid. Anyway, many things could have befallen my sister and kingdom. Our land isn't like here. Other atrocities might have happened. A dragon could have decimated it. I just don't know."

"A dragon?"

"Not every universe is like this one. Some parts of my world are at least a thousand years behind. Much of it is so beautiful. I miss it." I reached for his hand. "But I think I'll stop there."

"Why? It was just starting to get good!"

"If I don't maintain a bit of mystery, you'll get bored."

"I highly doubt that. Anyway, I thought I could ask you anything."

"You certainly can—and have. You now even know my sleeping habits. I promise that when the time is right, I will regale you with stories of my homeland—our warriors, magic, all of it. So much so you'll probably ask me to stop. But at this moment, I would prefer to stop answering questions."

"Why?" A traitorous blush rose in my cheeks.

"So I can spend my time concentrating on you, and how I want to do more of this."

He leaned over and kissed me, slowly, like he had all the time in the world. That wouldn't do. I kissed him back hungrily, like I had no time at all, because we didn't. Not really. And I didn't want to waste a moment.

He chuckled into my mouth. "You are a feisty one."

"You have no idea." With that, I slid over and straddled him, knocking over the cheese in the process. If he minded, he didn't say anything, because the next thing I knew, my shirt was off. The band holding his hair bit the dust as I threaded my hands through, pulling him closer. He kissed down the column of my neck, going lower as I arched my back in pleasure. His hands grabbed my hips and lifted me to better fit on top of him. I pressed my body against him.

His comm buzzed.

We froze, his lips just below my ear. He nipped my neck, then leaned back to retrieve the comm from his errant jacket.

"Hello, Counselor."

Oh shit. I sat perfectly still.

"Second Counselor, I need to speak with you. Please meet me here. Immediately."

"Yes, sir. May I inquire as to the nature of this conversation so I can prepare adequately?"

"If you must. With Dagna's last trip we were able to retrieve one of the missing pieces. The project is back on schedule. We need to discuss how you will best help with this."

"I understand, sir. I will wrap up this meeting and be back immediately."

The comm clicked off. Jyston rested his forehead on mine, his eyes closed.

"The Counselor, it seems, has horrific timing."

"It might be for the best."

"Are you sure about that?"

"Not at all."

I tucked his hair behind his ear. He turned his head so he could kiss the palm of my hand. "I have to take my leave."

"I know."

"I would love nothing more than to stay."

"I know."

"I cannot wait for the day when we have more than stolen moments." He kissed me once more. "Not yet. But soon. I'll let you know what I find out, but we will probably need to postpone another date until after the PITs."

"Jyston, I might not be alive after the PITs."

"You will be."

"You don't know that."

"I know that I will do everything in my power to make sure."

"I can take care of myself."

"Yes, Blu, you can." He reached over and grabbed my shirt from the other side of the blanket. "I don't say these things because I think you can't. I say them because I care, and sometimes just knowing someone is watching out for you is enough to get through this life."

He handed me my shirt as I stood.

"You know that you could leave now," I said. "You could come back with me. We can protect you."

"That thought alone gets me through most days. But you and I both know that I need to finish this."

I slipped my shirt over my head. "I don't have to like it."

"Neither do I."

26 FARA

I was nervous. While I was preparing for Ink's surprise, the plan had sounded like a good idea. Now I wasn't so sure. I wiped my sweaty palms on my miniskirt, adjusted my halter top, and checked my makeup one last time in the mirror. Styx had convinced me this was the outfit for this *mission*. I couldn't argue that I looked the part for what we were about to do, even if I had on less clothing than I was used to. I grabbed my purse and a sack of clothes. If it was going to work, we had to go now.

Ink's eyes widened as he took in the sight of me at his door. "You look amazing."

I shoved the sack of clothes into his hands with a grin. "Get dressed."

"I am dressed."

I rolled my eyes. "There are clothes in the bag. I'm cashing in your prize. You can leave your shirt on, but change the pants."

He walked into his bathroom to change. "What prize?"

"You won the bet, remember?"

"Oh yes. And winning means I have to change my pants?"

"Think of it like a disguise to fit into where we're going."

"And where are we going?"

"It's a surprise."

◊ ◊ ◊

"The Captain's all right with this?"

We were driving my POS, Voldemort, after having portaled out of Ink's room. Ink was checking the palmbox we'd brought along to make sure that Barrington and Dagna-times-two were both in their respective bad guy lairs, but mostly he was looking out the window at the city as I weaved in and out of traffic with abandon.

"It took some convincing, but eventually she relented. It might have something to do with Blu having a date tonight as well. Anyway, we have the night off. And tomorrow morning."

"You're still not going to tell me what we're doing?"

"Where's the fun in that?"

"You're starting to sound like me."

"I'll take that as a compliment. Anyway, it's the least I can do."

"What does that mean?" I could see him studying me from the corner of my eye.

"It means that the last time we had the night off, I made a mess of things. So I'm making it up to you."

"Is that what you really think happened?"

"It's what I *know* happened." I turned onto a side street. "But enough about that. I'm awkward enough as it is. My only goal is to show you a good time tonight."

"I'm already having a great time. Except for the pants, which are ridiculously uncomfortable."

"You'll get used to them. Or not. But once you see how the young ladies react to them? You won't mind."

We pulled into our first stop of the evening—dinner at one of my favorite restaurants. The hostess seated us, but not before taking a long look at Ink's ass, which I had to admit looked amazing in the jeans I'd forced him to wear. I glared at her anyway. I didn't appreciate that sort of lechery being forced on any person. He didn't seem to notice, though. He was taking in the brightly colored walls, and paintings—all of it. As long as I didn't get him drunk and make him cry, we might have fun tonight.

The waiter brought us menus and chips and salsa, which was a novel experience for Ink. Actually, from what Calum had told me about Blu's experience at this very spot, most of the Team had never eaten at a restaurant before, so all of it was new. Couple that with how he devoured the tacos Calum had brought, I thought he might enjoy this.

"I might leave my world behind and live here just to eat. This is the best surprise ever."

"The night's still young."

"There's more?"

"It's a surprise."

He tossed his napkin at me and I caught it. "How did you do all of this? I would have remembered that outfit . . ."

I told the blush on my cheeks to get a grip. "After the Captain gave me the go ahead, I snagged Styx to come back here for some reconnaissance with me."

"Styx was in on this?"

"I promised her shopping adventures."

I wanted him to have fun. I wanted him to know how much I appreciated him. How much it meant that he dealt with my craziness and was still my friend. And after running for my life yesterday, the worry Ink carried with him about dying young had really hit home. We had to do this now; we weren't guaranteed tomorrow.

"You won, even if you cheated. And you wanted to spend one night knowing what it was to be young and free. I'm going to make sure you have that night."

"I can never repay this, Fara."

"Seeing you have fun tonight will be payment enough."

"Whatever." He dipped his chip into the salsa. "So we're getting tacos. Then what?"

"Can't tell you."

"Can you give me a hint, at least?"

"Well, you'll get to meet Adora—other Styx."

"I'm assuming that Agent Jay is coming too?"

I started pushing down my emotions. It wouldn't be good to open a portal here. At all. But the question hurt because no, Jay wasn't coming.

"Not tonight."

As soon as Styx and I made it to our world, I had called Jay to ask him if he could come say hi. Not for long, but I wanted to see him. To hug him. To make sure he was all right. After he got over freaking out that I was back and telling me that I was taking unnecessary risks, he told me that because of the aftermath of my mission, he couldn't be seen with me for a while, just in case of blowback. We had convinced the government that we weren't an item, and we needed to keep it that way. Even though it hurt. Even though I wanted to stay with him tonight.

Ink stopped mid-dip of his chip. "Want to talk about it?"

"Not really. Tonight is about you and how many girls are going to throw themselves at you."

"As long as you are one of them, sweetness, then my night is complete."

"Fat chance."

"The night is still young."

27 FARA

"You look like a goddess."

Adora grinned at me. "I *am* a fucking goddess. As are you. And Ink, here . . . Well, he's—"

"Not in need of anyone feeding his ego."

Ink playfully nudged me. "I can't help it if you think I'm hot."

Adora rolled her eyes. "And he's modest. Are you ready? A guy I know got us on the VIP list at this club down the street."

It was the weekend, and the evening was warm for spring, which meant that people—particularly people our age—were out in droves. The bars, clubs, and restaurants that lined the brick sidewalks in this area of downtown were filled to the brim, people and music spilling out into the night.

I normally avoided this part of town. It was not that I didn't like it, but that crowds gave me anxiety. I would much rather sit at Rick's, drink beer, and eat tater tots than maneuver through throngs of people. But Ink wanted to know what it felt like to be young and carefree, and this was the best I could come up with. Any young person who wanted to see and be seen—and had money in their pocket to burn—was down here tonight. So, we took an Uber, which was another new experience for Ink, and came to join the party.

Ink had his hand on the small of my back as we walked through the crowds, helping me navigate the masses as he peered over everyone's heads. Every so often, he would stop and stare at this or that, but mostly he took it all in as we walked.

And people were taking *him* in. In his skintight black T-shirt and the jeans he complained about, he looked like a rock star. But it wasn't just his looks that were getting him noticed. Calum looked just like him but didn't seem to elicit the same response. It could have been the sexy danger Ink oozed, or the perma-smirk, or the confidence with which he carried himself. Whatever it was, he was getting noticed. A lot.

I squeezed his arm to get his attention. "We can stop at any of these places later if you want, but we need to get to the club or they'll give away our table."

"Whatever you say. This is . . . I'm not sure what it is. But I like it!"

"Just wait," Adora called over her shoulder. "The place we're going is lit!"

I could hear the music from the dance club before I saw the building, the bass reverberating in my chest. We turned the corner, and I spotted our destination. The building itself was lit in blue and green floodlights, which pulsed in time with the beat of the music.

When we approached the door, a bouncer the size of a mountain stepped in front of us. I gave the bouncer Calum's ID and mine, then paid the cover. The bouncer released the velvet rope, and we walked down the hall toward the curtain, and the pulsing music beyond.

Ink stopped just past the rope. "Did you just pay coin to get us in?"

I kept walking. "Yep."

"Fara! If I'd known that you'd have to pay for my night out, I wouldn't have suggested it."

"Don't worry about it, all right? I don't know when I'll come back here, and my money isn't doing me any good just sitting there. I can't think of a better use for it right now, so stop looking like you're going to argue with me, and let's go."

He didn't look convinced, but that didn't matter as we walked through the curtain at the end of the hallway. I'd never seen anything like it other than on TV. And by Ink's face, neither had he.

The giant room was made to look like we were underwater. Colored LED lights mimicked the ocean on the ceiling and walls, and the floor was painted to look like sand. The lighting and the paint and decor taken together gave the illusion of being at the bottom of a coral reef. Women and men, painted to look like brightly colored fish, were dancing in suspended cages high above the dance floor. Music thumped through the speakers as bodies pressed sensuously together.

Adora pulled out cash and handed it to the hostess. "VIP!" she yelled over the music.

The hostess nodded without a word and walked toward a round booth in the back of the room, her blue sequined dress catching the light. Ink had stopped to stare at, well, everything, so I grabbed his hand to pull him along. He laced his fingers through mine as we made our way through the crowd.

We reached our booth and slid in. "We've already paid for a drink—go ahead and order one," I yelled to him over the music.

"What should I order?"

"Not whiskey."

Ink laughed. At least one of us found that funny.

I looked at the menu and found something with some alcohol but mostly mixers for him and ordered myself something that had an exotic name—and price tag. Adora ordered us all shots, and some complicated cocktail for herself, then began her descent onto the dance floor. In her gold crop top and skintight jeans, she really did look like a goddess descending into the masses. She looked over her shoulder at us, eyebrow raised.

"Coming?"

I turned to Ink. "Want to go out there and risk the hordes?"

"I have no fucking idea what's happening, but it's amazing! You only live once, right?"

We made our way to Adora, who had already amassed a group of admirers. She winked at me, and I couldn't help but grin at her.

"What now?" We were crushed together in the throng of people.

"We're supposed to dance!"

"I've never danced!"

"Wing it?"

He started moving to the beat. I forced myself to do the same. If I pretended that I was alone in my apartment, I could just get myself to move. I wasn't a dancer. I didn't like attention. But with Adora and Ink, it wasn't scary. It was actually starting to be fun.

Of course, just as I felt like I was getting the hang of it, the DJ slowed the beat down to a sultry tempo. The new music incited the crush of sweaty twenty-somethings to grab the closest dancer to them and start to grind. Girls on girls on boys on boys on girls on boys on girls; the dance floor became an instant hedonistic playground. I realized I had stopped dancing to watch.

"This is crazy!" Ink yelled.

"I know! I've never been here before. We can go back and sit down?"

"Not on your life, Fara. I want to dance!"

He grabbed my hips, turned me around, and pulled me close, his body rocking in time with the beat. As our bodies moved together, I could smell his sweat and cologne. My pulse quickened as he brushed his lips against my jaw, his hands now gripped tightly around my waist, securing my ass fully against him. His breath was hot as he nipped my ear and laughed.

"Fara," he said, squeezing me closer into him, his hand just under the hem of my top, splayed on my bare skin. My name on his lips sounded just like the first time he said it—like he was tasting it. I shivered.

As we danced to the music, his hand inching up my torso, his breath coming faster on my neck, I *knew* that this was just Ink being himself. He was having a good time. He was allowing himself to be completely free for one night, which was the whole point of all of this. He oozed sex without even trying. He was the Compound's bad boy, and all of this breathy sexpot thing didn't mean anything to him.

But it did to me.

I wanted it too much. I liked it too much. I needed to stop this before I did something stupid—something we'd both regret. I was reacting to Ink like this because Jay didn't want to spend time with me . . . or at least, that's how it felt. And it hurt. I was reacting because I was feeling lonely and sad and confused with how my relationship with my boyfriend was going. But dirty dancing with Ink wasn't the answer to my problems. It was just going to cause more. So, I did the only thing I could think of: I turned around and swatted at him.

He raised an eyebrow. "What?"

"You know what!"

"I'm just dancing!"

"And being naughty! Knock that shit off or I'll leave you at Hewitt's house."

His perma-smirk was alive and well. "Fine. Whatever you say. But it looked like you were enjoying yourself too."

Wasn't that the problem? I dropped my eyes from his to give myself a second to get my shit together.

"Hey, what is it? I'm sorry. I was just—"

I pulled myself together, trying to put a smirk on my face to match his.

"It's nothing. Really. I'm so glad you're having fun. But you're gathering an audience. Don't you want to dance with some pretty young thing?"

"Only if you want me to."

"Ink, I—"

A young woman who had been eyeballing him since we walked onto the dance floor hip-checked me out of the way and planted her ass firmly against his pelvis. I forced myself to shrug and grin at him. I wanted him to have fun. He needed to let off steam, and he couldn't do that with me around.

I dodged a couple who were making out and doing various other things on the dance floor and finally made it back to the booth. I downed my shot and watched Ink dance as woman after woman tried to get his attention. Every so often, he'd find me and wave with a grin, and I'd wave back.

"You have a thing for him."

Adora had snuck into the booth when I wasn't looking. She looked at me over the rim of her gigantic drink, complete with umbrella. Only she could look amazing drinking out of what looked like a goldfish bowl.

"I don't."

"Girl, do not lie to me."

"I'm not! Anyway, I'm with Jay."

"Jay's not here."

"It's complicated."

She slid closer to me in the booth, waving at Ink when he looked over at us. "It's *not* complicated. I mean, it is with all of the alternate universe shit and running for your life and all of that. But underneath it all, it's not complicated."

"What are you talking about?"

"It's pretty obvious, Fara. The Hot Agent Man isn't here. By choice. And you're upset by that. He's not here because he thinks that you shouldn't be here. He thinks it's dangerous. He's not here because he's trying to do the right thing, even if it's wrong for your relationship. Wrong for you. Even though it's right for him. Even though you want him here."

"But he's probably right. I mean, this is reckless."

"Is it, though? From what I understand, you can take care of yourself pretty well now. So why is he insisting that you don't?"

"He could blow his cover if he's seen with me."

"And how long is that going to last? Until all of this is over? That could be months. Years, even. Are you willing to wait that long?"

I took a long sip of my drink. It tasted a bit like soap and was served in a weirdly shaped glass. For what we'd paid, there should have been gold flecks in it. But whatever.

"Fara, deep down, you know that you guys are mismatched. You're just discovering how badass you are—something I've always known, by the way—and he's trying to keep you from exploring that. You both were exactly right at the beginning of this, but not now. But you and Ink seem to be matched pretty well . . ."

"That's a terrible idea, Adora! Even if I had feelings for Ink—which I don't—but even if I did, it doesn't matter! He'll never settle down. He's a huge player—just look at that!"

I gestured in his direction with my weirdly shaped drink. He was grinding on some girl who was wearing what looked like a white onesie without underwear. He looked over at me again and grinned.

"He's only dancing with those girls because you told him to! So that's on you. But he doesn't matter. And the Hot Agent Man doesn't matter. And I don't matter. Not with this.

You matter. Fara, you have to decide what you want out of a relationship. Not what you settle for. What you *want*. Do you even want anyone at all? There's no rule that says you have to be in a relationship to be complete—Jerry Maguire was full of shit."

I laughed. She took another long drink out of her aquarium, waggling her eyebrows at some hunk on the dance floor. The guy beckoned her with a finger.

"Fara," she continued, "I have never seen you happier than since you left here. And I've never, *ever* seen you look at someone the way you're looking at that boy right now."

"It doesn't matter. It can never happen."

"You keep telling yourself that, but we both know it's a lie. You're afraid if it does happen and goes to shit, you'll lose him. But let's forget about that for now and get back on the dance floor. We're supposed to be young, wild, and free, right?"

28 BLU

The conversation I'd had with Jyston replayed over and over in my head. He'd left our date to meet the Counselor, then commed me after the meeting. During our conversation, he told me some very disturbing news. While the information shed light on questions the Team had been asking, it also caused me a fair bit of anxiety. Things were about to get ugly—or at least, uglier. If that was even possible.

I needed to talk to the Captain, but she was busy until our Team meeting after lunch. I stared at my ceiling, hoping that sleep would take me. But it didn't. With a string of curse words, I got dressed and decided to do the thing that I hated the most: go for a run. Fuck my life.

The gravel path hugged the tree line and encircled the portion of the Compound where we lived. I was glad it didn't go around the entire Compound. The property took up many square miles of treed land. If a longer path had existed, I'm sure the Captain would have made us run it.

The path was still over a mile long—which always felt like hundreds of miles—and normally the Captain made us run it three times unless she was feeling particularly vindictive. Then it was more. I promised myself to run it once, then decide if I was ready for coffee. Three times around seemed like two too many for this time in the morning.

I slowly began my jog, cursing internally as I did. Jack loved running and told me that if I just stuck it out, eventually I'd get a runner's high, whatever that meant.

Never once had that happened growing up, even though I'd had to run. A lot.

As I made my way behind the mess, the tech building, and the infirmary, I watched the glow of the sun crest over the horizon. People were starting their days with brisk efficiency, walking into and out of buildings, carrying tech or weapons or coffee, or all three. My lungs started to burn as I passed the barn, and pasture, the smell of animals filling my nose. I coughed at the stink.

Skirting the greenhouse, I headed toward the graveyard. Something flashed just past the tree line. I slowed my pace, trying to catch a glimpse. It wasn't unusual for random wildlife to traipse across our land, but I thought I'd seen the glint of metal in the gloom of the trees. A deer wouldn't be carrying a dagger.

My curiosity piqued, I ducked into the trees just outside of where I thought I'd seen whatever I saw. A tree branch cracked in front of me and I stilled. I could hear rustling. Where was it coming from? I stood, listening, when a robin abruptly took flight just off to my right, past a fallen tree. Whatever it was, it was that way.

Another flash of movement and the glint of metal. I dropped to my stomach and slithered through the mud in that direction. I finally reached the fallen tree and tentatively peeked my head over it.

Drake.

He was crouched low to the ground, studying something in the mud. I watched him. Why was he here? He was armed, which was unusual for him, even as the armorer. He also was up a lot earlier than normal. When I stayed with him, I usually left his place, trained, eaten, and bathed before he ever woke up. He preferred the night. Why was he sneaking around in the trees at this ungodly hour? I needed to find Jack.

I retraced my steps quietly, picking up more muck on my clothes as I did, and finally made it back to the path. I jogged toward our apartments, trying to make sense of what I'd seen.

"I thought you had the morning off."

I had been so lost in my thoughts that I hadn't noticed Iris jog up to me. Her hair was in a high ponytail, and she had not a bead of sweat on her. She actually looked like she glowed, unlike the red-faced drowned rat that I resembled when I ran.

"We do."

She looked me up and down, taking in the dirt and grime with only the barest hint of a frown. "Oh! Well, I run for fun too. Maybe we could run together sometime? It gets kind of lonely running by myself."

"I wouldn't be a good running partner, Iris. I hate running and will use any excuse not to do it."

"Then why are you out this early in the morning?"

"I'm asking myself the same question."

She giggled. We kept jogging.

"So, how's Ink doing?"

There it was. "He's fine."

"Is he—"

"I stay out of his personal business, Iris."

"Oh, well, OK." She slowed her pace. I wasn't going to gossip about Ink, so she'd had enough of me. "Well, hopefully I'll see you around. And can you tell your cousin that I'd still love to go shopping? You can come too, if you want."

I made a noncommittal noise and continued jogging. Jack was going to be pissed that I was waking him up this early, but he'd deal. I just wanted to know what Drake was up to.

◊ ◊ ◊

Jack was standing at his door, rubbing the sleep from his eyes, his brown hair curling up at the ends. It looked good even for having bedhead. With Ink's notorious ways, it was easy to overlook that Jack was cute. Although he wasn't cute now—he was glaring at me.

"Late night?" I asked.

"No, it's just really fucking early. We had the morning off, Blu. Why the hell are you at my door?"

"For fun?" He halfheartedly tried to shut the door in my face. "I saw something weird. Can I come in?"

He rolled his eyes and padded barefoot into his kitchen, turning on his coffeepot as he did. He had a new tattoo on his shoulder. It looked like something Ink would design. I'd have to ask him about it later when he wasn't plotting ways to kill me.

"This better be good, and from the looks of your clothes, I have high hopes. Does it have something to do with the list you gave me?"

"I don't know what it is."

He stopped rummaging around his cabinets and looked at me. "What happened?" I told him what I'd seen.

"It was luck that I found him, Jack. My guess is that he would have been gone by the time any trainees ran by there. Even if he wasn't, they probably couldn't have seen him."

"Well, it sounds like I'll be getting up early tomorrow too."

"Happy hunting."

29 FARA

I hadn't drunk that much. Maybe I was out of practice? Or maybe it was because I'd finally dragged Ink home as the sun started to rise. Regardless of the reason, I felt wrung out when I woke up.

I put on a pot of coffee and got into my bathtub, a sigh escaping my lips. The night had been fun. Surprisingly so. We'd danced for hours and ended up eating pancakes at 2 a.m. at some hole-in-the-wall greasy spoon. Ink and Adora shoveled down their pancakes while trading hilarious stories. I sipped coffee and laughed so hard that I couldn't breathe. It was one of the best nights I could remember. Until it wasn't.

It was dumb. I knew it was dumb. I'd texted Jay when we were about to leave the diner to see if I could stay with him. Maybe it was the alcohol. Or maybe it was because I'd been thinking about what Adora had said—about how long I was going to have to wait until it was safe for us to be together. That it was his choice. I wanted to see him. But really, I wanted him to want to see me.

In a way, I agreed with Adora. If Jay wanted to make this relationship work, he should help me figure out a way to spend time together. It didn't have to be much, just a little something. But he told me that I couldn't come over. That it wasn't safe. I tried to see it from his point of view, even if it hurt. How would I have reacted in the same situation?

I would have found a way to see him.

I dunked my head underwater, trying to clear it. If he didn't think we should spend time together until everything blew over (whatever that meant, and however long that took) then . . . what? What was I supposed to do? That was the million-dollar question.

There was a knock on the door, and I heard it open.

"Fara? It's Drake."

Shit.

"Hang on. I'm in the tub."

"I can come back?"

Well, this wasn't awkward at all. "Can you just step out for a second so I can grab clothes?"

I could hear him chuckling. "Sure. No hurry."

I heard the door close and rushed out of my bathroom to throw on something clean. Why was Drake here? I grabbed one of my last remaining unscorched shirt and legging ensembles and wrapped a towel around my wet hair. It would just have to do.

Drake was leaning against the wall across from my apartment, a small smile playing on his ridiculously gorgeous face. He pushed himself off the wall and followed me into my place.

"Your apartment is lovely."

"Isn't it?"

"It has to be far better than your accommodations at Jurisdiction."

"It's definitely a lot better than my last place." Not a lie. He chuckled. "Can I get you some coffee?"

"Rain check. I'm actually here to give you some gear." He handed me a package. "It's a prototype. Your request was . . . unusual . . . so please don't go running through fires just yet."

I opened the package to find a gray shirt and leggings. He'd made my fireproof gear.

"The unusual color is from the process the arm-techs put the fabric through to make it flame resistant. It fades the black to gray. I promise I didn't give you old material."

I didn't know what arm-techs were, but it didn't really matter as long as they were making sure my clothes didn't smolder.

"Mind trying them on for me? I want to see if we got the fit right."

"All right."

I walked into the bathroom and took a closer look at the clothes. The shirt was long-sleeved and formfitting, but not skintight. The leggings were, well, leggings, but felt thicker than the other pairs they'd given me. I moved a bit, and while the material felt different, it was far from uncomfortable. Now if only it wouldn't disintegrate when I lit my internal birthday candle, we'd be in business.

I walked out of the bathroom and gave a spin. Drake looked me over, his assessment completely professional, though still awkward.

"Do you make all of the armor?" I asked.

"No. We have a master tailor who I oversee, and a stable of tailors who make most of the clothes. I normally stick with weapons. But I also like to keep the special projects for myself. I'd get bored otherwise. How do they feel?"

"Good. Thank you so much, Drake. I don't have any coin—"

"This one is on me. I enjoy a challenge. Always." His grin told me that my clothes might not be all that he was referring to. I blushed. I couldn't help it. "Oh, I left you something on the table as well."

"Another present?"

"The first of many, I hope. I saw how you enjoyed the coffee I made, so I brought you some."

The good coffee? I was in heaven! "Thank you so much, Drake. How can I repay you?"

"You could always come over for dinner . . ." I shook my head but couldn't help the traitorous smile. "Very well, another time. You will let me know how the clothes hold up?"

"I promise."

Almost as soon as I turned to put the coffee away, I jumped at Ink's voice.

"What was Drake doing here?"

"Licking my face."

He stopped, his eyebrows climbing so far into his hair that I thought they might meet at the back of his skull. I winked for good measure. Was he always going to fall for this? Served him right for lurking.

"He was licking your—"

"Actually, he was dropping off his new fireproof clothing prototype. I just wanted to imagine that he licked my face."

Ink's perma-smirk returned. "If you need someone to lick your . . . face, I can obviously oblige."

I snorted. "Right. I'd have to get in line and wait my turn."

"I'd let you jump line anytime, sweetness."

"Whatever. Anyway, I'd prefer to go test out my new gear with you."

"You'd prefer that over—"

"—over you finishing that sentence. Are you up for it?"

"Always."

◊ ◊ ◊

Ink dropped his backpack on the ground and started walking to the center of the clearing. "It's sunny. I think we can practice your 'all-in-one' program first."

"And not worry about me short-circuiting in the process?"

"Yeah, that'd be helpful." The wildflowers were a riot of yellows, whites, and purples. The breeze was light, and the sun was vibrant. I loved this place.

"I was also thinking that at some point I want you to practice what you did on the guard during the OG palmbox mission. The basic 'stun' program—without passing out, preferably."

"How am I going to do that?"

"You're going to practice on me."

I stared at him. He couldn't be serious. "Abso-fucking-lutely not."

"We'll bring Sage."

"No."

Ink sighed. "OK, not today. But at some point. That's a really helpful tool, Fara. But only if you're able to consistently do it without passing out."

I wasn't going to keep arguing with him about it, but that didn't mean I agreed. The thought of purposely hurting him . . . I couldn't think about it. I followed him out to the center of the clearing.

"I thought we were here to test out my new gear?"

"We are. But after the OG palmbox mission, I was thinking that we need to get you used to as many offensive abilities as possible. If you can control the all-in-one, you'll be unstoppable."

"Or I could be a complete disaster."

"I have faith in you. I want you to do the all-in-one and hit our target tree."

The last time I did this, I almost killed him. I felt the panic rise.

"Fara, I'll stand behind you. You won't hurt me."

"Ink . . ."

He gave my arm a gentle squeeze. "You can do this. Time to get to work."

I hoped he was right. I was getting pretty good at using electric balls, and my aim was decent. But this? I wasn't sure. He was right, though. Time to get to work.

I pulled up my feelings and the program wheel. Before turning it to the right program, I looked at the tree. If I could focus enough on the target, then maybe I could—intend it? Will it? Use the force?—to get the lightning into the tree without hurting my friend. It was worth a shot.

I thought, *I intend for the lightning to hit the tree*, and dramatically threw my arms out like Emperor Palpatine. As weird as those words sounded in my head, it felt right. The electricity drained out of me, and it shot out, not as electric balls, but as bolts of lightning. They hit the tree with a boom.

"Holy shit! Fara, you did it!"

I did it! Maybe there was something to that intention thing to help me aim? Or maybe I was becoming a Jedi? I doubted it. This wasn't force lightning, but toxic palmbox lightning. But I wasn't going to complain.

"Again?"

I did the exact same thing with the exact same response. The poor tree was smoking and now thoroughly, irrevocably, and extremely dead. Ink ran over to it to make sure it didn't catch on fire—or catch the surrounding trees on fire. Then he ran back and put his arm around my shoulder.

"How do you feel?"

I swayed.

"Fara?"

He slowly lowered me to my knees. I was really dizzy. Nauseated.

"Just give me a sec." At least I hadn't passed out. That was something. Stupid side effects.

I could hear Ink rustling around in the backpack. He held out a granola bar and water bottle.

"I'm not sure why I'm dizzy."

"Maybe one too many all-in-ones?"

I sat all the way down and unwrapped my granola bar. "I have no idea."

"Me either. But what's our motto? Wing it?"

"Yep." I took a gulp of water, and the dizziness and nausea slowly faded into the background. "Why couldn't these abilities have awesome side effects instead of making me feel like I've been hit by a giant sledgehammer? Why do I have to feel like shit—emotionally and physically—to get them to work? It doesn't seem fair."

His bright green eyes searched my face. "Because, Fara, everything—*everything*—has a cost."

He spoke as if each word was weighted, as if an entire story hid behind that sentence. He turned his gaze to the dead tree, but I didn't think he was really seeing it. After a moment, he shook himself off and his perma-smirk returned.

"But," he continued, "I'm kind of bummed your head isn't in my lap. That's the upside for me." I snorted. "So, do you feel up for your . . . what do you call it? Your 'human birthday candle'?"

Did I feel up for it? The nausea was gone and I wasn't dizzy anymore, which was a bonus. Ink helped me to my feet. I guess I was as ready as anyone could be.

"I want to see if I can get the flame bigger."

"Like a fireball? Instead of an electric ball?"

I laughed. "I guess? I was trying to think of what this ability could be used for, other than burning down houses. When I was in the interrogation room with the government, crazy Dagna-times-two grabbed me, and my first reaction was to turn on my birthday candle and burn her hand off."

"She grabbed you?"

"Yeah. It actually worked in our favor. It gave Jay a reason to lose his shit and cause a commotion so I could switch the palmboxes. But that's not the point. I think this would be a good close contact defensive ability. But I'm not sure how it would help the Team, unless I can make the flame bigger."

"Not everything has to help the Team."

Wasn't that why I was doing all of this? To help take down Barrington Park? To help dismantle Jurisdiction so that they could live free, and I could, well, figure out what I wanted to do without running for my life? To spend time with Jay?

"Just . . . let's see if we can get it bigger. But we should probably get closer to the stream."

"Good thinking."

I pulled up my wheel. I already had a "fire" program. What was I actually trying to do? Bigger fire? Mobile fire? Fireball? "Human torch" popped up on the wheel. I guess we'd go with that.

I pulled up my emotions: the sadness of being rebuffed by Jay, how if things didn't straighten themselves out, I wouldn't be able to spend my birthday with him, which I had hoped. And . . . nothing. I tried again. Nothing.

"What are you thinking about?"

Ugh. I didn't want to talk about this with Ink. Or with anybody. But I guess that was part of the cost. "How the situation with Jay sucks."

"Maybe it doesn't suck enough for fire? I mean, it sucks, but—"

"I understand what you're saying."

"What did you use last time?"

"I was irritated. Angry? Not sad."

"Then try that?"

That might be a problem, if my initial portal training was any indication.

"I'm not sure how." I was hardly ever angry. Like, *really* angry. I wasn't the Hulk. Not even a little. Maybe the flame was small because I was only mildly irritated.

"What do you mean?"

I told him how Jay and Calum had tried to make me mad, and all I could muster was a giggle, back before I came here. It felt like an eternity ago. "Eventually I got angry enough to do it, but it took a while. At least, too long to make this ability worth anything."

"Maybe try irritation first? Like, irritated because I bet you that you can't do this."

"What?"

He smirked at me. "I bet that you can't create the birthday candle."

I shrugged. "OK. But still not irritated."

His smirk widened into a grin. "I wasn't finished. If you can't, then I get to tell Dev that he's your ex-boyfriend."

"You wouldn't . . ."

"I would." He winked at me. "I'll also tell him that he sucks in bed."

"No!"

"Yes."

"Asshole!" Now I was irritated. I knew Ink would do it too. That was completely unfair! "You can't! I mean, poor Dev! How would you like it if I went around saying you sucked in bed?"

"Wouldn't bother me, because I'd know it was a lie."

I snorted. "Every man thinks that, but most are wrong."

"I'm not."

"How can you be so sure?"

"Because"—he leaned toward me, so close that we were almost touching, and whispered in my ear—"I always, *always*, make it about you. Every inch of you. Now light your candle, sweetness."

Bastard. I was going to . . . Well, whatever I was going to do, it wasn't going to be pleasant for him. I took a final drink of water and channeled all of my warring emotions into the "fire" program. My little candle came to life, flickering in the spring breeze. I could feel my body heating up quickly, but Drake's clothes were amazing. No Mad Max repeats here.

Ink was grinning at me. "See? Now Dev doesn't have to worry. How do you feel?"

"Pissed!"

"But how do you feel?"

"Other than wanting to smack that smug grin off your ridiculously cute face with my birthday candle? Fine! I feel fine. Although I think my boots are starting to smoke." Those weren't fireproof. I blew out my candle and quickly ran into the stream, standing in the water up to my ankles. Steam rose around me. Once I thought it was safe enough, that I wouldn't set anything else on fire, I sat down on the edge of the stream and took off my boots. There were holes in the soles—melted. I showed them to Ink.

"Good thing it's time for us to go. It looks like I'll have to carry you to the car. You can't walk barefoot through here."

"I'll manage." No way was I going to let Ink carry me. Even though I was short, I wasn't a waif. The fragile grasp I had on my self-confidence couldn't take it if he threw his back out. Or grunted.

"Fara, don't be ridiculous."

"I'm not. Ink, you can't carry me."

"I have before."

"But I was passed out—"

"Why is this a big deal for you?"

"Because . . . because I'm not skinny."

"No, you're not. You're perfect. Put your boots in the backpack and hop on."

30 BLU

The Captain was just getting to her office as I approached.

The corners of her mouth turned up when she saw me. "You're early. Which means that I'm not going to like whatever it is you have to tell me."

"Probably not."

"All right. I'll put the coffee on. I'm sure we'll need it."

I told her about Jyston's conversation with the Counselor. Repeating what he'd told me out loud made it worse. We were very, very fucked.

"So, Dagna has been the one traveling between universes?" the Captain asked.

"Yep. Barrington has a second palmbox—a prototype—that can open portals. Since Dagna is the one to go through them, Jyston doesn't know many details about how and where they travel. Dagna obviously holds that over him. But he knows that she renewed Barrington's mission—picking up weapons schematics."

"Are the weapons fully operational?"

"No. But they're close to being completed."

Dagna had been struggling to get the components for the weapons over the years, but now they were only missing a piece or two. Once they found those, the weapons could be fully assembled. And used.

"They're using the prisoners—the kids—to put the weapons together."

"Does he know what kind of weapons?"

"No, but something at least as horrible as what the Counselor used on our world."

The Captain took a sip of her coffee. She looked pensive. And tired. "They must believe they need a lot of weapons, based on the number of kids they are bringing into the building."

"Unfortunately, that's not all Dagna is using the prisoners for. She also tests programs she finds in other universes on them."

I saw a flash of rage in the Captain's eyes. "I'm at the point where I would like to kill Dagna. Personally."

"I'll help." When Jyston had told me that, I'd come very close to leaving right then, heading to Jurisdiction's headquarters, and burning the entire thing to the fucking ground. I begrudgingly let him talk me out of becoming a one-woman demolition team. "Anyway, he said that he's been smuggling kids out as much as he can. That's how he knew about that trail. He's also been stealing weapon components and is going to turn some over to us to study. But even with his efforts, they're close to having all of the necessary materials."

"Can Jyston steal the Jurisdiction palmbox?"

"Not without the possibility of getting caught. But he said that will be the last thing he does . . . other than setting the entire headquarters on fire." It would probably be a suicide mission. I'd think about that later.

"Well, he certainly can do that too. But unfortunately, we still need him on the inside for now."

"We do. Until we get into the PITs, at least. Maybe longer."

The Captain steepled her fingers, her face determined. "Then we have work to do."

◊ ◊ ◊

"So, we've really lost our minds? We're entering the PITs?" Jack was not pleased, and I couldn't blame him.

To be fair, the plan really was crazy. In order to get into Dagna's building, we had to impersonate one of the drivers who made deliveries to the building itself. Unfortunately, Jurisdiction only gave those driving jobs out as prizes at the PITs, because they were assholes. Sometimes you could trade with the gangs before the competition to get one. As long as you had something worthy to give in return. We just needed to figure out what the other competitors wanted.

"How, do you suppose, are we going to do this?" Ink said.

"We have the invitation, and we have the way in. We need to plan for how we are going to get out."

"And how not to get you and Silver killed," Jack added. "I'm serious, Blu. I've only heard secondhand what the PITs are like. No prisoners make it out alive."

"We won't be entering as prisoners, Jack. The invitation Jyston got us is for the mercenary competition."

"I thought the PITs was just a way for Jurisdiction to kill prisoners for entertainment. When did they start letting gangs compete?" Ink asked.

"Jyston said that the elite got bored watching people with no actual skill try to ride motorcycles. The prisoners are as likely to die from a crash or falling off their bikes as they are from the obstacles or other prisoners. The elite whined enough that Jurisdiction came up with this."

"How altruistic of them. Will there still be obstacles?" Jack asked.

"Yes, although from what Jyston tells me, the obstacles—while still brutal—are less likely to kill us than when prisoners compete. It would be bad for business otherwise."

"Great. Flame throwers with a heart," Ink said.

I snorted. "Anyway, everyone who enters the mercenary competition is badass at this sort of thing. It's also why they offer up the driving jobs—it means whoever wins can handle whatever driving Jurisdiction throws their way."

"And you can do that?" Fara's eyes were wide.

"Silver can. I'll just be eye candy."

"You're starting to sound like me," Ink said. I could tell he wasn't happy about all of this either. "Do we even have a motorcycle that will work?"

"Jurisdiction provides the bikes for the tournament. That way they can keep it *fair*." Jack snorted. "Or as fair as people killing other people for sport can be. But we'll need to get a bike for Silver and Blu to practice on."

Silver nodded. "That would help a lot. Riding two-up is different from what I'm used to. And their bikes are different from street bikes too." She didn't look freaked out or worried. She looked determined. I really was beginning to like her.

"Any ideas where we can get one?"

She shrugged. "I know who we can ask."

31 BLU

First, we needed to meet Jyston. Styx, Fara, and I walked into the rendezvous place, an abandoned building. We needed him to help us with the OG palmbox; he needed Styx to look at something he stole from Jurisdiction. And I needed to kiss him. Unfortunately, that would have to wait.

I had told the rest of the Team about Jyston's secret during the meeting. While surprised, they were less wary of his duplicity than I had been. After a couple of questions, mostly about his home world (which I couldn't answer), they seemed to adapt to the new information and moved on. It just confirmed that these people were the fucking best.

Jyston rose to his feet as we entered. He was in his "Second Counselor" attire, his hair pulled back, his eyes gleaming.

"Holy shit," Fara breathed.

Jyston gave Fara a mischievous smile. "I have to say that is not the first time someone has greeted me with that particular phrase."

"I'm so sorry!" She looked mortified. "It's just that Jay— the you in my world—dresses in the exact same way when he's in 'business mode.' It's weird . . . but that's not an excuse for being rude. Sorry! Nice to meet you. I'm Fara."

Jyston gave a slight bow. "Jyston. It is my pleasure. And you are not being rude. It is a bit disconcerting to see someone who looks just like someone else." He looked at me with his eyebrow raised, and Fara laughed. "I'm assuming your . . . Jay . . . makes the same facial expression?"

"Usually when he thinks I'm doing something dangerous or whackadoodle."

"Whacka . . . Never mind. I can almost relate."

I snorted. "Whatever. Jyston, this is Styx."

He bowed to her as well. "I am very glad to meet you. You know, there are many in Jurisdiction who would defect just to learn how you do what you do."

"If they are willing to take down your horrible organization, send them my way."

With introductions out of the way, Jyston pulled something out of his suit coat. It was about the size of a palmbox, but I could tell it wasn't one, or at least, not one I had ever seen before. He handed it to Styx.

"This is one of the weapon components. Dagna retrieved it from an alternate universe, and I'm hoping you can figure out what it does, or at least how to disable it."

She studied it. "I have no idea what this is. I guess I can take it apart, but it would probably be easier if I could look at the schematics to see what it hooks into. What it's supposed to do. Is there any way you can get a picture of them? Or maybe get another part?"

"I will see what I can do. Dagna is currently away, so I have a little more freedom right now."

"For how long?" I asked.

The corner of his mouth turned up into an almost-smile. "Hoping for another date?" When I didn't answer, he chuckled. "OK, to business. Did you bring the palmbox?"

Fara handed it to him. He pushed some buttons, then shook his head.

"Can you decipher that?" I asked.

"Without a key, it will be hard, but I remember the basics."

"Was Barrington just trying to be an asshole?"

"Probably. He was always trying to be smarter than everyone else. Unfortunately, most of the time he was, so it fed his ego."

I peered over his shoulder at the palmbox. "But do you understand it enough to explain?"

"Let me see if I can make it more decipherable."

He began to describe the naming system Barrington had used for the programs, which was convoluted even by Jurisdiction's standards. What I was finally able to glean (with Styx's interpretation) was not only that his naming system was ridiculously complicated, but there were programs to open portals to dozens of other universes in the OG palmbox. The palmbox had programs *from* the other universes as well. Hundreds of them.

The enormity of what that OG palmbox was capable of slammed into me. I sat down on a piece of rubble, ignoring how it bit into my backside. "Holy shit." Whoever controlled this could go anywhere and do almost anything. In the wrong hands—Barrington's hands, the Counselor's hands—they could invade any world or take any technology. In our hands, we might have a shot at destroying Jurisdiction.

Jyston chuckled. "I don't disagree. That palmbox is one of two in existence that has parallel universe technology on it. Dagna and the Counselor have the other one. Barrington was never able to replicate it onto different palmboxes."

"So most of these programs are from other universes?" Styx asked.

"Yes. For example, the lightning program he was so fond of is from a different universe."

Fara's eyes were wide. "The lightning I can do isn't from my world, or this one, but another one?"

"I believe so."

She sat down next to me. "Holy shit is right. Do you think I can do all of them?"

He studied the OG palmbox, then shrugged. "It's hard to say. Without the key, I'm not sure what most of these do. I know 'L' is 'lightning' and 'P' is portal, but I have no idea what 'F' or 'U' do."

"'Fire' and 'Unlock' is my guess."

Jyston looked at her. "Can you do that too?"

"I'm learning to. So, in theory, we'll be able to open portals to specific locations with this?"

"I believe so."

Styx took the palmbox from his hand. "Let's see if we can get this baby to work." He showed her which program to start. And . . . nothing.

"What's wrong with it?" Styx looked frustrated. I didn't blame her. I felt the same way.

"It's as I thought."

"Jyston, what?"

"Fara's powers make it so she is the only one who can operate the portals."

"Well, that sucks. Do you know why?" she asked.

"Just a theory. Nothing concrete."

The worry on her face smoothed out. "I guess it's up to me, then."

Styx handed Fara the palmbox and showed her how to activate the program. The silver string began to form from her forehead. I stepped behind her to see the portal—and Calum's apartment. It closed and she deflated. Shit.

"That's the same spot that it normally opens to. I thought . . ."

"Don't despair," Jyston said with a lopsided smile. "I want you to try something. Barrington mentioned something once about 'intent.' Does that make sense to you?"

She nodded. "That's how all of my other abilities work."

"I'd love to see those some time."

"Once I can promise to almost not kill you in the process, you bet."

"That's exactly the opposite of what Blu would tell me. She would want me there just in case she could kill me." He winked at me, and I couldn't help but smile.

"Why don't you try to open it to Jay's apartment, since that is where we want to exchange information?" I asked.

Her eyes lost focus for a moment; then she pressed the button on the palmbox. The silver string began from her forehead again. The portal opened.

Through the portal was a low table made out of dark wood. Predominant in the picture, sitting on a plush, light-colored couch, was Willow. She was in leggings and a T-shirt that was three times too big for her. She held a mug, and her feet were tucked up on the couch, under the agent's leg. He said something to her that made her dip her head in a laugh. His arm was thrown over the back of the couch behind her.

It worked! We could open portals wherever we wanted, once Fara had some practice. This ability was a game changer! We could do so much good and cause Jurisdiction so many problems.

I turned to congratulate Fara but stopped. Her eyes lined with tears, but then they were gone. The window closed.

"As long as Barrington has been to the world, I can control where I open a portal?"

"Theoretically. And more. There's a program on here that allows you to go to new parallel universes too. I would have to study it more to figure out which one it is, but hypothetically, with this palmbox, you can go to anywhere in any of the universes."

"Is there a program to this world?"

He showed it to her. I could see the tears forming in her eyes again.

"I'm going to test it out, to go directly to the Compound."

Styx was looking between me and Jyston, a slow smile spreading across her face.

"Second Counselor, you said you had some free time?" Her grin widened. "Fara can portal you directly to Blu's room, if you want."

"It's just Jyston. And I'd love to."

Jyston had turned his gaze to me. "Tell me that you don't want me to, and I won't."

It was reckless, and stupid, and . . . and maybe not. No one would know he was there, as long as one of the principal Team members didn't barge in. Fara was probably going to train with Ink, and he would be the most likely culprit for an interruption. What was I nervous about?

"Remember, I can still kill you."

He chuckled. "How could I ever forget that?"

"Styx, be careful with my car."

"Of course. I'll see you when you come up for air." She waved and headed out.

Fara had already started the portal. My apartment was a mess. And I was really impressed that she was able to open it to the right place the first time. She was badass.

"It's weird," she said. "This is the second portal I've opened to your apartment. The first time, I just didn't realize that's where it was, and I accidentally borrowed a tank top. You can have it back, if you want."

32 FARA

A distraction—that's what I needed. A distraction so that the picture of Jay and Willow happily sitting on the couch didn't replay itself over and over in my head.

I knew that nothing was happening between the two of them—not yet, at least. He was too decent to do something like that. And I had a feeling that Willow wasn't that type of person either. In my heart, I knew that. They weren't doing anything wrong.

But that should have been me.

I should have been sitting on his couch in his T-shirt, warming my feet under his leg. Laughing with him as we watched TV. The first time I saw his apartment shouldn't have been through a fucking portal. I should have been sleeping there, curled up next to him. But I wasn't. I was here, standing in front of Ink's door, feeling as alone as I had ever felt. I was hurt. But mostly, I was angry. At the situation. At our lives. At all of it.

Ink opened the door before I could knock, like he was headed somewhere. "I was just going to come see you . . ." His green eyes searched my face. "What's wrong?"

I shook my head, unable to explain, unwilling to talk about it. "Do you have an hour or so? I'd like to train. Abilities, not weapons."

"Let me get some provisions."

I was silent on the drive, letting my anger pool in my stomach. If anger was what got my human birthday candle to light, I had plenty today. More than enough.

We made it to the clearing, and without a word, I walked directly to the spot near the stream, taking off my boots and socks as I went. I reached for my program wheel and turned it to "fire." A small flame appeared in the palm of my hand. But that wasn't enough to satisfy me.

I wanted to burn the world down.

I was so angry. Angry that I was stuck with these powers, even though I hadn't asked for them and didn't want them. Angry that Barrington and my own government had made it impossible for me to live a normal fucking life. Angry that I was in one world when my boyfriend was in another. Angry that I couldn't sit on the couch with him, kiss him, make him laugh. But I was alone. And with these unexplainable abilities, I would always be alone. I channeled all of that and turned my wheel to "human torch."

"What the fuck! Fara, are you OK?"

I let the rage and sadness and bitterness and all of it fill me up. It was easier than feeling empty and alone.

"No. I'm not OK."

"I can tell that, sweetness. But can you see yourself in the stream? I mean, are you physically all right?"

I looked down, and surrounding my bare arms was flame, about two inches tall. In the stream, I could see that the fire surrounded my head and shoulders too. I pushed my anger toward the flame, and it grew. Everywhere my skin was exposed was covered in flames.

I was on fire.

I *was* fire.

"Fara—your clothes . . ."

My shirt and pants were smoldering in tatters, but I didn't care. I let the fire burn, feeding my rage into it. Rage that had been pent up and boxed up and stuffed down because that was what I had been told to do—what I'd had to do to survive.

But not anymore. The flames got brighter, but it still wasn't enough. I turned my wheel to the lightning program and let the electricity form into spheres on my hands. I turned them over and over. I felt the lightning crackle behind my eyes as the fire raged on my skin.

Let it burn. Let it all fucking burn. Barrington. Jurisdiction. The government. Dagna. Hewitt. I would burn all of them to the fucking ground.

"Fara, not to sound panicky, but you're burning the grass beneath you."

The blackened spots beneath my feet were beginning to smolder. The clearing was my sanctuary—I couldn't burn it down. Wouldn't burn it down, even if the rest of the world deserved it. What had I done? I took a deep breath and shut it down.

"Fara?"

Not knowing what else to do, I sat down in the stream, steam rising off the water as I did. Ink waded into the water, careful not to touch me. I couldn't stand to look at him, so I buried my head on my knees. A sob escaped. Then another. Then I was shaking so badly I was causing ripples in the water.

"Fara, what happened?"

"Nothing happened."

"Hey—please, look at me." His green eyes were intense. "You can tell me to mind my own fucking business. You can tell me to get lost, or that you don't trust me enough to tell me. But don't lie to me. Never lie to me, OK? Something happened."

"It's just . . ." Through choking sobs, I told him what I'd seen through the portal. He listened, absently dropping water droplets on my arm and watching them sizzle. Eventually, they didn't, and he grabbed my hand, lacing his fingers through mine.

"I don't want these powers anymore," I whispered.

Ink squeezed my hand. "I know."

"I didn't ask for this."

"None of us did. None of us asked to be where we are. But we have to work with what we're given. You just need to ask yourself what you want to do."

I felt the tears starting again. "I can't . . . I can't get my mind to work. I'm a fucking mess."

"Maybe it's OK to be a mess once in a while."

"Ink, *please* . . . I don't know what to do. Maybe Jay was right. Maybe I should suppress them. If I didn't have these powers, maybe he'd look at me the same way he looked at Willow. If I didn't have them, then maybe that could have been me sitting on the couch. Maybe I could have a normal life, and go back home."

Ink met my eyes. "Is that what you want?"

I didn't know the answer to that. I looked out at our practice tree. It was the one thing in this sanctuary that showed the destruction of the world around us. It looked exactly how I felt. Burned and broken. And alone.

"What would you do?"

"I'm not you, Fara."

"That's not what I mean."

"I know."

Ink let go of my hand and took off his shirt, holding it out to me without comment. I slowly dragged myself out of the water, stripped out of my tattered tank top, and put it on. For as tight as it was on him, it was big on me and hung to my thighs. It smelled like him. I smelled like him.

"Thank you."

"For what it's worth," he said, as he tucked a piece of hair behind my ear, "I think that anyone who asks you to change for them, or to be smaller for them, or doesn't embrace everything you are, isn't good enough for you. You are exactly perfect, just as you are."

33 BLU

I dropped my daggers and sword on the floor in the corner and took off my boots. Now what?

Jyston walked around my apartment, his hands clasped behind his back. He had a smirk on his face. "So, this is where the fearsome Blu sleeps. It's—"

"A disaster? I know. It's really just a place to put my shit and sleep."

He made a noncommittal noise as I cleared off a space on the couch to sit.

"Jyston, why did you come here?"

"To spend time with you. Alone. We never get the opportunity." He made his way over to me and brushed a kiss on my lips. My toes tingled. "But . . . what did you call it? 'Getting in your pants'? That is not why I'm here, just so you know." I snorted, but he shook his head. "Blu, not to bring down the mood, but neither of us is guaranteed tomorrow— or so the saying goes. I like to take any opportunity I have to do things I enjoy. Like spending time with you. I want to do as much of it as I can."

"What if I just want to use you for your body?"

He raised his eyebrow at me, then chuckled deep in his chest. "I will take whatever you can give."

I needed to stop surviving. I needed to live. And I wanted this. I wanted him. I reached up and threaded my hands through his hair, pulling him down to me.

"Then what are you waiting for?"

"Tell me this is what you want." He kissed my neck, my mouth.

"This is what I want."

"That's all you had to say."

And the game was on. He grabbed my ass and lifted me up. I wrapped my legs around his waist. We crashed into the wall, all teeth and breath and hands and bodies. I wanted to touch and taste every part of him.

"Blu." He pulled back an inch from my face, holding me up against the wall. "I'll ask once more—is this what you want?"

"Yes."

"There will be no other for me, not after this. Do you understand?"

The words he said were almost formal, like it was an oath. My heart pounded in my chest. "There'd better not be. You're mine."

"Good. Now that we have that settled . . ."

I let out a laugh as he spun me around and gently put me on the bed. "While two hours will never be enough time to do what I want to do, I think I can accomplish *some* things."

🔥 🔥 🔥

Fara commed to tell me that she would be at my place in ten minutes. I drew lazy patterns on Jyston's chest as he played with my hair. I didn't want to get up but knew that this moment had to end. I didn't want it to. I didn't want to think about what that meant, either.

"Something is bothering you. I can tell." My ear on his chest made his voice even deeper.

"I was just thinking about how much I want to do that again."

"Ah. Me too. But that's not it."

"How do you know?"

He lifted his head and his eyebrow. "Because as much as you like to think of yourself as a closed book, I understand you. We're very similar, you and I."

"Then, if you know so much about me, what's bothering me?"

He looked up at the ceiling as he continued to play with my hair. "You don't like being vulnerable. It bothers you. Which I completely understand, by the way. In our line of work, it's a dangerous spot to be in."

"Except for the Team, I don't trust anyone. Well, except you."

"That I understand as well. You are the only person I trust in this world. And I promise you, I don't take your trust lightly."

He was right, and deep down, I knew it. I didn't like how vulnerable I was with him. It was easier for me to stab a minion in the eye than have a conversation about feelings, or lie here realizing I *had* feelings. For him. But I believed him when he said he didn't take my trust lightly. I looked him in the eye and saw . . . him. Not the Second Counselor, or the cold-blooded killer. Just him. He trusted me with that—so I could trust him with me. And I did. And I had. I would just worry about how much I cared about him later.

"I'm surprised you didn't ask Fara to open a portal to your home world."

His hand stilled in my hair. "I will be honest; the thought did cross my mind. But I cannot leave until my quest is completed. I must kill Barrington and see Jurisdiction destroyed. I cannot go home until this is accomplished. And I also know that you won't leave until those things happen as well."

"Leave where? Here? To go where?"

"I'd like you to come back to my world with me." He chuckled, the sound bouncing around my chest. "Don't answer yet. I can see the panic on your face. But I'd like you to think about it."

34 FARA

After my temper tantrum, I went back to my apartment to throw away my tattered tank top and pants and put on something that wasn't apocalypse-chic. In the process of figuring out how many more outfits I had before I had to beg Blu for replacements, I heard Calum knock at my door—the only person I knew who didn't just walk in. He told me that he needed supplies for the art class the Captain asked him to teach at the Compound, and asked if I would take him back to our world. He had already cleared it with the Captain. I guess now was as good a time as any.

I opened a portal directly behind his favorite art supply store. It was located downtown, in an area the locals called Little Bohemia. Really, what that translated to was "high-priced condos and coffee for hipsters," but it did have a good Vietnamese place that served amazing pho for cheap.

After we'd eaten pho and gotten the supplies, I sent him back through a portal and called Jay. We needed time. Then again, didn't we all?

He answered on the first ring. "Fara, what are you doing here?"

"I'm here for a bit because of a thing."

"You shouldn't be here—"

"Jay, please. We need to talk. In person."

"I'm coming to the meeting at the Compound in a couple of days . . ."

I could hear dishes clinking in the background. "No. I'd like to come to your place. Now, please."

"Fara—"

"I can portal directly to your living room. And out of it, now that I have the OG palmbox. Jay, *please.*"

He sighed. "OK. See you in a minute."

◊ ◊ ◊

"Hello?"

Willow peeked her head out from the kitchen, completely unfazed by my sudden appearance in Jay's apartment. "Fara! So good to see you. Just give me a second."

Jay's apartment was big. The living room was at least twice the size of my entire apartment at the Compound, with overstuffed, comfortable furniture, all in creams and beiges and browns. It was nice, and comfortable. It reminded me of him.

Willow walked out of the kitchen, wiping her hands on a dishtowel. Even injured, she was adorable—cute and pixie sized—accentuated by Jay's T-shirt, which hung to her knees. Her giant eyes were warm, her demeanor relaxed—she was completely at home here. I felt like the intruder.

"Some tomato sauce splattered while we were cleaning up, so Jay is in the bedroom changing." Jay had cooked for them. Italian, apparently. My heart thudded in my chest.

"Thanks, Willow. Mind pointing me in that direction?"

"Oh! Sure!" She pointed down the hall and to the door at the end. I counted to three and knocked.

"Just a second . . ."

"Jay, it's me." I opened the door without waiting for his answer. He was pulling a too-tight shirt down over his abs. His bedroom was also big. The bed was made, the furniture neat. It smelled of him: soap and clean laundry.

We stood staring at each other.

"Hey."

"Hey."

He walked over to me and pulled me into his embrace. I drank in his steady heartbeat, how safe I felt in his arms. He was a balm for my nerves—a rock-solid wall that I could lean on, hide behind. He was the person who made everything OK.

But I wasn't sure I needed that. I was beginning to understand that I didn't need someone to take care of me. I needed more. And I needed to tell him that.

"What is it?" he rumbled into my hair.

"It's just . . . We need to talk."

"I know we do."

I hadn't expected him to agree. "You go first, then."

He pulled back to look at me.

"I don't think I can do this anymore."

My heart thudded in my chest. I didn't want to know what came next. I hadn't expected it. It wasn't what I intended. I wasn't sure I'd survive it. But I had to ask. I had to be sure. "Do *what* anymore?"

"Live between two worlds. Our relationship. Us. I'm not sure I can do it anymore."

The weight of his words slammed into me as tears fought their way down my cheeks. My breath left me in a whoosh.

"Are you breaking up with me?" I whispered.

He looked confused. "Yes? No? I don't know! Shit, Fara— isn't that what you wanted to talk about?"

I slipped out of his arms and curled into a ball, crouching on the floor as if my legs had given up. I hugged my knees, trying to make myself as small as possible. I couldn't focus. I couldn't breathe. My heart began to ache.

Jay crouched down too—his face mere inches from mine. "Fara, wait. What is it? Talk to me. Please."

"I didn't want to break up," I choked out between sobs. "I wanted us to figure out a way to spend time together! I wanted to figure this out." He brushed a tear away with his thumb. "Is breaking up what you want?"

He grabbed my hand and pulled me to my feet, leading me to the bed so we could sit down. I wrapped my arms tightly around myself, as if they could protect me from what I knew was coming.

"Shit. I am so bad at this! I don't know." He stared out the window, his eyes sad. "I don't know what to do. Ever since I came back here, I've been losing sleep because of all of the crazy stuff you're doing."

"What crazy stuff?"

"What do you mean, 'what crazy stuff?' You're training with powers you can't quite control, burning people and passing out like it's nothing!"

"Jay, we talked about this. You said you understood why I was training with my abilities, and if you were me, you would choose to do the same thing."

"I know. But that was before I knew how dangerous it was for you. And for the people you train with. The Team laughs it off, but you could seriously hurt yourself—or them! Your powers are dangerous, Fara."

"Do you think I don't know that? It freaks me out! But I need to learn how to use these powers, Jay. Otherwise, I really could hurt someone. But if that's all it is, you can come with me to train. You can see the precautions I take . . ."

He scrubbed his face with his hands. "Fara, it's not just the powers. It's everything else too."

"Like?"

"Like, how you come back here and don't seem to understand, or care, how much danger you're in. You come back here to eat tacos and buy art supplies, for god's sake! It doesn't bother you to go to clubs or diners at 2 a.m., even though there are multiple people here trying to kidnap you! The Team has rubbed off on you, and not in a good way."

"That's not true, Jay. They are trying to help me . . ."

"You *ask* to go on missions!"

"Because I want to help!"

"It's dangerous for you!"

"Then come *with* me. We were a great team—"

"We can't spend time together."

"I'm willing to take the risk, Jay. I'm willing to do that. For us."

He was quiet, his eyes searching my face. "I can't risk us spending time together right now. Even for us."

"Is it because you'll lose your job?"

"I don't give a damn about my job."

"Then why can't you spend time with me?"

He grabbed my hand. "Because if they know we're together, it will be dangerous for you."

"I can protect myself."

"But I can't protect you!"

That was what this was about. I wanted him to accept all of me. To accept that I could control lightning. That I could become fire. That I could rip the membrane between universes. That I could unlock any door. That I could protect myself. But he still needed me to need him.

"Fara, I need to protect you. To be needed. It's who I am."

"What if I don't need to be protected anymore?"

"I can't help who I am."

But he *could* help who he was. It was a choice he was making, not something hardwired in him. Jyston was proof of that. But Jay didn't see it that way. And he wouldn't change.

But things changed.

I had changed.

I sighed and wiped my eyes. "I want you, Jay. I care for you, as much as I have ever cared for someone. But I don't need you like you need me to. Not anymore."

"Fara, I'm not even sure what to say to you."

"You don't have to say it out loud." I got my legs under me and stood.

"Please, don't go. Damnit, this sucks! Just—"

"Jay, don't. Just let me leave here with some of my dignity intact. I can't sit here with you, like this, knowing that it's over. Knowing that Willow is out there."

"She never would— She never said—"

"She never had to, Jay. But it still hurts to walk in here and see her in your shirt, sitting on your couch, eating dinner that you cooked, when I have done none of those things. I don't blame either of you. She needs you, and I don't. And I know that's not why we're breaking up. But, just—I need to go."

I opened the portal directly to my room, giving one last look behind me as Jay watched me walk through. I closed it with a hiss, lay down on my bed, and cried.

35 FARA

"Your apartment is actually messy. For you, I mean. Not for normal people. Although there still isn't enough to throw at you."

I knew the voice. I knew the smell. I knew Ink was lying in my bed. But I didn't want to open my eyes. I didn't want to face today. Because as soon as I did, I'd have to confront the fact that Jay had broken up with me. That I was alone. Again. I couldn't handle it. A tear slid out of my closed eyes.

"Hey." His voice was soft and closer than it had been. He wiped the tear off my face. "Fara. Hey. What is it?"

I shook my head and covered my face with my hands. I couldn't do it. I couldn't get up. Something essential was broken inside of me.

"Fara, open your eyes, sweetness. You need to go to training."

I shook my head again.

"Calum told me you were going to talk to Jay last night. Is that . . ."

I nodded and clutched my blanket. My heart was in pieces. How was I going to make it through the day? How was I going to put myself back together again?

"OK." I could smell his cologne and feel the heat coming off his body. "OK," he said again, quieter this time.

We lay there for a moment. I could feel his breath on my face. He wasn't teasing me or . . . anything. I opened my eyes to see what he was doing. He was mere inches away, watching me.

"I don't think I can do this."

It was his turn to shake his head. "I know you can. Your track record for living through horrible shit is a hundred percent. You don't give yourself enough credit. And it helps if you talk about it. It also helps to eat donuts and drink coffee— which I've brought you."

"Thank you."

"Always. Fara, what happened?"

"He . . ." *How do I put this? What do I say?*

Ink waited patiently. He was so close I could see a small scar right above his eyebrow. "He . . . couldn't handle what I've become."

"He broke up with you?"

I nodded.

"Then he's not meant for you."

"Maybe I'm not meant for anyone. Maybe I'm too fucked up and broken for anyone to love me."

"I think you're perfect, even if you are broken."

He wiped another tear off my cheek and stood up. "I have to wake up Blu. I'm trusting that I'll see you at the Quad?"

I sat up. He handed me my coffee, then headed for the door. My head was pounding from crying. He looked over his shoulder.

"You are literally made of fire and lightning. Don't forget that, OK?"

"Yeah, but like you said, everything has a cost."

🔥 🔥 🔥

I made it through training, and the Team meeting, and abilities training, and everything else, without having a meltdown or burning my clothes to bits. I plodded through, trying to not cry or blast things with lightning. It was a close call a few times, but I did it.

The highlight of my otherwise miserable day was that I was able to surprise Blu with a birthday present—her first ever. She appreciated the chips, salsa, hair dye, and finally knowing her true age: twenty-two. Styx appreciated the fact that I gave the "baddest bitch" she knew a giant pink birthday bag. My shopping expedition with Calum had paid off.

Even though I hadn't slept well last night, I was still restless when I got back to my apartment. Napping was out of the question, and so I drew a bath. The bathwater was so hot that at first, I was worried I'd burn my skin—but then again, I was made of fire. I might actually be fireproof. Wouldn't that be something? Maybe I could be a firefighter when I went back. If I ever went back.

I wasn't sure, now.

With my relationship with Jay over, and Calum here, what did I have to go back to? I could visit Adora any time I wanted. I could even go see Millie at kickboxing. Plus, after Jay's reaction to my abilities, I wasn't sure my world would ever accept me for everything that I was.

But they did here.

Even though I shot electric balls and opened portals and lit my birthday candle, Ink wasn't fazed by any of it. And actually, he was giddy with excitement when I recreated my lightning eyeballs and accidentally created a fire crown. He took it all in—took all of me in—without freaking out. Did I want to move back home, where I wouldn't be accepted for who I was? Or worse, where I'd be used as a weapon for the government?

I dunked my head under the water, trying to shake the malaise that had settled around me. I had hoped Calum would remember my birthday; he was usually really good about that. But I hadn't seen him. Not that there was much opportunity to. He was teaching his art class, and I was shooting lightning at dead trees. We were busy.

What was I going to do with myself? I couldn't just sit in the bathtub all night, as enticing as that sounded. Blu was with the Captain, and Styx was doing her tech thing. Should I see was Ink was doing? I hated using him as a crutch, always going to him when I didn't know what to do with myself. He had better things to do than help my fragile ego. But I couldn't sit here with my own thoughts. I had been keeping myself together fairly well, considering Jay . . . considering everything. But sitting alone in my apartment, I would probably have a breakdown. Ink's banter always got my mind off things. If I was teasing him, I wasn't thinking about the rest of it. Hopefully he didn't mind.

He answered his door while he was putting on a shirt, his mouth curved up in his perma-smirk, his eyes full of mischief as he took in my futile attempt not to stare at his body.

"Seriously?" I rolled my eyes for his benefit. I was here to get my mind off things, and I needed to remember that.

"I can't help it if you interrupted me getting dressed. I'd like to think that you did it on purpose."

"Don't flatter yourself."

"No need. You flatter me quite enough."

I was starting to feel guilty for coming over—he was obviously in the middle of something. I couldn't just come over here to distract myself. That wasn't fair to him.

"Did you come here just to stare at me? I wouldn't blame you for it . . . or did you want something?"

I snorted. "As much as I wish my social calendar allowed me the time to do nothing other than behold your amazingness, I came here to ask if you wanted to get some dinner. I'm . . . I just . . . I don't want to be by myself right now."

Understanding flashed across his face; then his perma-smirk returned. "Dinner? You know, one of these days you're going to knock on my door and ask for something else."

"Like to keep your girl de jour from being so loud? The other night, I literally slept with a pillow over my head to try to keep out the noise."

"I can't help it if they enjoy themselves."

"Right. I'm bringing back my white noise machine the first chance I get. Anyway, do you want to get food? I understand if you—"

"Fara, I'm teasing. You know that. Of course I'd love to get food. With you. I was actually heading to your apartment to ask you the same thing."

FARA 36

It was a perfect April night. The air was crisp, with the smell of early flowers blooming lingering on the soft breeze. The moon and stars shone brightly through the trees as we walked to our apartments from the mess. I stopped when we reached a clearing in the tree-lined path, tilting my head back.

"What are you looking at?" Ink looked up.

"Every year on my birthday, my dad would take me out into our backyard and lay out blankets, and we'd look at the stars. He showed me the constellations, but the only one I could ever find was the Big Dipper."

I pointed it out for him, pushing down the feeling of loss that pulsed through me. At least I had these memories.

"Your dad sounds great."

"He was. I miss him." Ink threaded his fingers through mine without taking his eyes off the stars. "Thank you, Ink."

"For what this time?"

"For spending my birthday with me."

"It's my pleasure. Although we aren't done yet."

"No?"

"Not even close."

We made it to our building, and he led me down the hall to Calum's apartment. The look on his face said he was hiding something, but his smile said it wasn't something I should be concerned with.

He opened the door. Blu, Styx, Jack, and Calum, and also Silver, Dev, and Sage were hanging out. The Captain was there too. Why were all these people in Calum's apartment?

Ink leaned down and whispered in my ear. "Surprised? Happy birthday, sweetness." He kissed my hand and let it go.

I couldn't believe it. A surprise party. For me and Blu.

Calum saw me from across the room, crossed the distance in two giant steps, and pulled me into a huge hug, swinging me around. "Happy birthday, Fara," he said into my hair.

"How did you . . . ?"

"I had some help." He set me down, but I continued to hug him.

"Calum, this is . . ." I didn't know how to put into words the gratitude I felt.

"It wasn't just me. Styx found me after your Team meeting this morning and told me her idea. Ink volunteered to keep you busy so we could plan, and Jack kept an eye on you so we could keep it a secret—although Blu forced us to tell her. She had figured something was going on."

I laughed. "Of course she did."

"But," he pulled me back into another huge hug, "every person here—even the Captain—wanted to make sure that you and Blu had a great birthday."

I smiled into his chest. "Thank you."

He pulled back and looked at me. "I know tonight is not the night you want to have deep and meaningful conversations, but . . . Ink told me about Jay."

"He did?"

"Yeah. He was . . . worried? It's hard to tell through his perma-smirk bullshit, but he said that you had a sort of breakdown, and since you wouldn't talk to him, maybe you'd talk to me."

That was a weirdly sweet thing for Ink to do. I didn't want to think about Jay right now. "It sucks, but for now it's in a box.

I don't want to accidentally 'human torch' my way through this party."

"Fair enough. But I'm here for you. Anything, anytime. Always."

"Thank you. Same. Want to get drunk?"

He laughed. "Not tonight. I'm teaching tomorrow and would rather not be hungover. But the Captain gave all of the Team the day off, so go find Sage. He's playing bartender, even though he doesn't drink."

I made my way to the kitchen, where most everyone had gathered. Sage gave me a hug, then resumed his post by the booze.

"OK, ladies. What can I get you?"

I walked over to look at the bottles. "How did you get all of this?"

"Calum said it was left over from his apartment. He brought it when he moved here."

Styx looked aghast. "He's been holding out on us!"

Sage's eyes twinkled, the closest to a smile we'd probably see tonight. "Apparently."

"I can forgive him, though, because I got the ale."

Blu looked around me to her friend, eyebrows raised. "Drake?"

"Yeah," Styx said with a grin. "I originally went there thinking I might want to get laid. I ended up leaving unsatisfied, but with ale. I actually invited him to come to the party, hoping Fara could have revenge sex, but he had something going on."

I blushed a thousand shades of red, then got myself together. I'd worry about that tomorrow. And tomorrow I'd worry about how everyone knew about me and Jay breaking up. I'd worry about all of it tomorrow. Tonight, I was going to try to enjoy myself.

"Let's do shots," I said. "Who's in?"

The rest of the night, we sat and drank and talked and laughed and had fun. A lot of fun. Other than Calum, I had only known these people for about a month, but they had gone out of their way to make me feel celebrated. For as horrible as last night was, and as horrible as things had been, they made me happy. They were funny, fierce, kind, and complicated. They made me want to be better, to be more. I was grateful that I'd found them, against the odds. And against the odds, I was having a happy birthday.

Eventually, the ale had its say, and I got up to go to the bathroom, wobbling as I did. Unfortunately, the bathroom door was shut and locked, and Calum and Silver were missing.

"Styx, can I use your bathroom? They're going to be a while."

She nodded, her head nearly touching Blu's as they talked seriously, as only drunk people can. I tried to maneuver around them, hip checking the table in the process. In my effort to have a good time, I had inadvertently gotten drunk . . . or at least drunker than I had been in a long time. I needed water, and probably to pass out.

"Where you off to, speedy?" Ink had my elbow as he steadied me.

"Other you is getting laid in his bathroom, so I need to find a different facility."

"I'll walk you."

"It's next door, Ink. I'll be fine."

"I insist."

"Whatever."

I turned on the lights to Styx's place, running into furniture and doorjambs left and right. I was a disaster but having more fun than I could remember. Actually, I could remember— when I went dancing with Adora and Ink. Maybe Ink was the fun one?

He was staring at Styx's painting when I made my way out of the bathroom. He quietly walked up to the wall, placing his hand on the tree. He was thinking something, but whatever it was, I interrupted it with a hiccup. Stupid ale.

"You're really talented, Ink."

It came out more slurred than I wanted, because I wanted him to know I was being sincere.

"Thank you."

"Do you wish you could teach art like Calum?"

He was quiet for a moment, then shook his head. "I'm better at destroying than creating; I have too much . . . *something* in me to teach anything other than how to kill people."

"Too much what?"

He turned to me. "Maybe you aren't the only one that's afraid they're broken."

"I think you're perfect." I couldn't believe I just said that, but I kept going, because . . . alcohol. He was standing completely still, staring at the painting. "Isn't that what you say to me? Anyway, I do. You're amazing and I love spending time with you and I'm so glad you're my friend and you handle all of the shitshow that is me—which is awesome— and the look you're giving me right now makes me want to rip your clothes off." I slapped my hand over my mouth, mortified, as if I could take back the words that had just fallen out of it.

He chuckled. "And you, sweetness, are drunk."

"I am!" I twirled for effect, because why not? "But can you tell? Because my mouth won't stop working and I really wish I could just stop talking. It's weird! It's like the opposite of my normal problem!"

"And because your cheeks are rosy. It's sexy."

"Ugh! Don't say that shit to me right now!"

He raised a perfect eyebrow at me. Bastard. "Why not?"

I let out an exasperated groan. "Because I know you're not serious and sometimes I wish you'd be serious when you say shit like that and I know you won't be serious with me so . . . ugh!"

"You . . . what?"

"Never mind! I hate men. I mean, not really, because I really like you, and Calum, and Jack, and Sage. And maybe even Dev, a little. But I don't think I'm ever going to date again. I think I'll just live in a cave. And I need to stop talking right now before I screw this up, like I screw up everything else in my life. I have sworn off men, so my naughty bits can just get a grip! And I can't stop thinking about you naked. Shit! I did it again!"

Ink grabbed my hand. "You are a fucking mess, which is entertaining to no end. But we need to get you back to the party."

"I'm not a mess—I'm a beautiful disaster! Sage said so earlier."

"Right. C'mon, beautiful disaster."

"OK. But I really do like you a whole lot, Ink. You're probably my favorite. Even though I've sworn off men forever and ever."

"You're my favorite too."

FARA 37

Styx was pounding on the bathroom door when I got back. "Silver! Get your pretty ass out here. We could hear that you're finished—and satisfied. We're going on an adventure!"

"Where are we going?" Ink asked and he led me back into the apartment. I was wobblier than I thought.

Styx shook her head at Ink. "Not you, pretty boy. Girls only."

"Yes!" I pumped my fist for emphasis. "Boys are dumb. No boys allowed!"

Silver came out of the bathroom, followed by Calum. Neither looked embarrassed at all. Good for them! I must have said it out loud, because Ink snorted.

Calum raised his eyebrow at me. "Drunk?"

"Yes! No boys allowed!"

He hugged me, then ruffled my hair. "I'm glad. Happy birthday, beautiful. Love you."

"I love you too. Glad you got laid on my birthday. Someone should."

We grabbed cups of ale and headed out the door.

"Where are we going, my purple-haired friend?" Styx asked, linking her arm through Blu's, then mine. I linked mine through Silver's, and we continued on down the path. If it were yellow, I'd have felt like Dorothy.

"It's a surprise."

We were heading in the direction of the Captain's office, giggling like crazy as we tripped over broken bricks, spilling ale here and there. Even Blu's face had lost some of its normal fierceness and had relaxed into a small grin.

"Getting laid has done you some good, my friend," Styx said.

"It's more than that, my naughty friend."

"She's in love," Styx stage-whispered. Blu rolled her eyes but didn't contradict her. My heart involuntarily clenched at the thought. That could have been me. I could have been in love. But tonight wasn't about that, I reminded myself. Tonight was about fun.

"I think I'm in love too," Silver said.

"You should be! My best friend is awesome." The last word came out in more syllables than it should have.

She looked at me askance. "I used to be jealous of you, you know. Still am, a little."

I snorted. The runway-model-assassin-ninja was jealous of me? No way.

"Silver, you are fierce and gorgeous, and from what I can tell, a-maz-ing. Why the hell would you be jealous of me?"

"Because," Styx said, "you are also fierce and gorgeous and amazing. Plus—"

"—plus Calum loves you," Silver added.

"He does. But not like that. He's family."

"Are you sure you don't . . . ?"

"No! Seriously, he's family. After his mom died—and I thoroughly danced on her grave, because she was a horrible, raging bitch—my family took him in. And when my parents were killed, he took me in. We're all each other has had for a really long time." I stopped so I could look at her, causing the entire train to stop too. "But, my runway-model-assassin-ninja-friend, he has never once looked at me the way he looks at you. So, no worries from this end. I'm *done* with boys! Done, I say!"

Silver snickered.

"He's not the only one that loves you, Fara," Blu said.

"Of course not! I love Fara!" Styx yelled. "She's awesome! I love all of you bitches!"

She pulled us in to a group hug, ale sloshing as she did.

"I have no idea what is happening here, but I think I just came across my fantasy scenario."

Drake was standing under a light on the path, looking for all the world like the cover of a romance novel. His shirt was unbuttoned to just above his belly button, which didn't make any sense to me—why wear a shirt at all, then? But it did show off his chest, which was nice. It was tucked into leather pants, which accentuated his package. And I was staring and awkward. I reminded myself that I had sworn off men forever and ever. But I could admire—right?

Styx snorted. "You missed your chance, Drake. I was hoping you'd give Fara a good roll in the hay to get her mind off breaking up with her boyfriend. But too bad—it's girls only now. No boys allowed."

"No boys allowed!" I yelled.

Drake walked up to me and grabbed my hand. He reminded me of someone . . . Aragorn! He was Aragorn from *Lord of the Rings*, and I wondered if he was going to offer me his sword. The thought made me giggle uncontrollably—his *sword*. Get it? No one else would get it, so I kept the thought to myself.

"I can see you all have been drinking my ale . . ."

"And it's de-lish!"

"I'm so glad you like it." He brought my hand to his lips, then pulled me closer. He wasn't that tall, which was a nice change from Ink and Jay, who were giants. "If what I am hearing is correct, you are now single?"

"She is!" Styx said. "She needs revenge sex!"

"Well, lovely Fara, you actually caught me otherwise occupied, but I will happily take a rain check." He kissed my cheek, smelling of woodsmoke and pine. I felt my face blushing. "Hope to see you soon."

He continued on toward the armory, Blu watching him closely. Did she still have a thing for him? Even with Jyston? Not my worry right now. Right now, I wanted to know where we were heading.

With a few more giggles and a lot more wobbling, Blu led us to a side door in the Captain's building. We crept up the stairs to the third floor and entered what appeared to be a meeting room—or at least, it had been at some point. Windows had been boarded up where they had been broken by vines, allowing the lights on the brick paths to filter in. A table sat in the middle of the room, with mismatched chairs. It smelled like dirt and dust.

"Why are we in the old Team meeting room?" Styx stage-whispered. I was asking myself a very similar question.

"We're not staying here," Blu answered. "Follow me."

She crept across the floor toward a broken door at the end of the room. She pulled up a board, motioning for us to sneak through to the room beyond. The next room was horror-movie creepy. Vines covered the walls, and the floor was littered with dirt and debris. Blu came in last, putting the board gently back in its place.

"Styx, I need a boost." She pointed up, and I could see a trapdoor in the ceiling.

Styx laced her fingers together and tossed Blu up as she stepped into them—which was one of the coolest things ever. Blu stretched and grabbed the trapdoor's handle midair, hanging from it until it lowered and a ladder slid down. She dropped down with a grin. If I'd tried that, I would have broken something—like my ankle, or the floor. We followed her up the ladder onto the roof.

The view was magical.

We could see the whole Compound from up here. The Quad, buildings, a pasture in the distance, and other open areas. Trees surrounded us for as far as I could see. The sky was clear, and without the light pollution, the stars and moon seemed closer.

"Ink told me that Fara's dad used to stargaze with her on her birthday. I thought we might resurrect that tradition."

A tear slid down my cheek as I smiled at Blu. I loved these bitches too.

"Thank you, Blu."

She gave me a one-armed hug and raised her ale. "Here's to new traditions."

Each woman raised her glass in turn, touching mine.

"Here's to beautiful disasters."

38 BLU

Fara was still sleeping when I slipped into her apartment to grab some of her headache medicine. I'd have to reconsider drinking if this was how it felt the day after. But, looking back on yesterday, it had been a good birthday. Fun, even. Worth the headache.

Fara made a noise in her sleep. She had the telltale silver string coming from her head; she was opening a portal. Would she do that the rest of her life? Or would that stop once we were able to take Jurisdiction's palmbox? Over time, would the membrane thicken back to its original . . . *whatever*?

She'd told me once that she wanted to stop opening portals while she slept. A new boyfriend would probably freak the fuck out when he woke up to find Calum's coffee table hovering over his face. Or if he saw whatever I was doing, which was usually way more horrific. I couldn't blame her for wanting that to end.

Curious, I padded over to the side of the bed, my socked feet silent on her floor. Calum's coffee table was in view, along with an envelope. I reached through and grabbed it, my hand meeting the water-like resistance of the membrane as I did. Barrington Park's name was on it.

Shit. I needed to make a pit stop at the Captain's office.

◊ ◊ ◊

Jack was with the Captain when I walked in.

"I'm glad you're both here," I said.

"I actually need to talk to you too," Jack answered. "I saw Drake this morning."

"Where?"

"In the trees by the graveyard."

"What was he doing?"

"Burying this." He pulled a comm out of his pocket. "It's like the one Jyston gave me."

"Only a handful of the Jurisdiction leaders have them. They're nearly impossible to make," I said. "Which means that the spy is more than likely talking to a top-level Jurisdiction official. Dagna or the Counselor, more than likely, although my coin is on Dagna."

"And," Jack said, handing the Captain the comm, "we know for a fact that Drake buried it out there."

"Yeah, that is weird," I said. "Captain, do we bring him in?"

She studied the comm in her hand, eventually handing it back to Jack. It would be the first time in as long as I had been on the Compound that we apprehended one of our own. If we were wrong, then the distrust that would spread could be catastrophic. But we couldn't have a spy running around.

"Jack," the Captain said after a moment, "can you put it back where you found it and set up twenty-four-hour surveillance? Only your most trusted. This cannot get out."

"Why are we waiting?"

"I just want to be sure. Some things aren't adding up. I know that look, Jackrabbit. I just want to give it until after the PITs. I have a feeling we'll know more then. All right, Blu. What else have you got?"

I handed her Barrington's envelope.

"Have you read it?"

"Yes."

"Has Fara?"

"No—she's still asleep."

The Captain read the note and passed it to Jack. His face creased in concern as he finished it.

"He still wants her."

"Yeah," I said, "and he's guessed that we planted a decoy palmbox. And that she's been staying at the Compound."

"It appears that he's put all of it together," the Captain said. "He now knows he just needs her to be able to travel here. And he's running for president, which is exactly how the Counselor began his rise to dictatorship."

"We need to talk to Agent Hanlon," Jack said. "When is he coming back?"

"Tomorrow. We'll need to accelerate taking down Barrington, but until we catch the spy, our resources are limited. Which is why, Jackrabbit, we need to be sure—a hundred percent sure—it's Drake."

FARA 39

"Why do I smell coffee? Why are you in my room? Why am I awake so early?"

"It's not early, Fara. It's almost lunchtime."

I rolled over to see Ink leaning against my table, sipping his own cup of coffee. His hair was wet, like he had just bathed.

"You know, they make shirts in your size."

"Why cover all of this up?"

I snorted and lay back into my pillows. I had a hangover, the size of which was probably proportional to the amount of alcohol I consumed. I felt like shit. At least I wasn't as sad as I had been. Silver linings and all.

"I thought I had the day off."

"You do. And with the way you guys were singing from the Captain's building at all hours, that's probably a good thing."

I pulled the pillow over my head. It didn't drown out Ink's chuckle.

"Nice underwear, by the way."

I was lying on top of my sheets, too hungover to even be embarrassed.

"Stop being a creeper."

"I'm not being a creeper. I'm just admiring the beauty before me."

"Ugh. Knock that shit off."

"That's what you said last night. After you told me that you wanted to rip my clothes off."

I buried my head into my pillow further. "Did I really . . . ?"

"Yep, sweetness, you did." He prowled over and sat on the bed. I peeked at him from behind my pillow. The smile he gave me made all reason go right out of the fucking door. "Is the offer still open?"

I swung the pillow at him, and he caught it with a laugh.

"You're the worst! I can never take you seriously."

"What makes you think I'm not serious now?"

"Because you never are with me! And even if you were—which you're not—but if you were—I'd be a one-and-done with you. And that's not how I am."

"Fara, I promise it would be more than once. I've had practice, you know."

"For real!" I groaned. "Why are you here, really?"

"I wanted to see what you were doing on your day off."

I had a thought. "You know, I might have a use for you yet." He raised his eyebrow at me, and I rolled my eyes. "I realized last night that I've never had a tour of the Compound. From the Captain's roof, I could see places I've never been before."

"Well, that's something we'll have to remedy, isn't it?"

🔥 🔥 🔥

Good to his word and backpack in tow, Ink gave me a tour around the Compound. It was a lot bigger than I had guessed, paths hiding behind trees or dipping beyond hills. Buildings bustling with life, even if they were deteriorating around the edges.

We paused at the greenhouse to pick apples and flowers, then made our way to the graveyard, which was so massive that I couldn't stop the tears from leaking down my face. I knew that the life expectancy for the Team was short, but the visual representation of *how* short . . . It put Ink's stance on relationships in perspective. He placed the flowers he'd picked on Robin's grave.

"C'mon, I have one more thing I want to show you."

He grabbed my hand and led me off the path through some of the dense trees. We reached a tiny clearing that hadn't been visible from the graveyard. It was just big enough for two rounded rocks on the edge of a little brook. Wildflowers were clustered where the light met the ground. It was another little reminder that the world could be a beautiful place.

Ink climbed onto one of the rocks, took off his boots and socks, and dipped his feet in the water.

I scrambled up the other rock and did the same thing, although my feet didn't reach the water. The trials and tribulations of being short. He handed me an apple and a purple daisy.

"For you."

"These are actually my favorite flowers."

The corner of his mouth curved up. "I know."

"Thank you."

The sun was out; the birds were chirping. I had a day off and could enjoy it without worrying about how to pay rent or when I was next going to eat. Even the hurt of Jay breaking up with me couldn't dampen this rare moment.

"This place is really awesome."

"Blu and I used to play here as kids."

"Calum and I used to play in the trees behind my backyard too."

"I wonder if other little Calums and Faras played in the woods in other universes." He took a bite of his apple.

"You're starting to sound like Sage."

"I'll take that as a compliment. But why am I starting to sound like him?"

"He's been after me to pay attention to all of the weird coincidences between our two worlds. He thinks there's some sort of Destiny-with-a-capital-D shit going on."

"Like . . . ?"

"Like how we both used to play in the trees with the other Calum/Inks when we were little."

"But that could really just be coincidence."

"True. But also how every person I'm close to in my world happens to be close to Blu here. Or how, when I'm dreaming in my world and open a portal, it actually shows what Blu is seeing. Or how Barrington's lair and the High Governor's mansion are the same building. Or how Blu and I were both . . . kissing . . . the same guy. Sort of. Although, that didn't last . . . but still." I explained what Sage had said about it.

He was quiet for a moment. I watched the water stream past, bubbling and happily full of the rain from earlier.

"Sage thinks that you are the fulcrum?"

"Or something. That it might be my *destiny* or something, not only to stop Barrington, Dagna, and the Counselor in these two worlds, but all of the Barringtons and Dagnas and Counselors in all the universes from doing their nefarious deeds."

"Do you think they are the bad guys in all of the universes?"

"I have no idea. I don't like the idea of destiny."

"Why not?"

I tossed my apple core in the same general direction Ink had. "I guess I'm just not a fan of believing that no matter what I choose to do, my fate is somehow tied to saving the universes. Don't I get to choose who I want to be, and what I want to do? What if I choose to ignore all of this and go live in a yurt in Patagonia?"

"Live in a . . . what?"

"A hut. In the wilderness."

"Ah. Do you want to do that?"

"No. But that's not the point."

"Obviously."

I sighed. "I guess I'm just unhappy with the idea that, even if I choose to live in the yurt, I will be dragged back into this mess because it's my destiny, or fate, or whatever. And the same thing applies to our current baddies. I mean, couldn't other universe Barrington decide that he was going to save the turtles or something, instead of being a first-class, warmongering prick?"

"I don't know. I mean, the other me that I've met is OK, I guess."

I reached over and punched him in the shoulder. "Hey! That's my brother you're talking about."

"Brother? Is that how you see us?"

"No, that's how I see him."

"Then how do you see me?"

"Currently? Like a giant pain in my ass."

"But normally?"

"Is there any normal with us?"

He snorted. "Probably not."

We were quiet, watching the birds flit between the trees and the sun dance on the ground. I had been thinking about what Sage had said for the past couple of days. How I didn't ask for these powers, and I didn't like the idea of being "chosen" by the universe. How I always thought Harry Potter got the crap end of the deal, and I'd much rather have been Luna, who ultimately had a choice in how she interacted with her world. How I knew I couldn't go back to the way it was, but I wanted the choice to do so.

"You know, the idea of this fate thing scares me." It came out quieter, smaller, than I intended.

"Why?"

"Well, if the fate of all universes rests with me . . . I can't even think about it. We're all screwed."

"Not at all." He looked genuinely surprised at my reaction.

"I'm not a warrior like you guys, Ink. I don't know the first thing about missions, or battles, or spies. I'm totally unprepared for this."

"That's why you have us, Fara. But really? You have something more important. You have heart."

"I'm not sure I'm brave enough to even take on the baddies I know about, much less the ones in worlds I know nothing about."

"You are. But if you decide to go universe-hopping to take on bad guys, I'll come with you." I looked up at him, expecting to see a smirk, but he was serious. "If you'd have me, I'd go with you. Anywhere. Anytime. To any universe."

BLU 40

"That's where my house used to be." Silver pointed to a burned-out wreck of a space between two houses as we drove slowly down the street. We were heading to meet Silver's contact in hopes of finding a motorcycle to practice on for the PITs. This neighborhood was poor but mostly still standing, thanks in part to the Mid-City gang. They might be thugs, but they protected their territory.

"It's weird," she continued. "I was worried about how I'd feel coming back here—that I might freak out. But I'm just pissed."

"That's actually good."

I parked my car on the street and looked around for cameras before I got out. Our meeting with the Mid-City gang was going to take place out in the open, which wasn't something I normally liked. But given my reputation—and Silver's growing one—it was understandable that their leader, Drift, wanted to be careful. Even if we were outnumbered, they'd have a hard time defeating us.

And we needed that bike.

"Remember the plan?"

"Yep."

We were both decked out in our armor, and we were carrying enough weapons for a two-person army.

"Styx?"

"Yeah." It was muffled.

"What are you eating? Wait a minute! Please don't tell me it's my chips and salsa."

"Then I won't."

"Styx!"

"Look, both you and Ink got chips and salsa. Jack and I didn't. It's only fair."

"Fine. Do you have eyes?"

"Yep! A group of angry-looking people in riding leathers are set to intercept you in about a minute."

"How many?"

"About a half dozen."

"Any cameras on this street?"

"You're clear."

"Any minions?"

"Not that I can see, but I'll keep an eye out."

"Thanks, my friend. And please leave me some of my birthday present."

"Can't promise that. Good luck and happy hunting."

Just like Styx said, a group of people, decked out in biking leathers and weapons, turned the corner, then stopped in the middle of the street in a V formation.

"That's Drift in the front," Silver muttered as we walked toward them.

Drift took off his helmet, which signaled the rest of his gang to do the same. The move looked practiced, like something they did to intimidate rival gangs. Unfortunately for them, I wasn't a rival gang and I didn't care about their coordinated helmet moves.

I took a moment to survey Drift. His white mohawk was slicked down, probably to accommodate the helmet. Tattoos adorned both shaved sides of his head. He was younger than I had expected, around my age. But his eyes assessed me, Silver, the street—everything—like a shrewd businessman. I could see why he was their leader. It didn't hurt that he was the best street racer in the entire territory.

"My, my, Silver. You look deadly."

Silver gave him a lethal grin. "And you look like you could use a haircut. How's the boyfriend? I always liked him better than you."

He snorted. "He ran off with some hussy. Typical. Well, here we are, like you asked. To what do we owe the pleasure?"

"We're here to negotiate," I said. "You have something we need."

He shrugged, the act nonchalant. "I have to be honest, I can't help but ask myself what could be so important that it brings Jurisdiction's most wanted person to our little street. You know we could buy ourselves new bikes just for turning you in, right?"

So we were going to play games before I had to kick his ass. "If that was how you were going to play it, you wouldn't risk being here personally, Drift. You'd let someone else do the dirty work."

"Maybe I just wanted to meet the infamous Blu."

"Well, now you've met me."

"I thought you'd be older."

"I thought you'd be smarter. Are the rumors that you're a clever businessman overestimated?"

"Hardly. Although I'm still not convinced that we want to make a deal with the Compound."

"You told Silver—"

"Of course I did. I wanted to see who the Compound would send and what you'd be willing to do to get what you want."

"That's brave of you."

"Not really. We hold all of the cards, Blu. As you already mentioned, we could call you in. We have something that you need. You're outnumbered and in our territory. Your piece of shit car can't outrun our bi— What the fuck?"

The handle of my thrown dagger had hit his hand hard enough that it forced him to drop his helmet. I let the deadly calm come into my eyes.

"Next time, I'll aim with the pointy end. I'm not here to banter, Drift, and I don't have time to deal with your adolescent games. Negotiate, or I'm leaving."

"I didn't think the Team threatened citizens."

"We don't. You're not citizens, you're thugs. I personally don't find your methods morally offensive, but then again, I don't give a shit. If it weren't for the fact that you have something I need, I'd slaughter the lot of you." That wasn't exactly true. Maybe sort of true? I was annoyed. "I need a bike. One like they use in the PITs. My guess is that you need a favor."

He shifted his weight. It was subtle, but enough that I knew we'd been right. He did need a favor, one that could only be taken care of by the Team.

"Why do you need a bike?"

"We have business relations with a new gang. I made a deal with them. This is part of the deal."

"What gang?"

"Doesn't matter. You'll probably be hearing about them later anyway. If you want in on the ground floor of this job, and to earn a favor from me, this is your chance."

Styx chirped in my ear. "Hey, B, half a dozen minions incoming. ETA five minutes or less."

"So, this has been fun and all, but we have company on the way."

His people, who had been standing still up to this moment, started to shift. They were afraid of minions, but Drift didn't so much as flinch. He'd known the minions would be coming. Interesting.

I shrugged. "Your loss. We're out of here."

I stalked right into his personal space. He wasn't that much bigger than I was, which was a nice change. He tensed but didn't move as I reached down to pull my dagger out of the ground. Then I forced myself to turn my back on them and head to the car.

"Wait." He walked toward me, hands up.

"You have exactly twenty seconds to get to the point."

"I don't like being strong-armed."

"Well, I don't like being ambushed and lied to. You have a spy in your gang, which is why you knew the minions would show. You set us up so I'd be forced to take care of your spy problem for you. I won't do it."

I began walking back to my car.

"Blu, please—"

"One bike for one favor. If you accept, let one of the vendors at the market know. They'll get the information back to me. My guess is that you'll need the favor sooner rather than later."

He was close enough that only Silver and I could hear him. "Will you take care of our spy problem?"

"Not today, but if I get a bike, then you might consider that to be your favor."

"What am I supposed to do about the minions?"

"I suggest running."

I turned on Jyston's comm as soon as we were in the car and out of sight. "You were right."

"Hello to you too. How was your day, dear?"

I couldn't help but laugh. "I got to threaten a bunch of young street thugs, which was fun. You?"

"Well, I'm currently standing in the bathroom of some arrogant elite's house, trying to find something with which to put myself out of my misery. The decorative soaps aren't that helpful."

"Probably not."

"Anyway, I'm right about a lot of things, Blu. To what are you referring this time?"

"Mid-City has a spy."

"Did you take care of it for them?"

"Not yet, although that's what they wanted."

"Well, my bloodthirsty girlfriend, please send the spy my way once you get the bike."

"I plan on it." From the corner of my eye, I could see Silver staring at me. "What?"

She was quiet for a moment, the rubble of the city slowly streaming by as we drove around potholes and debris. "Are you really going to let Jyston have Drift's spy?" I nodded. "Is he going to kill them?"

"No. He's going to help them."

FARA 41

Blu was leaning against her car as I shut Ink's car door. I didn't know if I'd ever truly get used to seeing myself in such a radically different way. She was decked out with enough weapons to look thoroughly intimidating. Her stance was completely casual, but like the rest of the Team, she had a coiled energy about her. Her purple hair hung loose on one side—as wavy and unmanageable as mine—but while it just made me look like I had escaped from an '80s music video, it fit her. How could someone who looked like me be such a badass?

"Where have you guys been?" she asked.

Ink smirked. "Nunya."

We'd been at the clearing. I had given Ink some colored pencils and a sketchpad that I'd picked up with Calum, and we'd headed there to enjoy the perfect weather for the rest of our day off. My intention was to read a book and eat chips and salsa while he sketched, but I fell asleep in the warmth of the sun. I woke up with my head in his lap. Neither of us mentioned it.

I sighed. "I wish I'd never taught him that. Anyway, what's up?"

"Something has come up . . . actually a couple of somethings have come up. Do you have time to chat? Ink, you should probably come too."

"I was going to insist."

In my apartment, I put the chips and salsa on the table for Blu and Ink, then sank into my bed. I was still a little hungover.

But by the look on Blu's face, I wasn't going to have the luxury of a second nap.

"Barrington left this on Calum's coffee table." Blu handed me a plain white envelope. "The general gist is that he has put the pieces of the puzzle together and realizes that he still needs you for the portal."

"How did you get this?"

"You opened a portal in your sleep while I was in here getting pain medicine. It sounds weirder than it was."

"Is it weird that I don't find that weird? Anyway, what do we need to do?"

"Well, for now we probably need to stop making random trips to your home world. Do you have everything you need?"

"I still need to get my paycheck from Douche, but other than that, I don't need to go back for a while."

"OK. When you do that, take someone with you."

Ink raised his hand. "I volunteer."

"Thought you might. Now that we have that horrible business out of the way, we have more horrible business. We're pretty sure that Drake's the spy." She told us about what she and Jack had seen. "Fara, I know he keeps asking you to dinner . . ."

"You think it's because he suspects something?"

"No, I think he thinks you're hot. But he also might suspect something."

"Then why don't we use that to our advantage?"

Ink stared at me. Blu grinned.

"What? I need to see him anyway to get more fireproof clothes. Maybe I'll accept his dinner invitation and see if I can find out anything. I mean, I suck at being a spy, but dinner shouldn't be too hard."

"That's not a bad idea. You're good at observing people," Blu said. "Jack has mentioned it more than once."

I blushed. "Thank you. So are you. Anyway, if I wasn't good at it, I would've starved. It's how I earned tips—knowing what a person needed before they did. That's what my old boss used to tell me, anyway. I just never thought it would translate to this sort of work. I'm still a horrible liar, though."

"You don't have to lie. Just have him talk about himself. Most men love that anyway."

Ink snorted but didn't disagree. "Are you sure you're OK with this, Fara? If he's the spy . . ."

"I'll be fine. It's just dinner. I don't plan on licking his face or anything."

"That makes me feel marginally better. When do you want to do this?"

"No time like the present, I suppose."

42 BLU

"Why is it," I said as I answered Jyston's comm, "that you always contact me the second I even think about getting ready for bed?"

He chuckled. "Luck, I suppose. Are you getting ready for bed?"

"No, but I was thinking about it."

"I was hoping you were free for a little adventure."

"What kind of adventure?"

"The kind that includes sneaking onto Dagna's property and snooping."

"Let me get my gear."

I parked the truck under the thickest clump of trees I could find and waited for Jyston. Because we were going to be sneaking around, I had minimal weapons, opting for daggers and a sword. I couldn't afford to clank when I walked. I had a palmbox and comm, but both were useless with the anti-tech that surrounded Dagna's building for at least a mile. The window of the truck was down, the sounds of the night filtering through the rain in puffs and bursts. I could hear the rumble of thunder in the distance and see far-off flashes of lightning here and there. I could smell dirt and leaves and . . . sandalwood.

"Jyston, while I appreciate your ability to sneak up on me, I'd prefer not to kill you by accident."

He emerged from the trees, his wet hair partially escaping the band holding it back at the nape of his neck.

His wet clothes clung to him, and a bit of dirt was smeared across his usually clean-shaven face. I hated to admit it, but he looked sexy.

"You might be the first person to figure out my ruse."

"I'm special like that."

"Yes, yes you are. I actually had to kill a minion on my way over here, so we might want to start our snooping."

"Are there any spikes of doom here?"

"That particular kind of nastiness only lines the main road. We should be fine in the forest."

Well, that was comforting. I rolled up the truck's windows and slid out onto the mud, my boots making squelching noises as I landed. The rain poured with a vengeance, lightning flashing across the sky. Although uncomfortable, it was ideal weather for spying.

Jyston began picking his way through trees on a path that only he could see.

"I'm glad you know where you're going."

His chuckle blended with the thunder that rolled above us. "We are headed back to the trail near the building. Unfortunately, Dagna has cut off all ways but this one."

"Why are we snooping tonight?"

"I thought you could use some up close and personal reconnaissance prior to dismantling the place."

"And . . . ?"

"I thought we could have an impromptu date."

"Jyston, really. Why tonight?"

"You really are all business, all of the time. Well, my beautiful Blu, Dagna has instructed her head of security, Nicolaus, to meet with someone tonight. I want to see who it is."

I didn't think he could hear me sigh over the noise of the incoming storm. "That's all you had to say."

He gave me a roguish grin. "What fun would that be? Plus, I want to see if the door is still unlocked."

"What door?"

"You'll see."

We broke through the trees and emerged on the trail the Team had been using for reconnaissance. This time, we were closer to the mass grave and gate.

"Where is Nicolaus supposed to be meeting this mysterious person?" I whispered.

"Under the awnings by the front door."

"Can we get close enough to hear?"

"Probably not. I just want to see who it is."

"Have ideas?"

"Lots of them, but not anything for this particular endeavor."

He silently made his way up the trail to the point where we were closest to the front of the building and still could remain unseen.

We squatted in the muck for what felt like forever, especially with the rain whipping itself into a frenzy, lashing across my face and making my hair swirl uncontrollably. Jyston reached over and tucked a dripping piece of hair behind my ear. His clothes were splattered with mud and blood. I had mud up to my shins, and god knows what debris stuck to me from crouching here.

"When we're done with this, I want a really hot bath."

"You know," he said, his mouth close to my ear, "the bathtub at my house is big enough for at least two people."

"Or to accommodate your armor?"

"Blu, I don't bathe in armor."

"That's not what I heard. Maybe I should check out your bath sometime."

"Tonight?"

"You know I can't go to your house."

"I know. But it's a pity. Someday soon."

A Jurisdiction town car pulled up the drive. The passenger door opened.

No way.

I felt Jyston shift next to me. "Well, that's interesting."

Gone were Warhorse's tattered clothes, replaced with standard-issue minion armor. What was he doing here? Well, that question was sort of superfluous. It was obvious he was on Dagna's payroll. But what was he up to? I wished I could hear the conversation. Too bad my tech didn't work.

Flanked by four other minions, Nicolaus walked out of the giant front doors of the building. Tall and broad, his dark hair was shaved close. Warhorse dipped his head to him, then handed over a roll of paper.

"Any ideas what that is?" I asked.

"Paper?"

Nicolaus unrolled whatever it was. Appeased, he nodded to one of the minions, who turned swiftly and went back inside. They appeared to continue their conversation, Nicolaus even smiling and chuckling at one point at something Warhorse said. It appeared that they had worked together before and could possibly be even allies. Interesting.

The minion returned, dragging a person by the elbow. It was the lady with the three sweaters from the first time I talked to Warhorse. She looked skeletal. The minion shoved the woman toward Warhorse. He dipped his head again, grabbed the woman by the elbow, and put her in the back seat of the car. He got in as well, and drove away.

"Well, at least we know that he's still a spy," Jyston said into my ear.

I snorted. "I wish I could find out what's on that paper."

"I'll see what I can do."

"What's next?"

"We're going to try to break in."

FARA 43

I was going to try to be a spy. I was also a terrible liar and hated the idea of being dishonest. So why had I offered to do this? That was the question I kept asking myself as I walked toward the armory.

Admittedly, Drake was hot, and I was single. And dinner was just dinner. And I really did need him to make me more fireproof clothes. How bad could it be? Other than the possibility that he could whisk me away to someplace dungeon-y? It might actually be pleasant. Sure. And the dark storm clouds on the horizon weren't a bad omen. Not at all.

I opened the giant wood doors to the armory just as the first raindrop dripped on my arm.

"Oh, hey Fara!"

Iris. Awesome.

"Hey, Iris. Drake around?"

"He's just in the back with some of the tailors. Want me to go get him for you? Or better yet, why don't I take you to him, and we can chat on the way."

"Oh, you don't—"

"I insist." She linked her arm through mine, and after initially being startled, I realized that I sort of felt bad for her. Maybe she was just lonely. Did she not have friends? I was still getting Froot Loop vibes from her, but maybe they were the "trying too hard" kind.

"How's Ink?"

Nope. They were still the "crazy ex-girlfriend" kind.

"He's good."

"Oh. That's good. Um . . . Do you know if he's dating anyone?"

"I try to stay out of his personal life."

"You do? I mean, you guys have been attached at the hip lately, so I thought—"

"We're just friends."

"Oh. OK. It seems weird though. He's always with you."

"He's usually kicking my ass in training."

"That sounds fun!"

"Sometimes."

"You know, if you ever want to do something, like get lunch, I'm game."

"I'll keep it in mind, I promise. The Captain just has me really busy right now."

"I thought you had today off?"

How did she know that? "I did, but I slept most of the day."

"With how much of my ale you drank last night, I don't blame you." Drake came out of one of the three doors we were standing in front of. He grabbed my hand and gave my knuckles a gentle kiss. "I'm sorry that I missed your party."

Iris's mouth formed a perfect pout. "You had a party?"

Drake caught my eye. "I was only invited because Styx thought, well . . . Let's just say, Styx owed me a favor. Otherwise, it was principal Team only, from what I understand."

I gave Drake what I hoped was a grateful smile. This girl might be on the crazy train, but she seemed sweet. I didn't want to hurt her feelings.

"It was for my birthday. I didn't plan it. I'm not good at crowds, so the Team kept it very small. Honestly, my head still hurts."

"Well, you're in luck, my lovely Fara. I just opened some more of my ale, which is the cure for all things. Come with me."

Drake put my hand in the crook of his arm and led me back through the armory. Iris passed us on our way, heading out the door without a glance at us.

"I feel bad for her. Does she have friends?"

Drake looked genuinely surprised. "I wouldn't worry too much about her, Fara. Although, that you do tells me something about you."

"What?"

"That you are kinder than your cousin."

"Not necessarily."

He gave me a look over his shoulder as I followed him around the corner.

"Welcome to my kitchen, such as it is." He was standing in front of a table that doubled as a kitchen counter, with shelving above and refrigerator off to the side. Drake started pouring ale into two mugs.

"You live here?"

"Yes. My bedroom is in the back of the armory, next to the tailoring annex."

Thunder rolled above us. Lightning flashed across the sky moments later; then rain started plinking on the windows. The storm wasn't here yet, but it was going to unleash itself soon. Either I had to leave now, or I was going to be stuck here for a while.

"So, Fara, I'm assuming it was not my delicious ale that brought you back. Was it my offer to take your mind off your current man troubles?"

"I'm actually here on business."

"Surely we can do both. Business and fun do not have to be mutually exclusive."

"True. Well, I came here to tell you that your armor is amazing."

"It worked?"

"It did! It was totally badass."

He rubbed his beard. "That is really good to know. It might be something that I incorporate into all of the new armor."

"I was hoping you could make me some more, but with modifications. And some boots."

"So, what modifications?"

"Well, before we get to that, I feel bad that I haven't paid you for the first set yet."

"That one was on the house. Like I said, I love a challenge." His light brown eyes sparkled golden in the light of the fire as he took a long draw of his ale.

"What about payment for the second?"

"How about I make you dinner tonight and you can tell me what it is you'd like? We can figure out payment later."

I knew what I'd like; I'd like to get my hormones in check. "That sounds really great. Thank you."

"I can't say that dinner will be much."

"It'll be amazing, whatever it is."

"Hungry?"

I was really doing this—I was really having dinner with a possible spy who just happened to look like the King of Gondor. "Can I help? It's the least I can do."

"No, but I'd love some company while I cook."

He put on an apron and threw a dishtowel over his shoulder, grabbing some ingredients out of his cabinets while he was at it. If I was going to be a spy, now was the time to do it.

"So, do you mind me asking you something?"

"Sure."

"Why do you live here in the armory instead of in the apartments or the dorms?" Was it because he needed to snoop?

"The apartments are reserved for Team members."

"As head armorer, I'm sure the Captain would make an exception."

"She has. But to be honest, I like the solitude. At night, I like to relax with a mug of ale and a book." He chuckled. "That sounds painfully boring, doesn't it?"

"No. It sounds perfect, actually." I took a drink of my ale. Something smelled really good. "What are we having?"

"If I knew I was going to have company, we'd be having something a bit more elegant. But you caught me on leftovers night." He raised the lid of a pot hanging in one of the fireplaces. "You're stuck with stew."

"Like . . . homemade stew?" Over a fire? Of course it was over a fire. Thoughts of slow blanket sex started creeping into my head. "That sounds perfect."

"Well, I'm glad that you aren't offended that our first date is leftovers."

"I've sworn off guys, remember? I'm not dating. Maybe not ever again."

His smile said that he didn't quite believe me. "The night is still young. So, Fara, it's my turn to ask some questions of the lovely lady who is currently in my kitchen, definitely *not* on a date."

"I'm not that interesting, Drake."

"Of course you are! Like I said, you've been the talk of the Compound since arriving here. Even more so than Ink's brother."

Ink's brother? Oh! He was talking about Calum. "I'm not very good at talking about myself. There's really not much worth telling."

"Well, I'll help. How did you end up at the Compound?"

That could be a normal question, or he could be doing a spy thing. What should I tell him? Why did he care? Was I being overly paranoid? I'd have to hug Jack the next time I saw him. This shit was *hard*. But I could do this. I stopped and *looked* at him, the way my old manager at The Grill trained me to do. He was relaxed, mixing ingredients in a bowl. He looked over his shoulder at me. His smile reached his eyes. But there was something else—something I was missing.

"My story is probably like most people's here. Some baddies thought I had information that I didn't, so they kidnapped me. I escaped and ended up here."

"How did you get away?"

"A friend sacrificed himself for me."

And there it was. It wasn't much, but his eyes darted to the door. Not once, but twice. He was distracted. Waiting for something—or someone. It might not be much, but my gut was telling me he was hiding something.

"I'm sorry to hear that, Fara."

He laid out some plates, bowls, and silverware on one of the workbenches, and served up some stew, flatbread, and a salad—the vegetables coming from the greenhouse. It was amazing, especially considering he'd cooked it all over a giant fire like a knight. Or a blacksmith.

We chatted in a way that was surprisingly comfortable. I told him what I wanted for my next armor and peppered him with questions about how he came up with new ideas and the process of making a weapon. I helped with dishes, and he showed me around the armory, explaining things as he did. I listened and tried to think of things to ask him. He poured me another cup of ale, which I was going to pretend to drink. The whole thing was actually very pleasant, as long as I didn't think of him being a backstabbing spy.

The storm finally decided to fully show up. The wind howled, and the thunder and lightning were almost simultaneous in their various displays. No sign of it clearing up anytime soon. But it was getting late. How long was this going to last? I missed my weather app.

Drake sat next to me on the couch, his arm casually slung across its back. The humidity of the storm made wild curls of the tendrils of hair around my face, or at least around the side that wasn't shaved.

Twirling a loose strand of my hair around his finger, Drake said, "You really are lovely."

"You really don't get out much."

"You don't believe me? You are, Fara."

In the dim light of the armory, mug of ale in hand and shirt unbuttoned to what I would now refer to as "Romance Novel Level," showing off his bronze skin and a tuft of brown chest hair, he made my hormones stand up and take notice. He would be a good time. A really good time. He was chivalrous and interesting. I was single. I could have a bit of fun, and it might do me good after all of the men crap I'd dealt with over the past year. The look he was giving me said that all I had to do was make the first move. But I couldn't. And it wasn't even that he might be a spy that stopped me from jumping on him. It wasn't that at all.

It was that he wasn't Ink.

That thought rocketed through me like the lightning that was throwing a fit outside. I couldn't think that. I shouldn't think that. That thought needed to go back under the mental rock it crawled out of. I'd make sure of it. I shoved it down as far as I could.

But I still wasn't going to sleep with Drake.

I moved my head to disentangle my hair from his more than capable hands, trying to look sorry about it.

"Drake, I shouldn't."

"Shouldn't? Or won't?"

I sighed. "Won't."

He looked genuinely surprised. "Can I ask why?"

"You are gorgeous and interesting, and in a different time in my life, I would have jumped at the chance to be with you.

But I literally just broke up with my boyfriend . . . and one right before that. I need some space."

"I'm not asking you to marry me, Fara."

"I know. But I'm not good at . . . just fun."

"Have you ever tried it? I'm pretty sure you would be. I know I am."

I laughed. He probably was, but that didn't change my mind. "Maybe someday, when I'm not dealing with monstrous amounts of man drama."

"I'll take a rain check then, as disappointed as I am. I have not given up hope, though."

"I should probably go."

Thunder shook the armory with a crash. The windows rattled and the wind raged.

"Fara, you can't go out in this. Stay here." When I opened my mouth to argue, he held up his hand. "Not like that. I understand and respect your decision. But this couch is very comfortable."

Should I risk staying here and accidentally opening a portal while I slept? Lightning hit so close that I jumped. I'd pretend to sleep and wait out the storm.

"Thank you, Drake. You really have been very kind to me."

"Fara, I can say this with all honesty: this has been really enjoyable. And even if you never decide to . . . Well, let's just say that even if you keep rebuffing my advances, I'd be honored to be your friend."

"Thank you."

He kissed my cheek, then headed in the direction of his bedroom. I pulled the blanket over myself and stared into the fire. The blanket smelled like him—woodsmoke and pine. I'd just stay here until the storm passed.

BLU 44

Jyston crept along the path, seemingly invisible in the chaos of the storm. I had trained for long enough that I could blend into my environment fairly well, but my talents paled in comparison. It was a first for me, one that I actually enjoyed. I'd risen through the ranks of the Team because I was better than most at kicking people's asses. And after my experience at the hands of Jurisdiction, I was determined to make sure I was the best. So, I trained as hard as I could. When I realized I had a talent for killing people, and sneaking around, and missions, I chalked it up to something that I was just born to do; that it was in my blood.

But after spending time with Fara, I wasn't so sure.

Would I have been more like her if the circumstances had been different? Maybe I had been, before Jurisdiction took me, but asking myself that now was useless. The real question was, did I *want* to be more like her? Now wasn't really the time to have an identity crisis. Even if a part of me wished that I laughed as easily as she did, or that my first reaction to someone in crisis wasn't to tell them to fucking get it together, I still had this mission to do. Once Jurisdiction had been taken down and I had the luxury of figuring out what I wanted to do with my life, I'd worry about that. And about Jyston's request that I go home with him. Now was definitely not the time.

Jyston threw a twig at the gate in the fence. It didn't fry, so he silently opened it, and we approached Dagna's building. He motioned that I should follow him, then ran crouched near the fence line toward the unmarked door I'd noticed earlier. I followed him exactly, not wanting to set off any random traps. We made it to the door, our backs pressed flat against the wall. Jyston grabbed the knob and turned. It opened. What the fuck? He slipped into the building, and I followed.

"Don't worry," he said once we were inside, "I have the cameras here on continuous loop. That was the only thing I was able to do before Dagna told the guards to keep me out of the control room."

"Don't you outrank her?"

"Technically, but the guards are loyal to her. They can't keep me out of the control room, but they report every time I'm in there. It has created quite the nuisance. However, since she is on the other continent, I have taken some liberties tonight."

"Won't they tell her when she gets back?"

"It's hard to have that conversation when you're dead."

"True. So, why are we here?"

"We're here to release some of the prisoners. Children. I thought that maybe you could bring them back to the Compound with you."

I hoped my grin was as feral as his was.

"However," he continued, "let's try not to burn the place down tonight—all right?"

"I can't promise anything."

"Fair enough."

We crept down the wide corridor and came to another door. Fluorescent lights buzzed overhead as we descended two flights of stairs, which ended in a gray metal door. It smelled like the infirmary down here—bleach and antiseptic. I didn't want to know why. I was sure the answer was something more nefarious than Jurisdiction's good cleaning practices. I also got a whiff of that cold, metallic smell that I associated with Jurisdiction.

Jyston listened at the door, then slowly opened it. I followed him down another hall lined with plain white doors. Each door had a tiny, barred window. The only sounds I could hear were the lights buzzing above me and muffled crying.

I stood on my tiptoes to look through one of the windows, but Jyston pulled me along with a sharp shake of his head. I hadn't seen much, but what I did see turned my stomach. Little kids were in these rooms. The sounds of screams and crying were coming from the kids. There were at least a dozen rooms in this hall alone, all filled with children.

I was going to kill everyone in Jurisdiction. Every fucking last one of them.

I promised myself right then and there that it didn't matter what I had to do—the PITs, or worse—I was going to save each one of these kids. Then burn the whole thing down.

Jyston jogged about halfway down the hall and stopped in front of one of the doors. He placed a palmbox against it, and it unlocked. What the hell? I thought technology was useless here. Or maybe it was just our regular tech that was useless. Now that I really looked, the palmbox did look different from others I had seen—it was bigger with some dials. It was also caked in blood. I'd ask Jyston about it later. He quietly opened the door, the two of us slipping in.

"Are you here to hurt us?"

A little boy, no more than eight years old, had put himself between us and the two even littler girls behind him.

Jyston crouched in front of him, hands out. "No, my fine man. We are here to bust you out of here. But we need to be quick and quiet about it. Can you do that?"

Another little boy was lying on the cold concrete in the corner. I bent down to wake him up. His skin was pallid, and he was stiff. He didn't have a pulse.

"He won't wake up," said one of the little girls. Her hair was a riotous mass of red curls that took up more space than she did. "We tried to wake him up, but he won't wake up. Can you wake him up?"

I subtly shook my head at Jyston, and his shoulders drooped. "No, sweetheart. He's not going to wake up anymore."

Her face scrunched up in an attempt to hold back her tears. The little boy turned around and gently grabbed her by the shoulders. "We're going to get out of here, Scarlett. So you can't cry yet. You have to get out first, and then you can cry."

She bit her lip, tears threatening to run down her face. But she nodded. "Sarah can't run fast. Her foot is hurt."

The other little girl was smaller and younger than even Scarlett. Her eyes, as big as dinner plates, surveyed the scene warily.

"Well, then it seems like Blu's going to need to give Sarah a piggyback ride. Scarlett, would you like one too?"

Scarlett looked at the boy for the answer. He turned back to Jyston. "You aren't going to hurt us? You promise?"

"What's your name?"

"Milo."

"Milo, I promise you that I will get you out of here safely, or die trying."

Milo sized him up, then gave him a curt nod. "All right."

"Milo, are you fast?" He nodded again. "I need you to keep up with us. Run as fast as you can. And if you see bad guys, you protect the girls while Blu and I take care of the bad guys. Can you do that for me?"

The little boy squared his shoulders as he prepared to protect these girls, the move making my heart break. I hated this. I hated Jurisdiction. I let the rage settle over me. It helped me focus.

I moved my sword scabbard so that it hung across my chest and bent down so that Sarah could hop up on my back. She barely weighed anything—just skin and bones and black hair that was in one remaining pigtail. Jyston scooped Scarlet up in his arms. She clung to his neck, her head buried in his shoulder. He looked out the door and whispered something in her ear, then nodded to me. We were off.

We had almost made it to the stairs when I heard shouting. "Fu—forks!"

Jyston smirked at me. "Yes, that. We need to make it up those stairs before they block our exit."

We sprinted to the door, Jyston ushering Milo, Sarah, and me through. I ran up the stairs as fast as I could without dropping the kid. Milo looked freaked out but determined as he climbed the stairs as quickly as his short legs would take him. We reached the top of the stairs, and he shoved through the door, only to be met with a wall of minions. Shit.

The minion closest to us spoke. "Second Counselor, what are you doing here?"

Jyston set Scarlett down by the door, and Milo stood in front of her. I set Sarah down too. Jyston took a step forward, putting himself between the minions and the kids. Then, he transformed right before my eyes. His eyes lost their humor. He pulled himself up to his full height and stood preternaturally still, cocking his head and appraising the minion like the guy might be dinner. It was his Second Counselor persona. It was chilling, and absolutely one of the coolest things to witness.

"I'm not sure why you are here, but your services are not necessary."

"Dagna's standing orders. If you are ever to be at this building, we are to escort you to her immediately."

"It's a pity you think that she outranks me."

"I don't, sir."

"Then let us through."

"I can't do that. That woman is Blu from the Compound. Our orders are to take her alive as well."

"Maybe I'm taking her in myself. Have you contacted Dagna?"

"She's not responding."

"Probably not. She's at the other continent right now. So, it appears that you can let us go and leave me to deal with these rebels myself."

"Then we will take you to the Counselor, and Blu to a holding cell."

"The Counselor is not here either. I am demanding one last time that you let us through."

"We can't do that."

"That's too bad. For you, actually."

Jyston drew his sword with a flourish and turned to me. "You know, I've always wanted to fight alongside you. I've heard rumors that you might even be able to beat me."

I grinned at him as I drew my sword. "It's possible, although swords really aren't my thing. I might beat you in hand-to-hand combat, though. I like that better. Or daggers."

"My bloodthirsty girlfriend. Leave none alive."

"I wasn't planning on it."

The two of us launched ourselves at the minions, Jyston taking out the first two without so much as slowing down.

"Show-off." I parried a guy who was trying his hardest to incapacitate me. Luckily for me, he wanted me alive for the reward money, and unluckily for him, I wanted him dead. I spun out of the way of his sword, plunging my own into his chest. The minion's new armor might have deflected my dagger, but it was no match for one of Drake's swords.

"Of course I'm showing off, Blu. It's what men do to impress women."

I snorted as I ducked under the sweeping blow of another minion. "No need for that. Just kill these fuckers quickly, please. I'm wet, dirty, and now bloody. I want a bath." The minion fell at my feet.

"As you wish." With that, he stabbed the minion behind him in the heart without a glance, then released his sword, and before the minion in front of him even registered what was happening, Jyston had stabbed him in the stomach. He moved with grace and power and seemingly little effort; it was the most impressive swordplay I had ever seen. It was like a dance. I needed to step up my game.

"Stop right there!" The minion in front of me was pointing his sword at me. I rolled my eyes and advanced on him.

"For real, you guys need to find something new to say. That never works." I saw fear register in his eyes as I went on the offensive. Soon, I found my mark and he stopped breathing. Permanently.

My arm was getting tired, and I had a gash on it. It was nothing deadly, but it hurt. At least it wasn't the same arm as the last time I got stiches. It reminded me that I needed to train with swords more. And probably wear my armor more. "Jyston, when this is all over, I want to challenge you to a duel."

He slashed a minion in the stomach and stepped over his body. "I think that is a lovely idea."

He turned to take on the last minion. I took out my dagger, flipped it in my hand, then threw it. It landed in the minion's eye socket before Jyston could land the final blow. He looked over to me, eyebrow raised.

"What's the prize?"

"I'll have to think about it."

45 FARA

Shit, shit, shit. The first light of dawn was coming through the windows of the armory. I had slept here all night.

Shit.

Had I opened a portal while I slept? Did I give myself away last night? How could I have been so careless? I sat up and grabbed my boots, quietly making my way to the door. I couldn't hear any movement from the direction of Drake's bedroom, so I slid through into the early morning air.

Shit.

The sun was peeking over the horizon as I hurried toward my apartment. My socks were snagging on the broken bricks. It would take too much time to put on my boots. Training would start any minute, and I didn't want to get caught out here doing the walk of shame. Even though nothing had happened. Even if it had, it wouldn't be anyone's business. But I didn't want to deal with it.

Which was too damn bad for me.

Ink's face was unreadable as he held the door to the apartment building open for me. "Late night? Certainly looks like you had fun."

"Ink, I—"

"Doesn't matter." He turned and stalked away. What the fuck?

Blu gave me a once-over while she closed her apartment door down the hall, taking in the total look of my hair, boots— all of it.

"Yeah. I'm a fucking mess."

"No, you're a beautiful disaster."

"It's not what it looks like. I fell asleep on his couch."

"It's none of my business, Fara."

"Tell that to Ink."

She rolled her eyes. "He's a pain in the ass. Just remember, if he gets too annoying, clock him in the jaw during training today. That usually knocks sense into him."

"I'll keep that in mind."

"Did you find out anything?"

"Nothing concrete. Just a feeling."

"Your feelings are better than most, so we'll talk about it at the Team meeting." She paused, her face softening a bit. She had a new and fairly nasty gash on her arm, complete with stitches. What happened?

"Fara, I know I'm not good at talking about feelings—or really, experiencing feelings. I ignore them, mostly."

"So do I. Mostly. Can't afford to electrocute someone for taking the last cheeseburger."

She snorted. "Right. But I know that the meeting today might suck more than normal for you. So if you want me to bash in Agent Hanlon's face, I'd be happy to do it."

I smiled. "No, thank you. But I appreciate it."

"Also, mind opening a portal to get Jyston here for the meeting?"

"He's coming?" I was actually interested to see how the two Jystons would get along. I could use some entertainment.

◊ ◊ ◊

It was hand-to-hand combat training today. Ink was distant as he barked orders and ran me through drills. He wasn't quite glaring at me, but he was obviously upset about what he assumed had happened between me and Drake. The longer we trained, the more he glowered, and the more pissed off I got. The double standard of it all! Even if he hated Drake, he had no right to be mad at me for doing something that was none of his business—or that he did with a myriad of girls during the week. Especially since I hadn't actually done anything.

He corrected my form with a grunt as we worked on punches and kicks. "Have fun with Drake last night?" He didn't even look up when he said it.

"I did."

"Did you forget why you went there?"

"No. But Drake reminded me that I could have fun and do my job at the same time. I'm good at multitasking."

I could feel the anger rising off him as we continued sparring. I was nowhere near where the rest of the Team were in terms of technique and speed, but I was getting the hang of it. Ink actually had to work to block me some of the time, which was satisfying. He opened and closed his mouth multiple times as he dodged my punches and kicks, like he was figuring out what he wanted to say to me next. I let him stew. I was pissed at him. Not a burn-down-the-world level of rage, but angry enough I had to shut down a portal before it started.

Finally, he stopped. The glare he was giving me fueled my anger. "Fara, I can't believe you did that! You shouldn't be with him like that. It's not safe for you—"

I hauled off and hit him in the jaw. I could not believe he just said that! I shut down another portal.

"What the . . . ?"

I stood on my tiptoes to get in his face. "That is what *every* person has said to me my *entire* life," I whisper-yelled. "Keep your emotions in check, Fara. Don't get angry, Fara. Don't train, Fara. Don't go on that mission, Fara. Because it's *not safe*. Except you. And now? Ugh!"

"Fara—"

"No! You don't get to explain away your idiocy to me! Not yet. And don't get me started on your double standards! I share a wall with you, remember? I can fucking hear them! And I never say a word. They could all be spies, for all I know, but I keep my mouth shut. I even have crazy Looney Tunes Iris stalking me because she wants you back! And once again, I never say anything. Because it's none of my fucking business. None! But here you are, throwing a fucking tantrum just because you think I slept with someone you don't approve of? That's bullshit! If you'd have stopped being an asshole for a second and listened, I would have told you that nothing happened with Drake. I slept on his couch because of the storm. But you didn't. I thought you were different, but you're just like everybody else."

I could feel the tears start, so I turned on my heel and left.

"Fara, wait."

But I didn't. I jogged back to my apartment, hoping I could get my shit together before the Team meeting. Before I had to deal with Jay. This day was starting to royally suck.

◊ ◊ ◊

Blu walked into my apartment, shutting the door in Ink's face when he tried to follow her in.

"No boys allowed."

I wiped my eyes with the back of my hand. She handed me a donut and some coffee. "Thought you could use some sugary goodness."

"Thank you."

"Don't worry about Ink. He'll pull his head out of his ass in a bit."

I shrugged. I knew my reaction was out of proportion to what he had done. And I knew why. I just didn't want to admit it to myself.

"You know, when the thing with Jyston started, Ink freaked out. But he came around to it."

"I don't even know why I'm so mad about it."

"I do. I know why he's mad too. But that's for you guys to fight about." She awkwardly patted my arm.

"It's just that most of the people in my life have made decisions for me so that I'd be *safe*. You guys have been different. But then he went and fucked that up."

"He didn't mean any of it. Not really. But I'll let him explain that. Anyway, you know what I've been thinking about?" I shook my head. She was smiling a real smile, although it was a little sad. "Everyone tells you to be safe, and I have the exact opposite problem. It's like, don't go killing anyone today, Blu. Don't burn down the building, Blu. Which is annoying. I really am not that impulsive. Or murderous. We're like two sides of the same coin."

I hadn't really thought of that. I saw her as this purple-haired badass who could take care of herself and didn't give a shit. But we were both more complicated than people allowed us to be. It probably bothered her as much as the safety thing bothered me.

"I could probably stand to be a bit more murderous."

"Well, punching Ink was a good start. How's the hand?"

"Hurts."

"Ice it—it'll feel better. But seriously, don't worry about him. And don't worry about Jay today."

"I'll try. I just . . ." I didn't know what I wanted. To get back together with him? To wish it had worked out? Neither of those felt right, but I was still sad.

BLU 46

How Fara had figured out how to use the OG palmbox so quickly was impressive to me. She landed us in Jyston's living room without a hitch.

I was also impressed by Jyston's house. Not because it was huge, but because it wasn't. It was out in the woods in the middle of nowhere. It wasn't even really a house; it was a cabin with log walls and plank floors. It only had two rooms: a living room/kitchen area with a bed in the corner, and what I was assuming was the bathroom, although I had no idea how he'd get running water out here. The space didn't seem fitting for the Second Counselor of Jurisdiction. Most of their leaders had huge houses in the city center.

"This is my secret hideout," Jyston said.

"Your lair?"

He chuckled. "Something like that. You two are the only people who know I have it. Other than me, of course. My other house is in the city center, and it's suitably ostentatious. I hate it. I found this place abandoned and renovated it. It gave me something to do other than be the leader of the shitheads, as Blu calls me. The only problem is that the bathtub here isn't as big as my other one." He raised an eyebrow at me, and I rolled my eyes. "How are the children?"

"Safe. Traumatized. Getting treatment and resting in the infirmary. Sage is having a hard time getting them to talk, but he's the best at it. It just takes time. I understand that."

Jyston moved closer to me. "I know you do. Well, unfortunately the Counselor and Dagna are returning soon, and so, my time is limited. I'm curious as to why I've been summoned to this meeting."

"Mostly so the Captain can ream your ass for bringing me along with you last night. Don't worry—she's already reamed mine."

"I will look appropriately contrite. Anything else?"

"You'll just have to see."

◊ ◊ ◊

Fara dropped us off in the Captain's office, then left to get Agent Hanlon. Ink tried to talk to her before she left, but she brushed him off. She was truly pissed. He deserved it.

She arrived moments later with the agent in tow. His eyes widened when he saw Jyston; then his face turned unreadable. He stuck out his hand. "I'm assuming you're the Second Counselor. Nice to meet you."

"It's just Jyston, but you know that. I would say that it was a pleasure to meet you, but then that sounds more egotistical than I mean. I will say that I need to give more credit to these folks for handling interacting with their doubles on a regular basis. It is quite bizarre."

I grinned. "You'll get used to it."

"All right," the Captain said after everyone got coffee. Ink had pilfered a couple of boxes of donuts from the mess. It was probably some attempt to apologize to Fara without apologizing to Fara.

"We have a full agenda today. The PITs are in a couple of weeks. Around the same time, Barrington plans on announcing his candidacy for presidency in Fara's world. Jyston has indicated that Dagna is ramping up the atrocities in her building. Plus, there's Barrington's note—"

"What note?"

The Captain handed the agent the note and continued as he read it. "The note that indicates that he understands Fara's abilities—at least, to a certain extent.

"As you've noticed, we have a couple of guests here for this meeting. Thank you both for joining us, Agent Hanlon and Jyston. I know that it's not ideal to have to sneak away like you do, but we could really use your help."

Jyston nodded his head. "It's my—our pleasure."

"I must ask," the Captain continued. "Next time, I'd like a bit of a heads-up before any night raids?" She gave Jyston a look that was equal parts chastisement and humor.

He dipped his head, looking contrite, or at least as contrite as he ever could look. "Understood. I find that, being in this position for as long as I have, I've lost some of my manners. I'll ask next time."

"No need. Blu can decide on her own, as long as she remembers our protocols as well."

"Hey! I told people where I was going last night."

Styx snorted. "You left a note taped to my forehead. I was sleeping. I'm not sure that counts."

"In any event," the Captain said, "I'm interested in why you rescued these specific children."

"And," Ink interjected, "if you could rescue these three, why can't we do the same thing for the rest?"

"Unfortunately," Jyston answered, "the children that Blu saw in the building are only a part of the group that are being held prisoner there. Most of the prisoners—adults and children—are held in a series of rooms at the other end of the building. If we tried to rescue them the same way, they would be slaughtered before we could get them out."

"Why are the prisoners separated like that?" I asked.

"The children we saw are the ones Dagna has decided to test new programs on. The three we rescued were next on the list. I heard some guards gossiping about a little boy who had hit Dagna to protect some of the other kids. I knew it would be ugly for him when she got back."

"So, we'll need to take their separate locations into account when we go in," Ink said.

"Yes. You will need at least two tactical teams to rescue the prisoners."

The Captain steepled her fingers. "Jyston, how many prisoners are there?"

"It's hard to tell. My best guess is that at any given point, there are between fifty and seventy-five prisoners."

That many? I knew Dagna was collecting prisoners, but I had no idea how many were there.

Jack's shoulders slumped. "Even if Blu and Silver don't die in the PITs, and we find a way to get into the building, and we can actually manage to get to the two separate places where the prisoners are held, and get them out without being slaughtered, we have no mode of transportation. We have nothing that can get that large of a group—even broken into small groups—out of there."

"We do." Fara looked up and met Jack's eyes.

"Fara, what do you mean?" the Captain asked.

"I can portal them out of the building. I'd need to work on getting my portals big enough so that more than one person at a time can go through. But if you can get into the place where the prisoners are held, I can get them out."

Jack looked at her. "That's suicide."

"It's not. At least it puts me at no more risk than the rest of you. We have to destroy that building, and we can't do it if the prisoners are in there. We have to get them out. I can do that."

The agent was staring at her. "Fara, these people are the experts. It will be dangerous. I don't think you should—"

"Jay, don't."

"It's just that—"

"I'm trying to hel—"

"I don't think—"

I felt the air in the room charge, like right before a storm, the hairs on my arms standing up. Lightning flashed behind Fara's eyes.

"I said, *don't*. This isn't even your mission, *Agent Hanlon*. That's up for the Captain to decide."

The room was suspended in a weighted silence. It was the first time most of us had seen Fara use her powers, and she did it to shut the agent up. I was so fucking proud. From Ink's expression, he was enjoying the show. He wasn't even trying to suppress his grin, even while Fara's glare alternated between him and the agent. It was Silver who finally spoke.

"If you can portal us out, do you think you could portal us in and we could avoid the PITs entirely?" Silver asked.

Jyston answered, "Unfortunately, that won't work. The anti-tech makes portaling in impossible. Or at least it blocks portals that are created with the . . . OG . . . palmbox. It was an unintended side effect of the anti-tech technology. That's why Dagna opens portals at headquarters. It won't work at her building, either in or out."

"But my abilities would still work there?"

"We'll just have to test it out, won't we?"

◊ ◊ ◊

Fara and Jyston were talking quietly as she opened a portal to usher him back to his lair. The rest of the meeting, with everyone updating everyone about everything, took so long that I drank at least a pot of coffee all on my own. Agent Hanlon gave us an update on Willow: she was going through some sort of treatment but was starting to feel better. But when Jack asked when she'd be ready to come back to the

Compound, he gave a noncommittal answer. I wasn't the only one who noticed.

After what felt like an eternity, the Captain released us.

"Fara, mind opening a portal back for Agent Hanlon?"

"I can do that. I also need to pick up my paycheck from my old job. Should I just do it now?"

"As long as you take someone with you."

"I can go," Ink said.

"Actually," the agent said, "I have to go that way anyway. I can take her."

Fara studied her hands, her face unreadable. "That's fine. I'm ready when you are."

"Say hi to Hewitt for me." I grinned at her. "And don't go burning the place down."

She smiled back, although it seemed halfhearted. "I can't promise anything."

FARA 47

Willow was tucked into Jay's couch, wrapped in a cocoon of blankets and pillows. Her face was pale; her smile was warm.

"Hey, Willow. How are you feeling?"

"Recovering, thanks! I had something called out-patient surgery, which is supposed to help with the pain in my stomach. I don't understand it all, but the doctor and Jay said that it'll help. I'm pretty useless until I heal."

"I'm hopeful it'll help."

"With Jay taking such good care of me, I'm sure I'll heal right up."

I gave her what I hoped was a kind smile, trying not to say anything, because everything that came to mind was pretty shitty. I didn't want to be that girl. Willow was sweet. A bit clueless about how awkward this conversation was for me, but sweet.

As I stepped out into the hallway, my heart ached for what could have been. I knew that it was going to take time to get over Jay breaking up with me, but I was still caught off guard by how much it hurt. My heart ached for the way Jay had gotten Willow a glass of water because he knew she needed it before she asked. My heart ached because that could have been me.

But everything has a cost.

And the cost of choosing the fire and lightning was that Jay and I couldn't be together. I was alone, and with everything that was me, I would more than likely continue to be alone. And I needed to figure out how to be OK with that. But it still hurt.

Jay made his way out of his apartment. Without a word, he opened my car door and I slid in.

"Fara . . ."

"What?"

He kept his eyes steadfastly on the road as he merged onto it. Eventually I gave up waiting for him to say something and watched out the window. He turned onto a main road, the cars of the city rushing by. This didn't feel like home anymore. I felt like an outsider in my own world.

Eventually, we pulled into The Grill's parking lot. I wanted to get all of this over with. I could feel my anger building again and shut it down. No use setting fire to Jay's car.

"Fara, wait." I waited. "I don't want us to be like this."

"Like what?"

"I understand that you're mad at me, but the way you're looking at me is . . . not like you."

"It is like me, Jay."

"You just . . . please. I hate seeing you like this."

"You broke up with me, remember? So excuse me if I don't trip all over myself to make sure that you're comfortable."

"That's not what I mean."

"I know. But it's what you expect of me. It's what everyone has always expected of me. I'm not trying to be rude or make you feel bad. I'm just trying to get through this."

"I miss—"

"If you say you miss me, I'm going to open a portal straight into Dr. Novak's office and leave you there."

"But I do."

I threw my arms up in frustration. "You had every opportunity to hang out with me and chose not to! I texted and called and begged, but you always said that it wasn't safe for me and acted like I was a nutcase for even asking!"

"It wasn't safe! It still isn't. I was trying to protect you. I couldn't let something happen to you."

"But *now* it's OK? Now that we aren't in a relationship? You don't get to make those decisions for me, Jay! What's safe and what's not. Where I go and where I don't. You can make them for you—and you did—and now I'm trying to come to terms with them. My choice to stay at the Compound and train in my abilities might have started all of this, but I tried to make it work. So don't tell me you miss me. Because that is on you."

"I know I'm not being fair. It's just . . . I hope that someday we might be friends."

I shrugged. "I like you. I like spending time with you. But I can't now. Not until the wound isn't so raw. Seeing Willow there . . ." I fought to calm my nerves as I felt a portal opening and shut it down. "Seeing her there is fucking *hard*. It sucks. It will continue to suck. Knowing that it could have been me. So for now, you're just going to have to deal with me like this."

His cool gray eyes searched my face. They were sad. I wasn't trying to make him sad. But it wasn't my job to make sure *he* was all right—it was my job to make sure *I* was.

"Now, can we go in there so I can get my paycheck? Then, if you wouldn't mind, I need to use your bank to cash it. I don't have a bank account anymore."

"Why did you close your account?"

"Because I'm not coming back to this world. Maybe ever."

◊ ◊ ◊

I stood in the lobby of The Grill, taking in its sights and sounds and smells, hopefully for the last time. The smells of things frying, the sounds of customers talking and dishes clanking. The dread that crept into my stomach at the thought of Hewitt. Yep. I wasn't going to miss this place at all.

We made our way toward the dining room. Carrie backed up a pace when she saw me, a terrified look on her face. Blu must have said something to her that wasn't along the lines of inviting her to lunch. Good. I wasn't in the mood for her today—not that I ever was.

"Agent Hanlon, I'll just be a moment. Good luck with her." I pointed to Carrie with my chin. "She's a treat." He was a big boy and could handle himself.

I headed through the dining room, hoping to see Douche. I didn't. Unfortunately, and for the first time in my life, I had to willingly go find him. I'd start by looking in the backroom. It was close to shift end, and that's where he could cause the most irritation to the staff.

I rounded the corner to the backroom, but instead of Douche, I found Hewitt. He had some poor girl pinned against the wall, and from the looks of it, he was trying to stick his tongue down her throat as he groped her.

I was well and truly going to kick his ass.

I didn't stop. I didn't think. I stalked up to him, grabbed him by the back of his shirt, and yanked him off the girl. She looked up, startled, and I motioned for her to get out of the room. But she didn't budge. She was rooted in place. I understood; I had been her, once.

"I've got this. Seriously. I don't want any witnesses for what I'm about to do to him."

After a moment's hesitation, she left.

The look of surprise on Hewitt's face turned into a sneer as he looked down at me.

"What are you going to do to me? I know exactly what I am going to do to you."

I pulled up every ounce of emotion that I had been bottling up for years. I let the rage and fear and helplessness and hopelessness and sadness and determination and *everything* flow through me, channeling all of it into a roundhouse kick right to his nuts. Maybe that would teach him to keep it in his pants, and his hands to himself. He doubled over, but I wasn't done. I grabbed him and pushed him up against the wall with my arm, pushing all of my weight across his neck.

"You bitch!" he gasped.

I pitched my voice to almost a whisper, letting Blu's deadly calm come to my eyes. Maybe it was becoming my deadly calm too; I really did want to make him pay for his horribleness in very painful ways.

"Don't you *ever* touch anyone without their consent. *Ever.* Do you understand?"

"I'm going to make you regret—"

"Not today, asshole." I lit my birthday candle and let my skin singe his neck.

"What the fuck?" He began to struggle harder, but I had been training with Ink, who was bigger, stronger, and deadlier than this bully would ever be. He wasn't going anywhere.

I whispered into his ear, "I'm not afraid of you, Hewitt. I'm angry. You have no excuse for being such a fucking worthless human being. I ought to just kill you." I met his eyes, letting the truth of my words sink in, realizing that I could. I, for one, wouldn't mourn him.

"Let go of me, you crazy bitch!"

"I don't think I will."

I felt blisters rise on his neck, so I turned down my birthday candle. It would still be hot on his skin, but it wouldn't burn him alive. Not yet. Now what? Unfortunately, I still needed to find Douche.

I headed toward Douche's office, dragging Hewitt along. Blu had taught me the hold I was using specifically for these types of situations, which, in retrospect, was weirdly prophetic.

"For years, Hewitt, *years* I have put up with your bullshit. How many others have had to deal with you? But not anymore. As of today, you are officially done being a predator." He struggled, but I held on tighter. "We're going to have a little chat with Douche. And if he doesn't do something to stop you, I will. Permanently."

"How will you manage that?"

"You can't assault anyone if you're dead."

"You wouldn't."

I got right into his face, letting the lightning cross my eyes, the air around us charged. "I could kill you and not shed a tear." His face showed fear for the first time. Good.

"Who the fuck are you?"

"I'm Fara Bayne."

The electricity in the air amplified. The lights flickered and the air stilled. Something was happening, something significant. Like those words were important—like they turned on some sort of invisible switch in me.

Like I had claimed my name, my place, in the universe.

I was Fara Bayne: daughter, friend, and now defender of those who couldn't defend themselves. I was scared and learning and clueless and a mess and complicated. But I was me, and I wasn't afraid of this shithead anymore. I was going to do whatever it took to make sure people like Hewitt and Barrington and Douche and Dagna and the Counselor stopped preying on people. I could be kind and sweet, and still burn them to the ground. I could do all of it. I just had to stop listening to people who said I couldn't and start listening to myself.

Douche stood from behind his desk, taking in the scene, and the slightly charred Hewitt I'd brought with me. Before he could open his big mouth, I cut him off.

"We have two matters to attend to. First, I need my paycheck. Now."

"I don't—"

I let the lightning cross my eyes again. "Now." He blanched.

I pulled out my phone. Jay answered on the first ring. "Agent Hanlon, can you please come back to Douche's office?" I hung up without waiting for a reply.

"While we're waiting for you to be arrested for paycheck fraud, I'm also going to have a little chat about this piece of shit—actually, all of the pieces of shit you let work here and harass people."

Hewitt had stopped struggling, but I didn't take that as a sign he'd given up. I saw it out of the corner of my eye just before he tried to launch himself at me. I took his legs out from under him with a sweeping kick, then pinned him to the ground, face first. I ignited for good measure.

"Hewitt, I am actually looking for a reason to kill you today, so it might make sense for you to stop being an asshole." The skin on his arm started to blister as his shirt smoldered, and I eased up, reluctantly. "It'll do you some good to know what it felt like to be totally helpless while you groped me and assaulted me and made my life, which was already hard, a living hell. But no more."

Douche was watching me warily.

"I found Hewitt sexually assaulting one of the new waitresses in the backroom, just like he's done to me and countless others. I also know that she won't press charges because she doesn't want to lose her job, mostly because you're an asshole. That's why I didn't call the police every time this weasel put his hands on me. But that behavior is going to stop, right now."

Jay walked in, his face unreadable. I stood up and yanked Hewitt off the ground, shoving him toward the agent. "Hi. Can you hold this for me?"

To his credit, he didn't question me. He grabbed Hewitt, who once again looked like a blade of grass next to the giant wall that was Jay Hanlon.

"This is Agent Hanlon from the federal government. He's going to help me monitor this restaurant to make sure that pieces of trash like Hewitt don't harass the waitresses anymore. He's also going to make sure that Hewitt is fired by the end of today. And if *one* person loses their job for complaining about being harassed by the remaining shitheads, then we will make sure that you pay."

"How do you plan on doing that?" Douche asked.

"I have already been a witness to multiple cases of felony sexual harassment involving this employee," Jay said. "My testimony alone can get both you and this little shit arrested. All it takes is one more of your employees to harass someone, and I'll contact the authorities to launch an investigation."

Douche looked like he was about to argue, but I held my hand up to stop him.

"And if that's not enough to scare you, then I have something extra special planned *just for you.*" I turned on my fire crown, another cool trick. "If things don't change around here, I'll turn the whole fucking place into a smoldering crater. You included. Do I make myself clear?"

BLU 48

"Ready to go?"

Ink was putting the training gear away in the shed. I had watched from the other side of the Quad while he worked with some of the Team on sword combat. His swords flashed with unnatural speed as he twisted and turned, showing the young Team members various techniques. I had to admit, for all of his pain-in-the-ass antics, he was better than anyone at training people. And his swordplay was equal to Jyston's, which was otherworldly—literally. Ink had chosen to wield two swords at a time, and while I could if I had to, I was nowhere near that level of skill. One was about all I could handle, as evidenced by my matching gashes and aching muscles.

He looked at me over his shoulder. "Where are we going again?"

"To intimidate a gang and borrow a bike."

"Oh, that. I'm assuming I need all my gear?"

"I'd appreciate it if you looked as scary as possible."

"Not possible with this face. Why isn't Silver going with you?"

"Why so concerned?"

"Because I'm afraid you're making me go so you can get me alone and berate me for being a first-rate asshole this morning." He closed the shed and brushed himself off. "If that's the case, then you don't need to bother."

"It's none of my business, Ink. But if you want to talk about it, I'd listen."

"No, you'd tell me to get over myself and apologize to Fara."

I snorted. "That too, but that's not why I asked. Silver has a personal connection with these thugs. I want to keep it that way. Drift can't blame her if we rough them up, and she can continue to use him as a contact."

"All right, then. You can go be scary. I'll be eye candy."

◊ ◊ ◊

Ink parked in the same place I had last time. We scanned the area.

"Dev, do you have eyes?" I asked.

"Six people about to intercept you in less than a minute."

"Bikers or minions?"

"Bikers, I think."

I sighed. It was easy to forget sometimes that Dev was new to all of this. "Are they wearing helmets?"

"No. The main guy has a white mohawk."

"Bikers. OK, thanks. Can you keep an eye out for minions?"

"Will do."

Ink sized up Drift and his gang as they came into view. "So, what's the plan?"

"We wing it, it goes to shit, and we run for our lives? Hopefully get a bike."

"Sounds about right." We got out of the car.

"I'm flattered, Blu," Drift said as they made their way toward us. "You must take me seriously, if you brought the infamous Ink with you."

Ink smirked. "Nah. I just didn't have anything better to do than run errands with Blu today."

Drift didn't even flinch, a similar smirk playing across his face. "I'm sure there's a member or two of my gang who wouldn't mind meeting you. Maybe even me."

"Happy to oblige." He winked.

"Before this turns into a singles' mingle," I said, "I happened to notice that there is a stunning lack of motorcycle here. The message I received was that you had one for me to pick up right now."

"Yes, but we have to take you to it. And if you're going to ride, you at least need to call it the right thing. It's a powerbike, not a motorcycle."

"Whatever. And why do you need to take us to it?"

"Because contrary to what you might think, we're in the business of making money. I can't do that if the fine citizens of this street believe that I'm dealing with the Compound."

"They'll think you've gone soft?"

He turned and started back the way he came. "They'll think I've sold out."

Ink snorted. "And you have a reputation to uphold?"

"You're not the only one people talk about . . . although I can see why they do." Drift winked at Ink over his shoulder.

"Drift, please don't feed his ego. It has a hard enough time fitting into the car as it is."

We followed him down the street, my eyes scanning for minions. There shouldn't be any, if reports of the last foray were accurate. After we'd left our last meeting, the gang scattered. The minions spent hours banging on doors, looking for me and Silver. Even if the spy had wanted to turn me in, I didn't think that they would do it knowing that we had eyes on the place and could leave before any minions arrived. The spy probably was going to report back about this meeting, though, so I needed to be on my toes. I also needed more information. We hung back behind the group.

"Hey, Dev, any sign of minions?"

"No. Where you guys headed?"

"No idea. Someplace they could hide a motorcycle—powerbike. Whatever."

I heard typing. "There's a building about a block away. Looks like there's a garage door in the back."

"How convenient. Any Jurisdiction cameras inside?"

More typing. "Not that I can tell. More bikers leaving the building, though."

I groaned to myself. Even with Fara's medicine, my arm still hurt like a bitch from my little night raid of Dagna's building. Plus, I'd just gotten the stitches out of my other arm, so that was sore as well. I really, *really* didn't want to have to sword fight. Again.

"Drift, tell me why you're leading us into an ambush, and I might let you live."

Drift stopped and rolled his eyes at us. I had to work to suppress a grin. "I'm not, though I appreciate your paranoia."

Ink stalked over and got into his personal space, casually placing one of his swords on Drift's shoulder. He was a full head taller than Drift, but that didn't seem to bother the biker at all. Drift took his time looking Ink up and down.

"My, my, you are sexy when you're threatening me."

The corner of Ink's mouth curved up. "I'm sexy all of the time. Even when I kill you."

"True. But let me tell you something before you lop off my head—although I find it tedious to repeat—I am a very shrewd businessperson. Even if I could kill you both in an ambush, which is unlikely, word would get out that I'd reneged on a deal. That is very bad for business. It would cost me money, and my other clients might go elsewhere for the services I provide. I don't ever lose money. Ever. Not to mention, the Compound would be pissed if we killed two of their favorite Team members, and I can't have someone come avenging you. We aren't going to ambush you. So, if you would be so kind as to remove your sword from my neck, I would appreciate it."

Ink and I exchanged glances, and Ink sheathed his swords. I had to grudgingly respect Drift; I even sort of liked his attitude. And the eyeliner that framed his almond-shaped eyes. And his mohawk. But not enough to want to do that myself. Yet.

"Fine. But I don't like surprises."

"Me neither."

We turned the corner, heading down a street toward the building Dev had mentioned. A handful of gang members at the door nodded to Drift as we made our way inside. They gave me and Ink a wide berth. One of the bikers was staring so hard at Ink that I thought her eyeballs might drill holes in his pants. He ignored her, which was unusual. What was that about?

The door led to what might have been an office lobby, remnants of cheap chairs and a sloping reception desk the only indication that this had once been used as anything at all. Drift vaulted over the desk, his gang following suit, and disappeared into the bowels of the building. We followed.

Behind the desk and around the corner was a giant, open room, ending with the garage door. Gang members were scattered across the open space, all working on motorcycles of various sizes, styles, and levels of disrepair. Parts and tires and makeshift machines littered the entirety of the room, illuminated by the huge skylight in the ceiling three stories above.

Everyone stopped what they were doing and stared at us. The room became so quiet that I could hear the faint buzz of fluorescent lights.

"Back to work, you hooligans!" Drift yelled. His voice sounded hollow in the open space. "Except Zach. Meet me in my office, please and thank you."

Drift made a sharp left and jogged up a set of metal stairs leading to a catwalk which encircled the room from a story above. At the top of the stairs, I hazarded a look down at the main level. At least twenty people were working on at least forty motorcycles. This wasn't some neighborhood operation—these guys were legit. Drift wasn't kidding when he said that he was a shrewd businessman.

About halfway around the catwalk, Drift opened a door. There was a desk, a couple of chairs, and all of the other accoutrements of a standard office, along with motorcycle parts that he appeared to be using as paperweights.

"I'd offer you a seat but considering you're a paranoid lot, I doubt you'd take me up on it. But please do not be offended if I sit."

"Our paranoia is why we're still alive," Ink said.

"As is mine." He looked up as a young man knocked on the doorframe. "Ah, Zach, please come join us. Shut the door, while you're at it. This is Blu and Ink, although they don't really need introductions."

"Why have you brought him in here, Drift?"

He paused. "I would like to negotiate a second part of the deal."

Zach was as tall as Ink but rail thin. His baggy pants hung onto his hip bones for dear life, showing the band of his underwear. His white tank top was dirty with grease, differentiating it from his almost translucent skin. I wasn't sure what his natural hair color was, but currently it was electric blue—I was a tad envious. And, unlike Drift's mohawk, which was standing up on his head in spikes, Zach had pulled his up into a topknot. His septum was pierced, as was his eyebrow, and he had gauges in his ears. I'd peg him at eighteen or nineteen years old. The most interesting thing about him, though? He didn't look surprised at all to be meeting with us. Drift had given him a heads-up.

"I don't like having a deal changed after it's been agreed," I said.

Drift and Zach had a wordless conversation; then Zach spoke. He had a thick accent. From the sounds of it, he was from the other continent. "It is because of me that the deal has to change. Do not blame Drift."

"I'm about three seconds from walking out of here—"

Drift sighed. "Zacharias got into a bit of a scuffle with Jurisdiction assholes yesterday, and now he's on the run. Unfortunately, he has become a liability to my business."

"I'm not an assassin for hire to clean up your *liabilities*," I said.

Drift chuckled. "As much as I'd sometimes like to kill him myself, Zach is my second, and I might even feel bad if he was dead. What I need is for you to take his sister to the Compound."

I don't know what I'd expected, but that wasn't it. At all. What were they up to? I really *looked* at Zach as he slouched against the wall near the door. His shoulders were hunched, and his arms were crossed over his chest. To the casual bystander, he didn't seem to give a shit about what was happening around him. But he also had dark circles under his wary eyes.

"How old is your sister, Zach?"

"Fourteen."

"Did you kill one of them?"

"Yes."

"Why?"

"Because he tried to—what is word?—assault my sister."

I felt the anger in my stomach rise. Fucking minions. "What do you plan on doing if we take your sister?"

He shrugged. "It does not matter. As long as she is safe, I will be happy."

Well, shit. I didn't want to like this guy. Just like I really didn't want to like Drift.

"What is it that you do for Drift?" Ink asked.

Drift answered. "He's the best mechanic in the territory. I'm going to miss this asshole."

I looked at Ink and he nodded once. "And what do we get if we take his sister into hiding?"

"I have contacts. I know who'll be competing in the PITs when your *new gang* makes their debut." He raised his eyebrow at me. He was obviously onto our little ruse.

"What the *new gang* needs is information on which jobs the mercenaries will be trading beforehand," I said. "If you can get that information, we will take Zach and his sister."

Zach stood up from the wall. "What?"

"We need a good mechanic at the Compound, man," Ink said. "Your sister will be safe, and you can earn your keep."

"Can you get us that information, Drift?"

Once again, they exchanged a wordless conversation; then Drift nodded once. "I can. Zach, want to go hang out with these two?"

FARA 49

"Am I interrupting?"

Ink stood awkwardly in my doorway, watching Calum and I eat tater tots on my bed.

Calum stole a glance at me. "Not at all." I glared at him. "Fara was just telling me how she roundhouse kicked Hewitt—other Jackrabbit—in the nuts, singed him a bit, then dragged him around."

"I had some pent-up anger." I looked pointedly at Ink, who for once wasn't smirking.

"I'm a bit sorry that you didn't kill the bastard." Calum kissed my head. "Well, it looks like you two need to talk."

"I can come back . . ."

Calum got up, leaving the tater tots with me. "Nope. I have to go anyway." He walked out the door with a wave, and I was left with Ink, who was looking very un-Ink-like as he lurked.

"Can I come in?"

I shrugged, shoving a tater tot in my mouth to keep the snarky comments at bay.

He sat in the chair, forearms resting on his knees, hands clasped, and stared at his boots. I waited. The silence stretched on; I didn't mind the quiet, and I wasn't about to try to make him feel comfortable. Finally, he caught my eye, no smirk in sight.

"I'm an asshole."

"This time, yes."

"I'm sorry, Fara." He ran his hand through his hair as he looked at his boots some more. "Everything you said to me this morning is true. I fucked up. All day, all I could think about was how much of an idiot I was. It's none of my business who you date or spend the night with. None."

"Exactly."

"And you never say anything to me about—"

"—being a playboy asshole?"

"Right. Are you going to forgive me?"

"I'm not sure I'm done being mad yet."

"I can't go another day of you not talking to me. I missed you."

I chucked a tater tot at his head. He caught it, but not without a look of bewilderment.

"You *miss* me? You know, Jay said the exact same thing today, which makes both of you idiots!"

Ink glared at me. "Do not compare me to him!"

"Fine!"

He was quiet for a moment, dropping his head to continue his staring match with the floor. Eventually, his shoulders drooped. "I didn't even mean what I said this morning. I was . . . I don't know why I was so mad."

"You don't just get to say shitty things because you're pissed, Ink."

When he looked up at me, his mask was completely gone. He was letting me *see* him. "I know. I'm sorry I hurt you. I'm just . . . sorry."

My anger deflated right there. I knew it would happen. Bastard. I got up and hugged him. He was almost the same height sitting down as I was standing up.

"Fine. Whatever. It's really fucking hard to stay mad at you, as much as I'd like to."

He squeezed me. "Good. I don't want to lose you because I'm an asshole. So, you forgive me?"

I pulled back, expecting to see his smirk, expecting to go back to our banter, expecting the weighted air to go back to normal. But instead, he was staring at me with the same unguarded look he had before. He searched my face, his gaze finally landing on my lips. I let him pull me into his lap. His eyes met mine as time seemed to stop, like the world was holding its breath. He brushed his fingers down my cheek. He leaned in.

"Oh shit! Sorry! I didn't—I'll just go."

Blu was standing in my doorway, looking mortified. She didn't realize it, but she'd just stopped a huge mistake from happening.

"It's OK."

"Are you sure?"

"Yeah. Ink was just apologizing for being a shithead."

"He should do that daily. Seriously, though . . ."

I stood up. "Yeah. No problem. Want a drink? Tater tots?"

"No, thanks. Although I'm not sure why I'd ever turn down tater tots. Anyway, I was just wondering if you'd mind helping me and Silver train for the PITs tomorrow? We got our practice bike."

"I'm not sure how I can help, but I'll certainly try."

"I hear that you throw balls of electricity. They'd make excellent obstacle practice."

50 BLU

If we were going to survive in the PITs, we needed practice. A lot of practice. Silver might be an amazing street racer, but this was a totally different animal. Participating in the PITs meant she would be maneuvering a death machine, with a passenger, in the dark, in an arena with thousands of screaming elites watching the mayhem. And obstacles—you couldn't forget about those. All while protecting the flag attached to our powerbike from nine other teams desperately trying to kill us and steal our flag. Like I said, we needed a lot of practice, and we only had a couple of weeks to get our shit together.

We were headed to a place Dev had suggested, about ten miles west of the Compound. Dev's grandfather was a farmer until he died. Dev's parents died shortly after, leaving Dev to fend for himself. He ended up at the Compound, leaving the land abandoned. Getting there was tricky, but it sounded like the perfect place to train for this madness.

Silver wanted to get a feel for the bike before having a passenger, so Ink drove us there in his car, Silver following behind. Fara, Sage, and I sat in the back seat, and Dev gave directions in the front.

The Captain had insisted that Sage come with us. Although missions and all of the other shit the Team did was dangerous, this was something none of us had tried before and had a higher probability of gruesome injury.

Silver had examined the bike before we left to make sure Drift hadn't screwed us. She assured us that it was all right, even if it looked horrific—and it did. It was neither a dirt bike nor a motorcycle, but like they'd had a very big and very scary baby. I understood now why they called it a powerbike. Its two wheels were wider and had thicker treads than a normal motorcycle. It also had a two-person seat, specifically designed for one person to ride backward, which was not awesome. This bike was meant for tough terrain and speed, not safety. I wasn't sure the helmets Silver had commandeered would be enough.

"Take a left here," Dev said, pointing to a road that was barely two ruts in the dirt. Ink's car was bigger than mine but still wasn't cut out for off-roading. Its shocks groaned as we bounced and maneuvered at a snail's pace.

Luckily, we only had to endure it for a minute before Dev told us to pull over by the remnants of a barn. The structure was still standing, barely, nature deciding it wanted to retake this spot. In front of it was a huge dirt area, peppered with divots and weeds. It would have been rolling pasture, had it not been left abandoned. Now, it looked dry and desolate—a stark contrast to the lush green of the Compound. I didn't realize the Compound being so close to the river made such a difference in the topography.

Silver parked the bike as we scrambled out of the car.

"How's the powerbike?" I asked her.

"It's going to take some getting used to, but not as much as I thought."

"Are you ready for me to get on?"

"As I'll ever be."

"I guess there's no time like the present. Let's just try not to die today."

51 FARA

The thought of deliberately throwing electric balls at Silver and Blu was freaking me out. I knew that they needed practice with obstacles for the PITs, but my aim wasn't that great yet, and I was petrified that I would hurt them in my attempt to help them. Weirdly, the thought of having electricity shot at them didn't seem to bother them at all. They just told me to aim at the dirt around them.

Easier said than done.

The wind whipped the dirt up into a puff, making my skin feel gritty. This place reminded me of the pictures of the Dust Bowl from history books. It was sad. And it reminded me, once again, why I needed to help the Team. This area used to be farmland. It had helped feed the country's citizens. Now people were starving, and we had to use it to train for a horrific blood sport. As much as I didn't want to throw electric balls at my friends, if it helped, then I'd figure out how to do it.

But how would I throw electric balls without killing someone while they were driving around on a crazy-looking motorcycle? I knew that I needed to *intend* for the balls to go where I wanted, but with the preternatural speed that Silver was driving the bike over the dried-out pasture around us, I still wasn't sure I could do it. My brain just took too long to process the programs, the intent—everything. And one mistake could kill them. This was a disaster in the making, for sure.

"Time to get to work, sweetness," Ink said.

"Any suggestions as to how to do this without taking someone out?"

"We wing it."

I snorted. That wasn't useful. I guess it was up to me to figure it out.

They'd told me I needed to create and throw electricity quickly in order to emulate the obstacles. I could do it with my "all-in-one," but that would drop me on my ass. However, the electric balls wouldn't. So, how could I get the balls to reload quickly? If I could keep creating them over and over without actively thinking about it, like a program running in the background, then I could focus on *intending* the balls to hit where I wanted them to. Like a pitching machine, but instead of throwing them out, they'd just show up in my palms. Something like a "reload" program. My brain liked that idea; "reload balls" showed up on my program wheel, between "fire crown" and "human torch."

I turned to Sage and Dev. "Stay behind me. I'm going to try something new, and I'd feel really bad if I screwed up and accidentally shot you with lightning."

"Yes, that would be a bit problematic." Sage grabbed Dev by the arm and led him behind me.

I walked across the dirt, in the opposite direction of Silver and Blu. They had enough to worry about without me accidentally shooting them too. I stopped at about twenty yards and drew a row of *X*s in the dirt, deep enough that they wouldn't blow away. Then I returned to the group.

"Here goes nothin.'"

I pulled up my "lightning" program (why did my brain refuse to name it "electric balls"?). I started the "reload balls" program, then focused on intending to hit the first *X*. I threw the balls at the *X*, which hit with a satisfying *crack*. Immediately, new balls were in my hands, and I focused on hitting the second *X*.

It worked! I had reloaded my balls!

My celebration was short-lived. Unfortunately, I couldn't throw them fast enough, and two more showed up. I now had four balls of electricity in my outstretched hands. Shit. I threw them. Two hit their mark, but two of them went careening wide. Luckily, there was nothing to hit, but before I could focus, two more balls appeared. I threw them at the third X. Then four more appeared, all going different ways. I turned off the program, panting.

Dev looked a bit shell-shocked. "What was that?"

"A disaster!"

Ink shook his head. "Fara never takes credit for doing cool things. What she meant to say was, those were her 'electric balls.'"

"That was a disaster of epic proportions, Ink! I'm so lucky no one got hurt."

"I have to agree with Ink," Sage said. "That was unlike anything I've ever seen. How did you do it?"

I explained the program wheel, the intent, everything. And while Sage asked questions, Ink's face was pensive.

"What?"

"I've never heard you describe your abilities like that before. I never knew how you did it—or that your brain created 'programs' on a wheel. It's really remarkable."

"My brain seems to do whatever it wants with the ideas I give it. As much as I'd like to say that I'm controlling the creation of these abilities, it's sort of a free-for-all in my noggin."

The corner of Ink's mouth turned up. "Maybe it's not a free-for-all, but that your brain is adapting the programs to suit you. What you're doing isn't exactly what the palmbox programs are—or at least, I don't think they are."

Huh. I didn't really know what a palmbox could do, especially what Barrington's palmbox could do. But my brain did seem to do whatever it wanted with the ideas I gave it.

"You can do fire too?" Dev asked.

"I can." I turned on my fire crown, which weirdly didn't incinerate my clothes. Or my hair. Blu and Silver had stopped practice to watch me, a huge smile spreading across Blu's face.

"That's so fucking cool! I wish I could do that!" she yelled across the dirt.

"You don't need it! You already look badass! I need a bit of help."

"You are badass too," Sage said. "But that's remarkable."

"She is pretty remarkable," Ink said with a wink. "She can also become a human torch—"

"But without the stream, or my fireproof clothes, I'd prefer not to. I'd rather not drive back to the Compound in just my underwear."

Sage smiled, a rare treat. "As disappointed as Ink might be, I don't blame you. Are you going to try your electric balls again?"

"I don't see why not."

52 BLU

We stopped practicing on the powerbike when dusk descended. At some point we would need to train with it in the dark, as the PITs were, but we weren't good enough yet. It would be embarrassing to die from stupidity at this point in my life. So, we came back to the Compound and headed straight for the mess.

I'd barely finished my food when the Captain approached me.

"What's up?"

"Drift seems to have gotten himself into a bit of trouble. If my intel is correct, you'll need all of you."

She continued, explaining that minions were on a rampage and looking for our new Compound residents— Zach and his sister. The minions didn't realize we had them, and so they were going to rough up Drift's gang to get the information.

Protecting thugs and killing minions was not how I'd planned to spend my night, but then again, I wasn't surprised. Shit always went to hell.

The Captain thought this mission needed the entire principal Team, which also meant it was going to be a royal cluster. It had been a while since the four of us had a mission together. Usually we split up, taking less experienced Team members with us. The Captain said it was good to spread out our talents, but mostly I thought it was because she got tired of the four of us squabbling. I couldn't blame her.

We crammed into Ink's car with only minor bickering, and I pulled out my comm.

"Jyston?"

"I was hoping it was you."

"Are you telling me other girls have access to your comm?"

He chuckled. "I've told you, there are no others. But I have a feeling that this isn't a—what did you call it?—a 'booty call'?"

"Sadly, no." I told him what was happening.

"Well, whatever Dagna is doing, it hasn't been sanctioned by the Counselor. Which means that I have no earthly idea how many guards will be there, or what they want."

Fuck. "I know what they want. Our new guest at the Compound killed a minion. They want him. And his sister."

"And I'm assuming you are not going to acquiesce to their request?"

"That's right."

"Good. Oh, and Blu? The spy in Drift's gang? If my information is correct, I know who she is, and her son is a prisoner at Dagna's building."

"Oh shit."

"Oh shit, indeed. As I said, I would love it if you could get her to me." He gave me a name.

"I'll try to get her out of there alive."

"I appreciate it. Tell your Team, who I am sure are eavesdropping, good luck."

"Tell your boyfriend that he sounds sexy over the comm," Styx said. I could hear Jyston laugh.

The four of us had planned as best we could as we drove toward Drift's building. Normally, we wouldn't bother with something like this. We couldn't act every time the Captain got word that a minion shakedown was going to happen. But the real reason we needed to bail Drift's ass out was that we didn't want anything about the PITs to leak. We had to plug the leak. If we took care of his minion problem, Drift would keep his mouth shut.

All of us were dressed for battle; even Styx had swapped her bright headband for black and her smile for a look that promised death. These sorts of missions sucked. It wasn't sneaking around stealing things or raiding things or rescuing people. It was a battle—a bloodbath. We only hoped that the blood shed wouldn't be ours, but Jurisdiction's. But we had no choice. Drift would sell us out in a heartbeat if it meant saving his hide, or his gang. He couldn't afford to take sides. Both the Compound rebels and Jurisdiction were bad for his business.

Dev had managed, with Styx's help, to loop the video cameras in the area for two hours, giving us time to kill the minions before they could get back up there. Minions didn't normally carry comms, maybe because Dagna saw them as disposable—the minions, not the comms. They were, however, heavily armed, which showed where her priorities were.

"Get in, get the spy, kill the minions, get out. Did I miss anything?" Ink got out of the car and drew his swords.

"Don't die," Jack added. His sword was thinner than both of Ink's. I was sure that the swords had names—and I was doubly sure Drake knew them—but I didn't, and I didn't care. All I knew was that mine was called a short sword, which had caused ceaseless amounts of teasing when I was younger. That is, until I kicked their asses with said short sword. Fun times.

"You've beaten the minions to the building," Dev said in our ears, "but just barely. They're about five minutes out."

"All right, Team," I said, "let's go save some gangsters."

BLU 53

"You know, you have minions on the way," I said by way of greeting.

The gang members stepped aside as Drift opened the door to let us through.

"Of course I do. How do you think word got to the Compound?"

We hopped over the reception desk and made our way to the repair shop. From what Dev had said, the minions were going to enter through the garage door. It would have been easier if we could bottleneck them by the reception desk I'd just hurdled, but no such luck this time.

"Are you in the habit of asking us for help?"

"You owe me a favor."

I stalked up to him and got in his face. I felt the entire room tense, except for him. "This is way more than a favor, Drift. Our bargain was to take the spy off your hands. I could do that right now, and leave you with the minions."

He sighed. "I honestly didn't think you'd show up; especially all four of you." He introduced himself to Styx and Jack, then gave Ink a sly once-over. Ink rewarded him with a wink.

"If you want us to deal with your problem, it's going to cost you."

"I figured it might."

"We'll negotiate the final terms in a bit. Just make sure your people either help or stay out of our way. If anyone so much as tries to look at us wrong, they're dead. As are you. Do I make myself clear?"

He nodded once, then turned to his people. "You might want to hide unless you plan on fighting. I will not look unfavorably on you should you choose to hide. But you need to decide now. Anyone that hinders the Team or helps Jurisdiction will answer to me."

Most of them left, but surprisingly, a couple stayed.

"So what's the plan?"

I whispered what I needed him to do. With a nod, Drift sprinted up the stairs to where most of his gang was hiding.

"Minions incoming," Dev said. "I count twenty, but it's hard to tell."

"I'll double-check." Jack slipped out into the darkness.

I exchanged glances with Ink and Styx, sending a little prayer into the universe.

"Leave none alive."

Ink got into position. "Wasn't planning on it."

I heard a panicked yell, then a chorus of shouts—Jack starting the melee in his assassin style. He was deadly in an open fight, but even more so in the shadows. Eventually he'd make it back to us, but for now, he was causing confusion and fear . . . and getting an accurate head count.

Ink stepped in front of the door as it opened, just to my right, his long arms and deadly precision the first line of defense. Anyone who got past him got my short sword. And if they got past me, Styx, positioned in front of the stairs with the two remaining gang members, would finish them.

After some more shouting, the minions came into view. The garage door was about fifteen feet wide. While less of a bottleneck than the reception area, it meant that they still couldn't come running in unhindered.

Their faces told it all: they hadn't expected us.

"Take the purple-haired one alive—I want the reward!" The tall minion in the back was the leader, sending his lackeys in front to deal with us, then hoping to benefit from the reward. I wasn't going to play by his rules.

"At some point, the bounty on my head will match yours," Ink said as he dispatched a minion.

"You need to burn down a building." I sidestepped a minion's sword and put him on the ground. Permanently.

"Dagna's, to be specific," Jack said, appearing out of the darkness next to me.

"She has more than a few to spare," I said as I stopped someone trying to stab me.

"There are seventeen minions left, by the way."

"Thanks for the info."

"Can you guys stop gabbing and start killing faster, please?" Styx was taking on two minions who had slipped past me. I threw a dagger into one's back, dropping him.

"Sorry, Styx!"

She snorted as she took care of the second minion. The gang members were standing behind her, not moving, eyes wide. I guess they had never seen us do this before. I'm sure we were quite the sight. I had forgotten what it felt like to fight with these three. How we were a well-oiled machine of death and destruction. How we had been doing this for so long—too long. How we couldn't keep this up forever. And how I didn't want to fight forever. Maybe there was more to life than this. There had to be.

Though we were holding our ground, we were still outnumbered and starting to lag. We might be the principal Team, but bashing minion after minion took its toll, even on the best of us.

"Man, these assholes just keep coming!"

Ink was surrounded. They saw him as the biggest threat, so they were focusing their attention on him. They weren't wrong, but even he could use help sometimes. I avoided one minion who was valiantly trying to incapacitate me as I made my way to Ink, killing another who was rudely standing in my way. I only had one more to deal with before reaching Ink when he fell to his knees, dropping his swords. His hands reached for his neck. Blood was starting to ooze from it.

"Shit! Jack!"

"I see it! Go protect him, I'll take care of these assholes."

I ran through the minions, stopping a killing blow before it could take Ink out. His face was wan, and he dropped to his haunches.

"Didn't move fast enough," he said through gritted teeth.

"We need to get you out of here. Dev!"

"What? What's going on?"

"We need Fara to portal here. Now!"

"What happened?"

"Ink's really hurt."

"Oh shit! OK. Know where she is?"

"At the armory. Tell Sage she's going to portal Ink right into surgery, so to get the rooms clear."

"Do you guys need backup?"

"There isn't time."

FARA 54

My comm buzzed just as Drake and I were sitting down for dinner. I had stopped by to pick up my daggers, and he had asked if I'd like steak. Who doesn't like steak? He even promised that he would be on his best behavior, and he had been true to his word.

"Sorry . . ."

Drake smiled over his steak and roasted potatoes. "It's fine. I understand how the Team works."

"Please don't wait for me. Your steak will get cold."

I walked toward the front door to give myself some privacy.

"Fara!"

"Dev, what is it?"

"You need to portal Ink out of a battle."

"What?"

"Ink is dying."

My heart stopped. "Where?"

Dev told me everything he knew as I grabbed the OG palmbox off my belt. No, no, no. Ink couldn't be dying. It wasn't possible.

Drake was watching me from the table. "Something happened."

"Yes." I looked away before the tears lining my eyes could fall. He might be nice, but he still might be the spy. I couldn't let him see how freaked out I really was. "They need backup."

Before he could answer, I walked out of the door and into the surrounding trees. Ink was dying. That couldn't happen. I wouldn't let that happen. I'd apologize later for leaving.

Once I was secluded enough, I tried to open a portal. It didn't work. No! I was always shutting them down. Why wouldn't it work now, when I needed it most? I tried again, but I just saw Calum's place. Shit! I started to panic. I needed to get to Ink, to help him. To rescue him. But he was somewhere I'd never been, so I had to *intend* it—but I was freaking out, and my brain just couldn't *intend* on going somewhere I knew nothing about. My heart was racing. Tears started to fall. I had to get to him. I had to. I couldn't lose him. I needed to open a portal. Now.

In a last-ditch effort, I thought about Ink. Just him. Not a place, but a smell. A smile. The tone of his voice. His eyes. Him. He was my location. I *intended* to open a portal to him. This had to work.

The portal flickered to life, and through the window I could see Blu holding Ink's neck—trying to stanch the blood seeping between her fingers. He turned his head slightly. His eyes glazed over. I didn't have time to feel relieved as I jumped through, to chaos.

Jack and Styx were back-to-back, holding off minions as Blu tried to give Ink first aid. They were a mess. Jack had blood smeared across his face, and Styx was limping. A tall minion was pacing around them. His eyes caught mine.

"Well, well," he said with a sneer. "It looks like Dagna's not the only one with a little secret. They'll reward me handsomely for Blu. And for you."

He licked his lips. "Don't hurt her, boys. I'm going to take this one back with me, along with Blu."

Ink's face filled with rage as he struggled to get up.

"Knock that off!" Blu whispered to him, holding him down. "You can't help her if you're dead."

The minion, who apparently was the leader of these shitheads, watched Ink struggle, a smile lighting on his face.

Jack tried to intercept him, but because he was also fighting two minions, the head shithead dodged and grabbed me. He looked me up and down like I was a sandwich. It was Hewitt all over again. His hand gripped me harder as he reached to touch my face, recognition and desire in his eyes.

No.

I felt something crack in me. I wasn't scared—I was angry. More than angry, even. Rage pulsed through me like a heartbeat. I let it fill me up and fuel me.

"I'm going to kill your boyfriend and make you watch."

The electricity grew, and I let it come across my eyes. Blu nodded to me once.

"Leave none alive."

I knew right then that I would do whatever it took to protect them.

"You will not *touch* him!"

I drew on all of my anger, and fear, and every emotion that I had bottled up, and allowed my program wheel to open wide, giving it free rein. I became a human torch, flames leaping off my skin. The head minion let go of me and stumbled away.

"What the fuck?"

I couldn't focus on him right now. I had to save Ink. I would not let these assholes hurt him, hurt them—my friends. I turned and grabbed a minion who was trying to get to him. My flames set his armor on fire as I pushed electricity through him. When he screamed, Styx plunged her sword into his chest.

My shirt and pants were starting to smoke, but I wasn't done yet. I had to protect my friends. The fear of losing Ink fed my fire as I pulled the electricity into spheres and threw them at two more minions. I was pure flame. I was avenging death. I was Fara fucking Bayne and would leave none alive, if it meant keeping those I loved safe.

Another minion swung a sword at me, but Jack parried it. I dropped the minion with a set of electric balls to the chest. I turned to see the head guy trying to get to Ink.

No.

I let the lightning cross my eyes again. I could feel my hair floating away from my body.

He stumbled away from me. "Who are you?"

I didn't answer. I didn't need to. I knew who I was.

Lightning snaked over my arms as two bolts left my outstretched hands, hitting his chest. He crashed to the ground, twitching and smoking. Blu pulled his head back and slit his throat for good measure.

I shut down my powers, dropping to my knees. "Did I get them all?" I was panting, but I didn't care.

Jack walked up and put his hand on my shoulder, then pulled it back with a slight hiss. "You OK?"

"I'll be fine. Are they all dead?"

"Yes."

"Good." I crawled over to Ink. His eyes were slowly closing. I couldn't control the sob that escaped. I couldn't touch him for fear of burning him, but I got as close as I could. "Ink! Ink, you can't die on me. You're my favorite, Ink. That means you can't die."

"I'm your favorite?" His voice was barely a whisper. I sobbed again.

"Yes. You're my favorite. But you knew that already. Stay with me, OK? I'm getting you help. You can't die. *Please.*"

"You are a magical badass, Fara."

His eyes closed and didn't open again.

BLU 55

The portal closed behind Fara and Ink. Ink's blood stained my hands, and I tried to wipe it on my pants, sending a prayer to the universe that he'd be OK, that we had been in time.

"I ought to just save myself the trouble and kill you right now," I told Drift when he came down the stairs. His gait was casual; his eyes were wary. My arm ached. My best friends were hurt. Yeah. I was pissed and ready to take it out on someone.

Standing beside me, Jack and Styx knew exactly what our current problem was—other than the twenty dead minions. Everyone here had seen Fara unleash herself. They might not have understood exactly what happened, but with how brightly she burned, and how loud her lightning was, there was no mistaking something fucked up had transpired.

Drift looked me in the eye. "I didn't see anything."

Jack moved closer to him, just inside his personal space. "What didn't you see?"

"I didn't see someone come in here through a magic window and lay waste to multiple Jurisdiction assholes like an avenging goddess of old. I didn't see someone call fire and lightning to do her bidding and who could destroy anything in her path. I didn't see someone that, should I fuck up, could be unleashed on me and my people. And I will continue not to see that until my dying day. As will anyone else here. We didn't see anything."

Interesting. He saw Fara as a weapon. I guess she was, in a way—although anyone who talked to her for three seconds would know otherwise. He was scared of her. Good.

"As long as you continue to not see anything, then she will continue to ignore you. As will we. Clear?"

His shoulders dropped just slightly. "Crystal."

"Now, we need to talk about what our payment will be for rescuing your gang's collective asses."

"I owe you a favor, at least."

"Yes, a big one."

"And removal of the bodies."

"Yes."

"And getting a story circulated that will cover your tracks."

"Yes."

"Anything else?"

"I'm sure we'll come up with something. You owe us. Big time. So, let's chat."

When we concluded our negotiations, he sighed. "We still have the spy problem, Blu."

"Where is she?"

FARA 56

I curled up in the chair in Ink's room in the infirmary, grateful I was watching him sleep instead of . . . well, I couldn't think about the alternative. He had almost died. Sage said that if I hadn't shown up when I did, Ink wouldn't have made it. I cried when he told me that. And now, knowing how close he was to death, I didn't want to leave him. I couldn't leave him.

So I sat.

I watched his chest rise and fall. I watched the medics when they came in to check his wound, his temperature. I watched as the rising sun slowly peeked in through the gaps in the curtains. Morning was not far off. I watched and waited. And thought. I had a lot of time to think. I replayed last night in my head. Last month. Last year. Everything that had happened. Everyone I'd met.

But mostly, I thought about Ink, and how his belief in me was showing me how to believe in myself. And how I wouldn't date Drake because of him. It was something more than friendship or gratitude.

Ink's brows knitted together in a dream, and I finally admitted to myself something that I had known for a while but refused to acknowledge, hoping it would go away. But no matter how hard I ignored it, it was no use.

I was in love with him. And that was a problem.

Having just gotten out of two relationships, I wasn't ready for another one. I needed the time and space to figure myself out, without it being in relation to someone else. And Ink would never settle down. We could never have a relationship.

But I loved him anyway.

I knew he cared about me, that he enjoyed spending time with me. And that had to be enough. He was the ultimate bad boy. Nothing I could do or say would change him—not that I wanted to. It wasn't my job to reform him—to tame him—to *anything* him. He had to decide that he wanted something more; I could never, and would never, force that. It was all on him.

And I didn't want him different. Well, to be honest I'd prefer he didn't take a girl home every other night. But everything else? I loved him as he was. And I could never tell him. I didn't want to do that to him—to us. I couldn't force him to tell me that he didn't want the relationship. It would be awkward; I'd risk losing him as a friend. Instead, I just had to tuck my feelings into the box and put it in my heart. It was better to carry a torch than burn down a house. He could never know.

"Hey, sweetness." His eyes heavy, he licked his dry lips.

"Hey. How are you feeling?"

"Like someone slit my neck open."

"Oh, just that?"

He chuckled, then winced. I handed him the water next to his bed. The room was so quiet I could hear the birds chirping outside, the sounds of morning filtering through the window.

"I thought I was dead."

"We wouldn't let that happen."

"Apparently not. 'Thank you' seems inadequate."

"Not dying is enough thanks for me."

The corner of his mouth turned up. "Fara?"

"Mmm?"

"I . . ." He grabbed my hand, lacing his fingers through mine. "I . . . It's just . . ." He sighed. "You're my favorite, OK?"

With that, his eyelids drifted closed, his long eyelashes resting against the pallor of his cheeks.

"You're my favorite too," I whispered.

57 BLU

The weeks leading up to the PITs were hell. I fell into my bed every night, battered and sore and hating Jurisdiction more and more. I'd known this mission was going to be the hardest I had ever attempted, but I didn't think the preparation would almost kill me.

Silver and I were spending every minute we could on the powerbike, working ourselves to exhaustion. Fara shot electric balls at us as Silver navigated through the tough terrain of the dusty farm. Seeing how well the human body responded to Fara's electricity had given me a new sense of purpose for not getting hit.

After some near misses and one fairly embarrassing crash, Silver was good enough that I was certain we wouldn't die a fiery death within the first two minutes of the PITs. That was really all we could ask for. We didn't need to win. We actually didn't want to win. We just needed to negotiate the right job prior to the PITs, and then not die.

Easier said than done.

Jyston had told us the winners were personally commended by one of the lower-level leaders of Jurisdiction and given their prize, while the rest of the competitors usually left the arena in a hurry. We wanted to leave in a hurry.

We also spent hours refining our plan, such as it was. Because of how the arena was guarded, Fara couldn't portal us in without us getting captured immediately. We still needed Jyston to get us in. It was dangerous for him—more dangerous considering if he got caught . . . Well, we'd just make sure that he didn't get caught.

Finally, the day of the PITs arrived. I was worried, a lot more so than normally. Each day I was a Team member, I knew that it might be my last. But something about the PITs made me think about my own death more. Perhaps it was because the odds were horrific, or because Ink had been so close to death. Maybe because I was starting to realize that there might be more to life than surviving. Whatever the reason, I was worried.

I ran to the mess to grab food for me and Ink, then headed to his apartment, letting myself in without knocking. Although awake, he was still in bed—a testament to how close to dying he had been just a couple of weeks ago. He usually woke the rest of us up, but now he was barely awake.

He sat up as I shut the door, the blanket pooling over his hips. There was always a risk that he wouldn't have clothes on. Or be alone. Or both. I had seen more of Ink—and some girls—than I ever really wanted to. My luck was good today, however; he was wearing shorts.

"Why are you bringing me food?"

"Why so suspicious?"

"Because you never do this."

"Can't I just be nice?" I handed him his container of hashbrowns, bacon, eggs—the works. He patted the empty space on the bed, and I climbed up with my own food. "I just want to spend some time with you is all."

"Tying up loose ends before you die? That's not morbid."

The smell of pancakes hit me as I opened my food. "I guess. I don't know. I have a bad feeling about tonight."

He put down his container and pulled me into a hug, which was weird but not uncomfortable. We weren't big huggers—we usually took the more direct "punch you in the face" approach. Fara was rubbing off on us.

"It's going to suck," he said, "but you're going to live. OK? No dying on me."

"Says the guy who almost died. Listen." I took his hands in mine. I needed him to pay attention to what I was going to say next. "The mission is to secure one of the driving jobs. If we don't make it out—"

"You'll make it out."

"—you'll still have the job. Save those kids. Burn down the whole building, Jurisdiction, *all* of it. Promise me."

He pulled back, his green eyes catching mine. "You'll make it out. We'll burn them down together, Blu."

"But if I don't . . ."

"But if you don't, I promise. Just make sure I don't have to keep that promise, all right?"

I nodded once, then began eating my pancakes. Ink wasn't eating. He was still staring at me. "What?"

"B, I can't take another Hastings. You're all I have left."

"That's not true."

He sighed. "You know what I mean. You're my family."

"You're my family too." I reached over and squeezed his leg. "I know I don't tell you enough—or at all—but I love you. Even if you are a pain in the ass."

He was taken aback. I'd never said that to him. He shook his head, a smile playing on his lips. "You're an even bigger pain in the ass than I am, but I love you too."

I couldn't help but smile back. "You know, I'm not the only one you should tell that to."

"Styx and Jack already know."

"That's not who I mean."

"Can we not do this right now? Don't you know that I'm worried fucking sick about tonight? About all of you? And I can't even be there."

"So tell her."

◊ ◊ ◊

"You sure you can't sneak a palmbox?"

"I don't want to fight about this again, Styx," I said. "The other gangs wouldn't have access to the tech. It'll give us away for sure. If we get caught before going into the room, this whole thing's for nothing."

"And it would also cause problems for that hunky boyfriend of yours."

"Whatever. Believe me, I want one too. It just doesn't make sense."

"Fine."

She was worried. We all were. Not only would we be without palmboxes and comms, but Silver and I were also going in with relatively few weapons. Officially, entrants were each allowed a single dagger. Drake had also outfitted each of us with a set of knives, which we tucked into our boots. Jyston told us most entrants carried them illegally. We'd practiced with them too, but not nearly enough. My accuracy throwing them was not close to what I could do with my daggers. But then again, throwing anything at a giant powerbike in the dark while dodging flamethrowers was probably not the best plan anyway.

"Nice gear," Ink said as he walked in. The bandage was finally off his neck, although the gash still looked gruesome, the stitches sticking out of his skin. They'd come out tomorrow.

"Yeah, it's pretty awesome, although I'm sweating already."

"Better to sweat than to die," Styx quipped. "Plus, you look intimidating as hell."

I didn't know how Drake had created the riding leathers in the time he did. The pants and jacket fit over my armor perfectly. It would literally save my skin should we crash. Looking badass was just a side benefit.

Silver and I weren't the only ones decked out. Jack and Fara were both in armor—although Fara's was gray; something to do with the fireproof treatment the arm-techs put on the material. Neither of us understood the reason, but it didn't matter—the gray fit her. She stood with shoulders back, her eyes alert—a far cry from just over a month ago when we'd saved Agent Hanlon from Barrington Park.

Ink was trying, and failing, not to stare at her. She smiled at him.

"I wish I could go," he said.

"Being nearly headless has its drawbacks," she replied.

"Nearly headless? What does that even mean?"

"It's from a famous book . . . Never mind." She sighed. "Anyway, you need to stay and hold down the fort."

"Just make sure you come back in one piece." He meant all of us, but he was looking at Fara.

FARA 58

I portaled the four of us into the designated alley, giving Ink one last look through the window before shutting it and forcing myself to clear my head and focus. It wouldn't do to die because of unrequited love. I'd leave that to Shakespeare.

Jyston stepped out from behind the dumpster, hands in his pockets. The way he was able to appear seemingly out of thin air always impressed me and, without exception, made me jump. I wasn't the only one. Although their reactions were less dramatic than mine, Silver and Jack tensed when he came into view. The only person who didn't seem fazed was Blu. I'd have to ask her how she did it.

"The people guarding the holding room are loyal to me," he said by way of greeting. "They have been paid handsomely to turn a blind eye to whatever happens prior to the PITs."

"Doesn't that just give us away?" Silver asked.

"Jurisdiction is used to shady shit," Blu said. "This won't even register with them."

"Correct. They will just assume that I have coin riding on the negotiations."

Jack and I checked our gear one last time. "We're ready when you are, Jyston."

Blu walked up to the Second Counselor and drew him down for a kiss. Eventually he pulled away.

"Remember, no matter what you see," he said, "there is only you. I promise."

"This isn't my first mission, Jyston. I understand how this works. However, I have to ask. Who is she?"

"The daughter of a petty lord of the area south of the territory. I need their support."

"Fair enough. I promise not to kill her . . . today."

He gave her a smile that was as lethal as hers. "I appreciate your restraint. Do you have the map?"

"I do."

"I'd prefer you didn't die today, if you can help it."

"That's the general plan."

"We'll celebrate tomorrow, when this is over." He kissed her again, then turned to us. "Ready?"

Blu looked at me. "You've got this. Light them up if you get caught. You can't get taken by them."

"Understood."

Jyston nodded to her once, then led Jack and me farther down the alley to an unmarked door. He pulled out a palmbox.

"Can they tell if you used your palmbox to unlock it?" I asked.

"If they are looking, then yes."

"Allow me."

I focused on the unlock program, undoing both the knob and deadbolt.

"I have to say, that's pretty useful."

We entered a small room with no windows. Straight ahead was a staircase leading down, and not much else.

"These are the stadium's maintenance tunnels. This is one of two exits—the other is directly opposite of us, through the arena."

Jack looked around. "Where are the minions?"

"I killed them."

Well, then.

"Will there be more?"

"Undoubtedly."

We crept along the tunnel, which eerily reminded me of the Department of Weapons Technology's underground interrogation area. Why was it that all really horrible places had fluorescent lighting? Villainous stadium tunnels, traitorous federal government buildings, cubical farms—they all wanted you to look your absolute worst as you met your demise.

We reached a turnoff. I could hear voices coming from straight ahead. Jyston stopped.

"This is where I must leave you, and rejoin Blu. There are guards up ahead. Leave the bodies in the maintenance room where you'll be hiding. I'll dispose of them later."

The voices grew louder. Jyston turned to me. "Fara, please do not get caught. Generally, because it's a bad idea, but selfishly, I need your help in getting to Barrington."

I pulled up my electric balls, earning a cocked eyebrow from him. "I won't."

59 BLU

We left the alley, heading down a few side streets and into the throngs of people surrounding the stadium. The air had a festive feel. Vendors were selling fried foodstuffs on a stick, the smells making their way through my helmet. Something smelled like donuts; my stomach growled.

Other vendors were peddling glowing sticks of various colors, blankets with the Powerbike Inground Tournament logo emblazoned on the front—anything a member of the elite would want but didn't need, you could buy. I didn't know if there was this sort of fanfare when the prisoners competed, but for the mercenary tournament, it felt like a party. It would have been fun if they weren't making money off people's deaths.

"Over there," Silver said, motioning with her head to a space just outside of the stadium. An area had been cordoned off with a velvet rope, and other contestants were making their way behind it. Jurisdiction liked to hold the contestants outside of the stadium, to eventually be led, with much pomp and circumstance, in a parade of sorts. Members of the elite paid a ton of coin to join the parade. I guess it let them feel like they were part of the festivities without having to risk their own asses. The whole thing was ludicrous.

According to Jyston, there would be ten teams of two riders. Most of them had already shown up and were milling around, trying hard to ignore the gawking elites and each other. They all wore riding leathers in varying shades. Most were dark like ours, but a few were dyed in reds and whites and blues and yellows. Everyone was wearing their helmets, some designed to look like gruesome creatures—monsters or demons with gaping maws. Charming.

"What are the hash marks on the back of their helmets?" I asked Silver as we approached.

"It's how many people they've killed."

"In the PITs?"

She shrugged. "Just generally."

A burly minion stood at the ropes. Whether he was keeping riders in or others out, I wasn't sure. Without comment, he let us in with the rest of the group.

"Well, well, well, if it isn't the new kids." The voice coming through the helmet sounded like a man who'd gargled with gravel most of his life. Roughly the size of a truck, he wore black leathers with green patches on the elbows. His helmet, matte black like mine, had at least two dozen hash marks on it. I tilted my chin to him in acknowledgment.

"I heard you guys were doing some pretty risky shit," he said. Another contestant snorted.

I shrugged. "People say all sorts of things."

"True." I got the feeling he was studying me behind his helmet. "Do I know you?"

"Doubt it."

He stuck out his hand, surprising the hell out of me. "Stratton."

I shook his giant hand. "Riley. You're the leader of the North-City gang?"

"Something like that."

Someone snickered behind me. "They call themselves the Trenches, which is about right."

The body the voice belonged to resembled an inverted triangle. His giant arms and shoulder muscles strained against his bright blue and yellow leathers. His helmet was in similar shades but had a grotesque depiction of some sort of monster or demon on it. There were hash marks on it, but less than half as many as Stratton's.

He stood in my personal space and flipped open his visor, his bloodshot eyes twitching a bit. Fara would call this guy a Froot Loop. I tended to agree. Before he could say whatever brilliant thing came next into his brain, we were interrupted by a voice I knew all too well: Jyston.

"Contestants, the parade will begin momentarily. During the parade, you are to follow me through the stadium. I need not remind you of the penalties for disrupting the proceedings."

The contestants were murmuring, and I caught words here and there. They were startled that Jyston himself was presiding. His eyes were cold, his face bored. He was the Second Counselor right now. It put everyone on edge. Everyone, that is, except me.

"Remember," he continued, "you are here only by the generosity of Jurisdiction. You are our guests. If you do not play by our rules, you will suffer the consequences."

A giggle. "You sound so intimidating when you talk like that."

A young woman sidled up to Jyston, her waist-length auburn hair swishing as she walked on the highest heels I had ever seen. Her skintight leather pants hugged her thin frame. Her top—no more than a thin piece of fabric—had the PITs logo on it. It seemed like a weird outfit to wear to a stadium where people were trying to kill one another on powerbikes in the dirt. But then again, what did I know?

"Ah, Aurora, I see you've found me. I was just giving a bit of a pep talk." He took her hands in his and kissed her cheek. I was glad I had a helmet on; I knew my face would say everything I was thinking. I *knew* he had to do this. I actually felt bad for him that he did. But I didn't like seeing it play out in front of me.

"Should we begin the parade?"

"We're really going to lead it?" She squeezed his arm and got as close to him as she could without wearing his skin. Silver pressed her arm into mine.

The burly minion walked down the rope, taking each team's invitations as he went. Silver handed him ours and he looked it over.

"New team?"

Silver answered, "Yes."

"Piece of advice: put on a good show."

I could hear the smile in her voice. "We plan to."

60 FARA

Jack opened his mouth to say something, but I cut him off. "I know. Don't get caught."

"Actually, what I was going say is, if you can take the minions down from a distance, I'll make sure they stay down."

"Oh, sorry."

"Are you going to pass out on me?"

"I don't think so. As long as I keep it to my electric balls, I should be all right."

"Good, because here they come."

At the far end of the tunnel, four minions came around the corner.

As Ink would say, time to get to work.

The tunnel was long but narrow, forcing the minions to be staggered. I had already created the electric balls, so I threw them at the minion closest to me. He crumpled to the ground in a twitching heap. I set my reload program and threw the next two, unintentionally hitting the same guy.

Jack had pulled out his sword. "I think he's down."

"I know! Sorry! My aim is off."

"I'm not complaining . . ."

The other minions were looking around, confused. They had no idea how their guy had been electrocuted in a tunnel underground.

I now had four balls in my hand and couldn't get rid of them fast enough. I threw them, missing the second minion but hitting the third, all the while trying to turn off my reload program. It finally shut off, but not before I threw three more electric balls—all of which hit around the minions, making way too much noise. Shit.

"Can you get the last two?"

"I'm trying!"

He grinned at me. "You're doing great. Seriously. I was just asking . . ."

I finally got myself together and brought up two more balls, throwing them at the two remaining minions. One dodged, but the other crumpled, smoke coming from his twitching body. It was starting to stink in here—like burned hair and smoke. I stifled a gag.

"Thanks for the assist. That's my cue." He advanced on the last standing minion, who parried Jack's sword with his own. The minion didn't stand a chance. Jack was so fast, I couldn't track what was happening—and neither could the minion. He fell to the ground, a nasty gash in his chest.

Jack made sure none of the minions moved ever again. "You all right?"

"Yeah, sorry about that. It's just . . . I'm not used to this."

He patted my shoulder. "You did great. OK, we need to move these guys, or we're in a heap of shit."

Jack ran down to where the tunnel turned, looked around the corner, then ran back. "No one is coming. At least not yet. The maintenance room is just around the corner. Can you drag one of these guys?"

After many sweaty minutes of hauling smoking minions into the maintenance room, I had one last thing I needed to do. Jack and I crept to the end of the tunnel and up the stairs, adding a minion to our pile as we went. When we approached the door at the top of the stairs, I could hear an announcer riling up the crowd, and the crowd responding with a roar. With a prayer to the universe that Blu and Silver had better luck than the gladiators in Rome, I unlocked the door with my brain, and we crept back to the maintenance room, where we'd wait.

BLU 61

The crowds outside dwindled; most had entered the stadium to find their seats. It was a brisk night. The moon was out, the stars blinking brightly in the night sky. Vendors were milling around, talking among themselves. They would wait until after the PITs ended, hoping that the show was so good, people would buy more of their wares. I couldn't fault the vendors. They had to eat too. But it didn't make me like the situation any more. People making money off others' deaths was something that made me angry. I shook my head, trying to clear it. Getting pissed all over again wasn't going to help me focus.

I could hear the master of ceremonies leading the crowd in chants and cheers, or providing them with snippets about the contestants to pique their interest. Some of these riders were celebrities in the arena, if the rising clamor of the crowd was any indication. Many people were wearing blue and yellow or carrying black and green pendants. Some even wore jackets emblazoned with the monsters from the bikers' helmets. It was nuts.

The burly minion got us all in a line of sorts, Jyston and his date at the head. The beginning of slow, rhythmic clapping filtered out into the street from the stadium. The clapping got louder and faster, and Jyston led us toward the noise. They began to stomp as we approached the giant double doors of the stadium. The doors swung open slowly; the clapping and stomping fell apart into a frenzied pandemonium of screams and cheers and whistles.

There must have been close to twenty-five thousand people crammed into the stadium.

I knew this was a place to see and be seen, but this many people wanted to watch others fight to the death?

"Holy shit."

"You get used to it." I hadn't realized that Stratton had walked up beside me.

"I'm not sure I want to."

The crowd lost their collective minds as Jyston and his lady friend walked into the stadium. Jyston waved at the crowd, his eyes continuously scanning everyone and everything. Aurora's face broke into a huge smile as she grabbed Jyston tighter with one arm, blowing kisses with the other. The crowd ate it up.

But they were just the warm-up act. As soon as the first of the contestants came into view, the crowd erupted. They screamed and yelled and tried to get our attention as we walked in. Dread started to spread through my stomach. Competing in the PITs was scary as fuck in theory, but seeing all of these people? This was a nightmare of epic proportions.

Jyston led us around the circumference of the stadium floor, nodding or waving every so often as Aurora continued to blow kisses to the crowd with fervor. The stadium was massive, every available space in the lower and upper tiers filled. About halfway around the arena was a platform with chairs, separated from the masses by ropes. It was guarded by minions, like ridiculous numbers of them—then I realized why: The Counselor was seated on the platform, and by his side was Dagna.

Shit.

Silver nudged me with her elbow just enough to let me know she saw them too. We couldn't run away now. Too much was depending on this mission. But still. We were so, so dead.

"I wonder why they're here," Stratton asked, mirroring my own thoughts.

"It's probably nothing good."

After all of the elites in the parade had made their way around the arena and gotten their fill of the limelight and fanfare, they were escorted up some stairs to a special section of seating where they could watch the death close up.

The contestants, however, weren't so lucky. Jyston led us in front of the main doors, where a stage had been quickly erected during the festivities. Jyston helped Aurora up the stairs onto the stage; the rest of the contestants followed him.

Stratton turned to look at me over his shoulder as he made his way up.

"A piece of advice?"

"Sure."

"Stupidity is what will kill you. Don't be stupid, and you can survive this."

As he mounted the stage, the crowd's screams rose to deafening levels. They were chanting his name. Stratton waved at the crowd, then dipped his head toward the viewing platform. Silver and I did the same, then positioned ourselves behind him. As he was about the size of a brick house, it wasn't hard.

Jyston approached the microphone. "Esteemed Counselor, may I present your contestants."

The Counselor rose from his seat and approached a microphone as the crowd cheered. Even across the arena, this was the closest I had ever been to him. He looked like a slightly older version of his brother, Barrington. He wore an expensive dark blue suit, and like Jyston, he wore a pressed white shirt with no tie. He was still fit for his age, which had to be close to seventy years old. But most striking were his eyes. Even through my visor, and at this distance, I could tell that they were such a light shade of blue that they were almost translucent. He was scary as fuck.

Dagna stood just behind the Counselor's right shoulder. She surveyed the crowd, her face blank until it reached Jyston and his lady friend. She gave him a look that could have meant she wanted to kill him, or sleep with him—it was hard to tell. Either way, I didn't like it. Jyston ignored her.

"Second Counselor, thank you for the introduction." The Counselor surveyed the contestants on the stage. They shifted as if uncomfortable with his attention. It must not be normal for him to show up. Great. Did Jyston know he'd be here? Was I going to have to kick his ass for not telling me?

"I see there are some crowd favorites here." He paused to let the crowd scream and cheer again. "And I see that we have some newcomers." He looked directly at me. I continued to try to hide behind Stratton. "It is customary for new contestants to remove their helmets at the end of the competition. A bit of pomp and circumstance—should they survive, that is. I'll look forward to your performance."

What the fuck? Having to reveal ourselves to the Counselor and Dagna was a pretty big thing for Jyston to have "forgotten" to tell us. Regardless, I now knew that Silver and I had to get out of here before the tournament concluded.

"Remember," the Counselor said, looking at each contestant in turn, "you are here at Jurisdiction's invitation. Give these people what they want."

"And what do you want?" the master of ceremonies yelled into a microphone. I couldn't tell where it was coming from.

"A good show!" the crowd responded.

The Counselor's smile was magnanimous. "That's right. Put on a good show and you will be rewarded."

Or killed. But they didn't care about that.

As the master of ceremonies continued to rattle off the riders' information and rules, I took the opportunity to look around the floor of the arena. To the right, about forty feet away, was an unmarked door. That was our escape route. We just needed to give Fara enough time to get there and unlock it.

Silver nudged me, her head turned toward the dirt below and to the left of the Counselor. At first glance, I couldn't tell what she wanted me to see. Then I saw it—or them—to be more precise. Just under the dirt's surface was a slight hint of metal. With the lights out, we would never have seen it. The assholes had added pressurized spikes of death to the arena floor. That was next-level fuckery.

"Good luck," the Counselor said, his smile beatific. "For the glory of Jurisdiction!"

"For the glory of Jurisdiction!" the crowd yelled.

The master of ceremonies began speaking, thanking the corporations for sponsoring this and that, as Jyston led us back down the stairs and across part of the arena. He stopped in front of a dugout, where the powerbikes were parked. Behind the dugout was a door. That must be the holding room.

He opened the gate to the dugout and ushered us inside.

"Good luck"—he looked directly at me, and I saw concern in his eyes. I looked away; now was not the time to worry—"to all of you."

62 BLU

The holding room was surprisingly bleak, with no windows at all. The floor was concrete, the metal girders exposed in the ceiling. The only way in or out was the door that led to the arena floor. A few mismatched chairs were scattered throughout, along with some cheap tables. This room wasn't meant for comfort; it literally was just a place to keep the contestants before the tournament began. I also noticed anti-tech. How did they confine it to this space? I'd have to ask Jyston. If I lived.

"OK, who's the new kid?" A woman had taken off her helmet to reveal short cropped black hair. A skull tattoo stood out on the pale skin of her neck.

"I'm Riley."

She walked over to me. "You and I both know that's bullshit. As were the papers you used to get in here, although they were good forgeries. I'm wondering how you got them." She gave me a slow once-over. "What are you up to, little bird?"

"I came to negotiate with you assholes."

The inverted triangle guy stepped forward. "We don't negotiate with newbies. Not good for business."

The woman sprawled into one of the chairs like she owned the place. "Plus, I can't imagine that you have anything I want, *Riley*. So go sit on that chair in the corner and let the grown-ups do some business. We only have about thirty minutes before we have to go out there. Chirp chirp."

"I think you might be mistaken, Bri—"

"How do you know my name?"

"I know a lot of things. I know what deals you have, and I know what you're offering. I might be new to the PITs, but I'm definitely not new." I paused for dramatic effect. Silver positioned herself behind me, just in case. "I know that you need someone to transport some drugs through the city to the settlement outside of your gang's territory, and that you can't do it because Jurisdiction is onto you and will steal your stash if given the opportunity. If that happens, your dealer will stop contracting with you and give the run to someone else. So, you're here to trade."

"How do you—"

"I know that Simon's gang was trying to make a move to overthrow the Mid-City gang until the debacle a couple of weeks ago, and if he wins, he'll request the release of two of his gang members. I also know that Jeffes, over there, won the PITs last month, and his prize was a huge gig transporting supplies to the Jurisdiction headquarters in the north territory. However, he doesn't have enough drivers to do it."

The biker in red leather stood up and took off his helmet, his long braid falling down his back. "*Pequeña ave*, indeed. How do you know that?"

I shrugged. "I know that the leader of each gang competing is in this room. I know how many gang members you each have in the crowd, and how many you have stationed around the arena. I could keep going, but as you mentioned, Bri, we're running out of time."

They gawked at me.

"It appears that I've underestimated you, little bird," Bri said.

The first guy wasn't having it. He strode directly into my personal space. He'd taken off his helmet, and his brown hair hung in greasy strands over his pockmarked face to his shoulders. His right eye was twitching something fierce. "We should just kill this bitch now for knowing too much," he said through two rotting front teeth.

A biker stepped up next to me. "You don't want to do that, mate."

"Why the fuck not?"

The biker lifted off his helmet, revealing his slicked-down white mohawk and eyes lined in black. "Because she could kill your dumb ass in about forty-five different ways with just her helmet." Twitchy looked like he was about to interrupt, but Drift held up his hand. "You want her on your side. Trust me on that. She has resources we can only dream of." I had to love Drift's flair for the dramatic.

Stratton quietly placed his helmet on the table. Everyone stopped talking. He was the obvious leader of this group. His hair was shaved close, and the goatee he was sporting over his dark brown skin was sprinkled with gray.

"What is it that you're looking for, Riley?"

"Dagna's new building. I need one of the jobs driving there."

"Why would you need that job?"

"I plan on raiding that building."

Bri snorted. "You're fucking nuts."

"Maybe. Maybe not."

"What if whoever has that job plans on doing the same thing?" Stratton asked.

"No one here can do it. I can."

"You sound pretty confident."

"As Drift said, I have resources. You all don't. At least not the kind I have."

Stratton, Jeffes, and Bri exchanged a wordless conversation. Eventually Stratton spoke. "I won't deal with you until we know who you really are."

The Team had known that it would probably come to this. If I could free those kids, destroy those weapons—it was a risk, but I had to take the chance. I might not get out of the PITs, but Ink could finish the mission as long as I got the job.

I took my helmet off. The room went completely still. They obviously weren't expecting me.

"Are you fucking kidding me?" Bri started to laugh. "You've got balls of steel to come here, Blu."

Stratton was giving me a look I'd seen before—the one the Captain had when she steepled her fingers and weighed her options. "What does the Team get out of this?"

"Jurisdiction is running experiments on children in that building. They're also building weapons, like the ones that won them the war years ago. Obviously we want that to stop."

"Experiments on kids. Are you sure?" Bri asked.

"Yes."

"Fuckers."

"And what's in it for us?" Stratton asked.

Silver took off her helmet. "If you come with us when we bust out the kids, you're free to take whatever loot you can carry. I'm sure there's all sorts of shit that you want in that building. You keep anything you take before we bring it down. Plus, you'll take a cut of whatever Jurisdiction pays."

He studied Silver, a sad smile on his face. "I thought you were dead," he said.

"I would have been, if the minions had their say. The Team saved me." And I was so glad we did. She was becoming someone I actually liked, which was saying something. I didn't like most people.

"I don't give a fuck who you girls think you are. You know too much. I think we should still just kill you both now." Twitchy grabbed my arm. I let the deadly calm come into my eyes and smirked. It would've been cool if I'd had Fara's ability to lightningify my eyeballs too, but I didn't need it. They all backed away—everyone but Twitchy.

"I'm going to give you to the count of three to let go."

"Or what?"

"One."

"You won't do it."

"Two."

"You're bluffing."

"Three!" Drift grabbed Twitchy's arm, causing him to let go of me. He threw him to the ground and grinned at me as he put his boot on Twitchy's neck. "I was never good at waiting."

"Let me up, you fuck!"

"Tsk tsk. Drugs must've eaten your brain, asshole. Otherwise, you'd know that trying to kill a principal Team member is bad for your health. Anyway, I like having Blu owe me a favor."

"I don't—"

"You do now."

I sighed. "Whatever."

"I believe that we have intersecting interests, Blu," Stratton said, "and an agreement would be mutually beneficial. Although there are certain items that will need to specifically be addressed."

"I'd expect nothing less."

He pulled up a chair to a table, and indicated I do the same. "All right then. Let's negotiate."

FARA 63

The maintenance room was about as big as my ex-apartment, which was to say it wasn't very big. The walls were lined with a bunch of machines that didn't seem to do much other than blink lights every so often. Other than those lights, it was completely dark. Jack and I waited. I tried to breathe through my mouth as much as I could, as the smell of the dead, flambéed minions stacked in the corner clung to the air.

"Are you all right?"

I couldn't help the snort that came out. "In what way?" The roar of the crowd was deafening even this far below the stadium. It also would cover up our talking . . . or someone coming our way, which could be problematic.

Jack chuckled. "That's fair. It's just that you're breathing hard."

"It's the smell."

"You know, Blu is sensitive to smells too, although she'd never admit it."

"Really? That's oddly comforting. It's one of the first things I notice about someone."

"Hopefully I don't smell bad . . . ?"

I chuckled. "No, although your doppelgänger wore so much cologne that it would rub off on me. It made my eyes water."

I could hear him shift his feet. "How bad was he?" His voice was quiet.

"You're not him, you know."

"I know. But . . . You don't have to spare my feelings. I want to know."

I'd never really talked about how Hewitt treated me with anyone. Shame was the main reason. The thoughts that wormed their way into my head, telling me that I was somehow to blame for Hewitt acting the way he did. That I was too weak, or too nice, or led him on. That if I had just done something else—anything else—then he wouldn't have assaulted me day after day. But that wasn't true. Hewitt was the only one to blame. I could say that now and believe it. Maybe I felt safer talking about it in the dark. Or maybe it was because Jack was a testament to what Hewitt could have been. Whatever the reason, it was time to get it off my chest.

"It started with lewd comments, then escalated from there," I said. "By the end, right before I came here, he would trap me in the back room at least once a shift and . . . Well, let's just say that I was lucky that either Calum or Adora started walking me back there. I'm sure it would have gotten worse than it already was. He was horrible with all of the girls, but singled me out. Maybe because I didn't fight back. Or maybe it was something else. I don't know. But it took moving here for me to realize that it wasn't my fault. It was all him."

"Please tell me you kicked his ass the last time you were there."

"I kicked him in the nuts and singed him a bit. I'm not sure it will make a difference, though."

Jack was so quiet I could barely hear him over the noise of the crowd. "My dad used to do that to my mom." I could hear the pain and rage in his voice. "He'd beat her, burn her, and worse. And me. When my big brother died, it escalated. He wasn't there to protect us anymore. One day, I walked into the kitchen to see him beating my mom so bad that I knew he'd kill her. I grabbed the first thing I could find—a frying pan—and hit him in the head with it. It killed him. The next week, my mom killed herself. That's how I ended up in the Compound."

I took the two steps separating us and hugged him. "I'm so sorry, Jack."

He squeezed me, then stepped back. "I'm just glad that you can see past my doppelgänger and be nice to me."

"You're not him, Jack."

"No, but I could have been."

"But you chose not to. You chose to be awesome instead."

He smiled sadly in the dim light, then cocked his head. "It sounds like the competition is starting."

How he could hear what the announcer was actually saying was crazy. It just sounded like Charlie Brown's teacher to me. As soon as he said it, the machines that had been quiet came to life, blinking and beeping and whirring.

Jack's head whipped around. "What the fuck?"

He pulled out his palmbox and turned on the flashlight, pointing it at the machines that had all lit up like Christmas trees.

"Styx, you there?"

Nothing.

"Styx? Shit. We're too far underground."

"What are you thinking?" I asked.

"If we can reach Styx, maybe she can talk us through what these are—and see if they're something we should be worried about."

I had an idea. "Hang on." I opened a portal. The Captain didn't so much as flinch when she saw my disembodied head appear in front of her.

"I'm glad to see you alive."

"Me too. Sorry to bother you, but could you get Styx or Dev?"

"I'm here." Dev, eyes wide, was staring at me.

"Can you come with me quick? I'll bring you back in a minute."

"Uh, sure?"

"Brilliant!" Jack said as Dev stepped through the portal. "Can you take a look at these machines and tell me if you know what they are?"

Dev looked freaked out, although to be fair, I had just pulled him through a portal into a room filled with machines and a stack of dead bodies, so I couldn't blame him. To his credit, he got himself together as soon as he started to inspect the machines.

"How long have they been on?"

"Since the competition started. Just a minute or two."

Dev took out his palmbox and turned on the flashlight, shining it this way and that on one of the machine's panels. "Well, this one seems to control some sort of hydraulics. It's on a timer." How did he know that?

He looked at one of the other machines, and put his ear to it. "This is some sort of combustion system—I can hear the hiss of gas being released . . ." He pressed some buttons on his palmbox, walking to the door as he did. Jack grabbed his arm before he made it into the hallway.

"We probably shouldn't go out there."

Dev looked up, chagrined. "Sorry. But it's really weird. From what I can tell, the gas is going through a pipe under the flooring, and igniting about fifty feet that way." He pointed in the general direction of the stairs.

"What's fifty feet that way?" I asked.

"The door to the arena," Jack answered.

Dev scratched his head. "But I'm not sure what they're for."

"I do," Jack spat out. "These are the machines that control the PITs' obstacles."

"Oh shit. Flamethrowers—" I said.

"And something on hydraulics—which can't be good," Jack supplied.

"Blu and Silver are out there." Shit. "Dev, is there any way to stop these from working? Could you break them?"

"Probably, but it would take a long time."

"Too long," Jack said.

"There has to be something we can do to help them out up there! Could I just burn them down?"

"I wouldn't do that," Dev said. "You'd blow up the entire place."

Jack snorted. "I'm generally not opposed to that."

"Still wouldn't recommend it."

"What about electricity?" I asked. "Would that short-circuit them?"

Dev ran his hand through his hair, making it stand up like Beck's did. Ugh, Beck. "Probably? Maybe? I don't know. You'd have to hit the right spot for it to work."

"Show me where."

He walked over to the hydraulics machine and opened a cabinet underneath. Inside was a jumbled mess of wires and gizmos. He held up some sort of circuit board.

"I'd start with this."

"All right. And the other one?"

He opened the cabinet below on the other machine, searching around inside it. "There's a tank of something, probably flammable. Stay away from that. Really, you just need to shut it down. It shouldn't take a lot of electricity."

"Good to know," Jack said. "Let's get you back first. I'm sure when they stop working, someone will come down and wonder why."

"If you wouldn't mind?"

I smiled to myself. I couldn't blame Dev for wanting to get out of here. Hell, *I* wanted to leave with him. But I couldn't. Not yet.

"Think you can short-circuit it?" Jack asked as I closed the portal behind Dev.

"Let me start with the non-flammable one." I walked over to the machine and opened the cabinet again. "You might want to stand back."

I was absolutely winging this. Ink would be proud, and a little mortified. Why was I thinking about him right now? I needed to stop that. I pulled up the tiniest electric ball I could manage and lobbed it into the open cabinet, onto the circuit board.

"Is it supposed to smoke like that, Fara?"

"I doubt it."

Electricity began snaking over the machine like some sort of cartoon as smoke billowed out of the cabinet. Jack and I backed as far away from it as possible while it shimmied and shook. Then it just died. A tiny fire broke out on the face of it.

"Shit! It's going to burn the . . ."

Without giving it too much thought, I walked up to the machine, cupped my hand around the flame, and scooped it up.

"Well, that might come in handy." I couldn't help the smile on my face. I really was fireproof. I smothered the flame between my hands. Now, how to deal with the other one? I might not be flammable, but Jack was—and I didn't think my abilities covered saving me from getting blown to smithereens.

"Jack, does your palmbox have a 'disable' program?"

"Oh, shit! Why didn't I think of that?" He walked over to the machine and placed the palmbox on it, pressing buttons as he did. Nothing happened.

"I don't think my palmbox has enough power to disable something this big."

But maybe I did. "You might want to stand back."

"What are you doing?"

"Well, if the 'disable' program is pretty standard on a palmbox, I probably have it too, right? It's worth a try. But I'd also rather you not die in the process."

He snorted. "I appreciate that. I don't want you to *die in the process either*, though."

It was my turn to snort. "Here goes nothing." I pulled up my program wheel and added "disable machine" to it. My brain didn't like that, and before I consciously realized what was happening, a "disable and destroy" option was added. I felt a weird sensation go down my hands, not quite unlike the electricity, but . . . softer? The electricity felt like glass shards, and this felt like hot smoke. Neither felt awesome.

There was a pop, and the machine died. Then I felt electricity go through my hands. Just a jolt, but enough that the machine started to smoke.

"What the—"

64 BLU

Silver and I put on our helmets as a minion opened the holding room door. Luckily, no one had bothered us while we hammered out the deal with Stratton, but our luck couldn't hold out forever. We needed to get out of the PITs as soon as we could.

"Contestants, follow me."

The lights were still on in the arena, the master of ceremonies stirring the crowd into more of a frenzy, if that was even possible.

I hazarded a look at the viewing platform. Dagna was talking into the Counselor's ear; he nodded every so often, although he never took his eyes off us. It was like he was looking for something. I had déjà vu. The last time I'd had this feeling was when Jyston cornered me at the masquerade ball. That time, he had been looking for *me*. I hoped this time my instincts were wrong. Where was the *tug* I relied on? I hadn't felt it in a while.

Jyston was sitting on the platform as well, his arm casually slung over the back of Aurora's chair, her hand resting on his knee. His head was tilted toward hers so that he could hear whatever she was saying. Jealousy like I'd never known slammed into me. It didn't matter that he'd warned me. It still sucked seeing him up there with her. I turned away and focused on the arena floor. I had more to worry about than jealous girlfriend feelings. So much more.

The arena floor had transformed into a pit of nightmares.

What must have been a fake floor had been removed to reveal a pit that ran the length of the arena, complete with twists and turns, like a maze. It was just wide enough for a powerbike or two to drive through, and deep enough you couldn't see anyone who was in it. Why the hell would anyone ever go down there? Ah yes—to avoid the flamethrowers that were shooting out at ground level. Great.

Metal ramps bridged the pit at various points, but they moved at seemingly random intervals. Some sort of hydraulic mechanism. If they moved while you were still on them, it was likely you'd fall down into the pit with your powerbike. Which didn't sound appealing. At all.

On top of that, the ground was a wet, muddy, soupy mess—nearly impossible to drive on without crashing. And then there were the pressurized spikes of doom that I could no longer locate. Were they only in that one spot? Once the lights went out, there was no way of knowing.

We were so, so fucked.

I'd known there was a chance we wouldn't make it out of this alive. But now, it was almost a certainty.

Drift came up behind me and leaned in to talk.

"The powerbike maintenance guy is on my payroll, so the bikes are clean. Keep an eye out for the asshole in yellow and blue. He's a big, fat cheater."

"Twitchy? Need me to take him out?"

"I'd love that, but wouldn't it draw too much attention to you?"

"Unfortunately, it would. Drift, I need to get to that door over there as soon as possible. Think you can create a distraction?"

"Me, a distraction?" I could hear the smirk in his voice. "It'll cost you."

"We've already established that you still owe me."

"Whatever. I want in on the deal with Stratton."

"Fine. Just help us get out of here."

"Contestants," the master of ceremonies boomed, "take your marks!"

Each set of riders approached a powerbike, having seemingly done this dance many times before. Since this was our first time, Silver and I let them get situated. It didn't matter to us what powerbike we had. We didn't plan on riding it long—just until Drift created a distraction.

The bikes themselves looked like the one we'd practiced on, until the lights turned off.

"Whoa."

"Yeah," Silver replied.

They looked like something from outer space. The bikes were covered in fluorescent tubing: on the body, along the side, around the wheels, on the spokes, on the handlebars. Each bike was a different color, and in the sudden darkness in the arena, they shone like a fluorescent rainbow. Bikers were choosing the powerbikes that matched their riding leathers. The purple was the last remaining. I guess that was ours.

"Purple is bad luck, chica," Jeffes said as he mounted his red bike.

"I kind of like it."

He shrugged. "Don't die, all right?"

"Wasn't planning on it." I retied my boots and made sure my knives were still in place. "But why do you care? Wouldn't it be better for you if we did?"

"For me personally? *Tal vez si, tal vez no,*" he said. "But for the rest of the world? No."

"Why's that?"

"You represent hope." He opened his visor and nodded to me. "To many. The Wolves are with you. Remember that."

He shut his visor and said something to his riding partner, then started his bike. It roared to life.

"Making friends, I see," Stratton said. He was on the dark green bike. "But I agree with Jeffes. Don't die."

"There are pressurized spikes at eleven o'clock," I replied.

He nodded once. "Stay out of the pit. It's a death trap."

I would have said it looked worse in the dark, but it was almost impossible to see. The entire arena was eerie. Small lights lined the stairs between tiers of seating and circled the walkway, but otherwise the only light came from the moon, the stars, and the bikes.

I double-checked that the flag was securely attached to our powerbike. It glowed purple with the fluorescent tubing as well. All of the powerbikes had them. We had to protect our flag from the other teams; that was what this was about. A *game*. Fucking entertainment, all for the enjoyment of the rich and powerful. The cost of a ticket would have fed a family in Drift's neighborhood for a month. The crowd cheered and drank and waved their glow sticks and flags, while people were down here about to meet their death. Though these bikers were thugs and criminals, they deserved better than this. We deserved better than this.

I stopped being scared; now, I was angry. "I want to destroy this place."

"Join the club," Silver replied. "But we need to survive, first. We don't need to win, Blu. Then we come back and take it down."

"Every last one of them."

"For the glory of Jurisdiction!" the master of ceremonies yelled.

"For the glory of Jurisdiction!" the crowd replied. My stomach knotted.

"Let the tournament begin!"

65 BLU

Silver and I had made it out of the gate into the arena in one piece, which was harder than it sounds. The light green and pink powerbikes had crashed into each other while making their exits, causing the riders on each bike to fall off. Other teams scrambled to grab the bikes' flags while minions raced out and grabbed all four fallen bikers, marching them to a row of seats on the edge of the pit. They didn't check for injuries, but then again, why would they care?

Additional minions were stationed to guard any bikers who fell off. While these contestants may have crashed on purpose to avoid the worst of the PITs, Silver and I couldn't afford to do that.

We also couldn't afford to have our flag taken. That's where we'd end up if that happened. So, we needed to avoid, well, everything until we made our move. It was going to be harder than it sounded, and it sounded hard.

"Orange bike on our tail," I yelled to Silver over the din. We had barely made it out of the dugout and we were already fucked.

"I'm on it."

I held on while Silver punched the gas, fishtailing as she did. Mud splattered up onto my clothes as she sped past the escape door. I took a look at the viewing platform, which was illuminated by soft, glowing lights in all of the bikes' colors. The Counselor was looking right at us.

"We can't—"

A spear of flame, a foot across and at least ten feet long, shot out from a mechanism right next to the door, blocking our path. Silver swerved to avoid it, but the orange bike wasn't so lucky. The crowd cheered as the orange bike crashed into the wall, minions already descending to clean up the carnage.

"I'm going to keep circling," Silver yelled over her shoulder.

We skirted the pits, avoided the spikes, and ended up on the opposite side of the arena from the escape door. I could vaguely see other bikes through smoke billowing out of the walls. Bri was on the gold bike, perched on top of one of the hydraulic ramps, waving to the crowd.

"I can't see shit!" Silver yelled.

"Unfortunately, I can."

Out of the smoke, Twitchy's bike appeared like something out of a bad dream. In this lighting, the monster on his helmet looked like his real face. He looked like a demon.

"Get us out of here, Silver! Go! Go!"

Silver turned and sped past him. His partner made a grab for my flag, but I slashed down with my dagger. I didn't cut off a digit, but it had to hurt. I could barely hear the scream of rage over the crowd.

Twitchy made a cutting motion across his throat as he revved his engine. Asshole. I flipped him the bird in response. The crowd let out a cheer, enjoying the theatrics of what just happened. They thought it was part of an act. I only wished it was.

"Are they still back there?"

"Yeah—and pretty pissed off."

Twitchy's yellow bike was letting off an eerie glow, casting weird shadows on its riders. They looked like monsters from another realm. Maybe they were. Or maybe they were just drugged-out thugs. Either way, they were gaining on us, and we needed to get our asses in gear.

We wove in and out of the other bikes, dodging the pit and another flamethrower. Nothing we did lost them. They continued to get closer, and eventually Twitchy was parallel with me.

"I'm going to fucking kill you!"

"Get in line, asshole."

His passenger tried to grab the flag again. I lashed out with my dagger, then realized belatedly it was a feint—instead of the flag, she grabbed my arm. She was going to yank me off the fucking bike. I held on for dear life, trying not to lean too much and cause us to crash.

"Silver!"

"Hold on!"

"I'm trying!"

The girl's grip was like a vise, and I knew where they were leading us: the pressurized spikes. She was going to throw me onto them. Fuck.

I struggled, but it caused Silver to lose balance, fishtailing in the mud. We almost went down. But by some miracle, and Silver's amazing driving, she got us righted. It didn't matter, though, because we were headed directly for the spikes, and we couldn't stop it.

I was going to die, but Silver could save herself.

"Jump off!"

"Not a chance! We go down, we go down together."

She aimed straight for where the pressurized spikes were. I used my other hand and grabbed onto the passenger. If we were going to be impaled, so were they. I didn't want to die, but I would, knowing that we had completed the mission. Stratton would make sure the Captain got the information about our deal. That was part of what we negotiated.

Then I heard the passenger scream.

A knife was sticking out of her chest. Where did that come from? She let go of my arm.

"Silver!"

"Turn, turn, turn!" Silver chanted as we leaned as far as we could. Spikes, at least four feet high, popped up from the ground—close enough that my foot brushed up against the side of one. Twitchy wasn't so lucky. I turned my head to look away. Even in the dark I could make out the slaughter: Twitchy—his passenger—his bike—impaled and dangling. It was gruesome. The crowd cheered. Fuckers.

"Well, that was dramatic."

Drift, driving the bike with the bright white lights, pulled up next to us.

"Thanks for the assist."

"Now you really owe me."

"Whatever."

The crowd gasped, then let out a cheer. Minions scrambled over to the pits, hoisting the blue riders out. One more down. We needed to get out of here before we accidentally won by attrition.

Drift followed us as we made our way toward the door. Our luck wasn't going to hold much longer.

"We have to get out of here, Drift."

"Yeah, I'm working on it!"

"Not hard enou—"

And that's when the world blew up.

66 FARA

Jack peeked his head out of the door. "Holy shit."

Holy shit was right. We ran down the hall, Jack taking the stairs three at a time, up to the hole where the door to the arena used to be. Smoke was billowing into the hall, and I tried to make sense of what I saw. Right in front of the hole was a powerbike on its side, white lights blinking on and off. It was beyond mangled. A few feet behind it was a purple powerbike, also on its side. A person was trying, and failing, to stand.

Blu.

"Jack! Get down!" I threw two electric balls at the minions a few feet behind Blu, barely missing Jack's head as he hit the dirt. The minions dropped, twitching.

Jack got up and ran to Silver as Blu finally got herself upright and wobbled over to the white bike. She knelt down next to the person lying there and took off his helmet. Blood was trickling out of his nose.

"Was that your distraction?" Blu asked. His slight shake of the head was the only indication that he heard her. She turned to me. "We need to get him out of here."

I wasn't sure the two of us could lift him, but we had to try. At least a dozen minions were running toward us.

"Minions!" Jack was hauling Silver to her feet.

"I see them!" Blu reached for her dagger, then staggered. She was in no shape to fight. Jack had his hands full with trying to get Silver out of the way, taking out a minion as he did.

It was up to me.

I pulled up my "reload" program, sending a prayer into the universe that I could control it, then shot the two minions who were closest to us, managing to hit both of them. They crumpled, giving me a straight shot at more minions behind them. I hit two more. Then the one behind them. Then the next two. My hands started to shake from the strain. We really needed to get out of here.

A man the size of a bulldozer was approaching us, along with a guy in red riding leathers.

"Fara! Don't fry those two!" Silver was making her way toward the duo.

"Need an assist?" the truck-sized guy asked.

I shut down my reload but kept two electric balls out just in case.

Blu was trying to lift the guy with the mohawk. He wasn't moving. "We need to get to that hole, Stratton. We'll take Drift and get him patched up. His rider's dead."

Another bike approached, glowing golden. The rider and passenger got off and nodded to the other two. The bulldozer-sized man spoke to the other riders. "It's time." Then he turned to Blu, and said, "Don't forget us."

"Never. Thank you. The Compound owes you all."

"At some point, you can tell me why someone who looks just like you shot lightning out of her hands."

The bikers all turned to face the minions. I didn't know what they planned to do, but I couldn't worry about them right now. We had to go.

With Jack's help, we got the guy with the white mohawk on his feet. He couldn't stand on his own, so Blu put her arm around his other side, and they started to drag him toward the gaping hole in the wall. Silver wobbled, then righted herself. They were a mess.

"Ladies and gentlemen, my name is Stratton." The crowd cheered. "Tonight, Jeffes, Bri, and I are announcing our retirement."

The huge guy—Stratton—and the other riders were standing on a stage. They were creating a distraction for us to get out of here. The minions had stopped following us and watched the stage. It wasn't going to last long, but hopefully long enough to get us to the hole.

Stratton continued talking as we shuffled toward the hole. A voice interrupted. A voice I knew. It sent chills down my spine.

"I see you, Blu." Dagna—the real one, not the one from my world—was at the microphone on a viewing platform and looking directly at me. "You are mine! Lights!"

The minions stopped watching the stage and saw where Dagna was pointing—she was pointing at me.

"Shit! Jack, go, go, go! I'll hold them off."

All six riders came off the stage, creating a wall between me and the minions. Stratton pulled out his dagger. "Run!"

I ran, catching up to the group. We made it a few feet inside. It had to be good enough. We couldn't make it back down the stairs, in the shape these people were in. I opened a portal directly to the infirmary, hoping that no one was there.

"Go!"

I stood in front of the portal so they could make their escape. I could feel my powers draining as I hit minion after minion. I'd never felt that before, but I couldn't worry about it now. I kept going until the last of the group made it through.

"Come on, Fara!"

With one last look over my shoulder, I jumped through the portal.

BLU 67

Fara had portaled us right into a surgery room. She got on her comm as soon as the portal closed.

"Styx, we're back. Need a medic. Or a few."

"Oh my god!" I could hear Styx yell through the comm. It was quiet; then I heard her chirp again. "Where are you?"

"Infirmary."

Jack and Fara had lifted Drift onto the table. As soon as Drift was situated, she wobbled, then slid onto the floor, passed out. Nauseated, I sank into a chair. Silver had already slumped into a corner. The room wasn't that big, but it was filled with hot messes.

After some time—I couldn't tell how long—the door flung open and Ink rushed in. He dropped to his knees in front of me, palming my face. His eyes were worried but he was smiling. "You're a fucking mess."

"A beautiful fucking disaster."

"With a concussion, it looks like."

"Ink, please stop accosting my patients." Sage was standing in the door. "What do we have here?"

Jack spoke. "There was an explosion at the PITs."

"Drift took the worst of it," I said, my words slurred. Yeah, definitely something was wrong with my noggin. "Silver and I took some of it. I think we might be . . . concussed? Is that the right word?"

Ink had made his way to Fara, who was lying on the ground. He scooped her up and cradled her in his arms. "Did she use an 'all-in-one'?"

"I'm not sure what happened. She saved our asses, though. She was badass."

"Hey. Thanks, Jack," she said. One eye opened, then shut again. "Ink, you can put me down. You'll strain your back. I weigh too much for you to carry me, you know. I'm fine . . . Just need to rest my eyes." Her arms went around his neck, even with all of her protestations.

Sage shook his head. "This Team is going to be the death of me. If you insist on manhandling my patients, Ink, there's a room down the hall where you can put her."

"Thanks. And I'm really glad you all made it back in sort of one piece. You even brought an extra person, which is fun."

He left, carrying Fara to a bed. I needed to find one too. I'd just close my eyes for a minute . . .

"Blu! No you don't!" Sage was glaring at me. "No sleeping for you, or Silver, either! At least for three hours." I started to whine, but he held up his hand. "You cannot have survived the PITs only to die from stupidity. You have a concussion."

Jack pulled me to my feet. "Let's go find you a room to not sleep in."

◊ ◊ ◊

Even if I wanted to sleep, there was no way I could have, with everyone coming in and out and wanting to talk. My brain started to clear up a bit, but I still felt like I'd been hit in the head with a giant explosion. Because I had. At least I wasn't dead.

Silver sat on one bed and Fara was in another. She was awake now and laughing at something Ink said, sprawled next to her.

Styx rushed through the door, tears lining her eyes. "I'm just so fucking glad you assholes are alive!" She flopped into a chair.

Calum walked in right behind her, his face breaking out into a grin when he saw Fara. "You OK?"

"Yeah."

"I'm glad."

He headed over to Silver and kissed her so thoroughly, I wasn't sure they remembered—or cared—that we were in here. Good for them.

Dev came in, looked around, then stood awkwardly next to Styx. The Captain came in last and shut the door. Jack offered her his chair, but she waved him off, choosing to stand by the door instead.

"I, too, am grateful that you all made it out alive. I'm anxious to hear what happened, if you're feeling up to it?"

"Silver and Blu have concussions, so they might not make much sense," Jack said.

"I'll be OK in a minute," I said.

"All right. Then, why don't we have Fara and Jack start?" And so they did.

When they got to the part about disabling the machines, Fara said, "I feel awful. My 'disable and destroy' program blew up the flamethrower by the door. I messed up. I could have killed you."

"You also gave us the diversion we needed," I said. "Without you, we might not have made it out."

Ink grabbed her hand even as he rolled his eyes. "What she's trying to say is stop beating yourself up, Fara. You learned that you're fireproof. You can also disable big machines. So, for the thousandth time, please give yourself some credit."

"She also took out at least a dozen minions," Jack said.

"Did anyone see it?" Styx asked.

Jack snorted. "Only about twenty-five thousand of our closest friends—and the Counselor and Dagna. But they think she's Blu." He filled us in on the rest of what had happened. It sounded like Fara really had saved our asses. Badass didn't even begin to cover it.

"Jackrabbit," the Captain said when he'd finished, "I think we need to get out on the street and see what rumors are floating around."

As Jack and the Captain talked about how to approach getting intel, I heard a buzzing. The Captain smiled and handed me a comm she'd pulled out of her pocket. Jyston's comm. "I think this is for you."

"You're alive," he said. "How did you get out of there so fast?"

"Just got my bell rung, is all."

"I was worried."

"Seriously, I'm OK," I said. "Are you in danger?"

"No, I have ways. But I have some information that I don't believe can wait."

"Fara's here. Need a lift?"

FARA

Jyston didn't so much jump as tense when my head popped through the portal. I couldn't help but grin.

"I understand why you like sneaking up on people."

"It is fun to see their reactions," he said. "Although in my defense, you are a floating head, which I'm not sure anyone can prepare for."

"The Captain didn't even flinch."

"She's made of sterner stuff than I."

I grabbed his hand and pulled him through.

His eyes landed on Blu. "If you might give me a moment, Captain, I have something I must do first."

Without waiting for a response, he walked over to Blu's bed and knelt down beside it. "I didn't know. About the Counselor, or revealing yourself at the end of the PITs—any of it. I didn't know. I never would have put you or the Team in that sort of peril if I had, Blu. Please believe me."

"How is that possible?"

"Your mole. Whoever it is knew about the PITs, and that you would be there. I tried to minimize the damage—"

Before he could finish that sentence, Blu grabbed the back of his neck and pulled him in for a kiss. Why was everyone kissing publicly all of a sudden? It must be affirming life after a near-death experience or something. I knew I wanted to do that with the person lying on my bed and holding my hand, but I couldn't. Now wasn't the time to focus on that.

Jyston cupped Blu's face. "You before all others. Always. I swear it."

She sighed, resigned. "OK, I'm not pissed at you anymore. So, you have something to share?"

He perched on the edge of her bed and turned his attention to the rest of the room.

"I have news about your mole. Dagna revealed some information that might help in identifying them."

"How do you have information about that?" Styx asked.

"Dagna's desire to become Second Counselor has become an obsession. One tactic she uses is . . . Well, I guess you'd call it bragging, although it's more gauche than that. This time she was bragging to my . . . date. She said that it would be anticlimactic if the most notorious assassin in the world was captured because of a set of 'mundane' riding leathers."

Drake had made their riding leathers. He must have put the pieces together and guessed Blu and Silver were entering the PITs. Ink released my hand and jumped up. As did Jack. They must have come to the same conclusion. The Captain held up her hands.

"It is the middle of the night. We do not drag people out of their beds for questioning like Jurisdiction does." Ink looked like he was going to argue, but she cut him off. "I need you all at your best. We can't afford to screw this up. Please get a few hours of sleep. Jack, have someone keep an eye on him tonight. We'll deal with this in the morning. Jyston, thank you."

"I have more information for you as well, but I need to be getting back."

"Is this information about the PITs?"

"Yes, and then some. Fara put on quite a show. I wasn't the only one who noticed."

◊ ◊ ◊

Blu and Silver were spending the night in the infirmary—Sage's orders. Because of their concussions, a medic needed to check on them regularly. And it was my fault.

Ink kept sending glances my way, his face pensive as we walked back to our apartments. I didn't know what he was thinking, but I was too tired to worry about it. I wanted a bath. I wanted sleep. I wanted to cry from relief that we'd made it out of the PITs relatively whole. Tomorrow was a new day, and we were all alive to enjoy it. That was something to celebrate.

He paused at his apartment, leaving his key in the door and taking a step toward me.

"What?"

"Fara, I . . ." He stopped and looked over my shoulder, his perma-smirk reapplying itself. A young woman was heading our way.

I sighed before I could help myself. "Go on. I'll bury my head in a pillow."

"You know, the offer is always open to you."

"I'm sure there's not enough space on your bedpost for a notch for me."

"There's always room for you."

"I've sworn off men, remember? But even if I hadn't, Ink, I will never be one of your many. I'd have to be the only one. And we both know that's not happening."

The young lady was wearing what might be casually called a nightgown, held together with gauze, ribbon, and men's fantasies. She ignored me totally, snaking her arm around his waist.

"I was hoping you could use a bit of company," she purred.

Right. That was my cue to go. I couldn't take watching this play out.

"Fara?"

The look he was giving me was one that I still couldn't place. "Yeah?"

"Could you do me a favor tomorrow? I'm supposed to meet the kids in the open space by the greenhouse, to play king of the mountain. I'll more than likely be busy with Blu . . . with the other thing. Can you go in my place?"

"Of course. Good night."

"Good night."

BLU 69

Sage finally gave us the go-ahead to sleep, but with medics coming in and out to check that we weren't dead, it wasn't *good* sleep. I should have been grateful that they were keeping us alive. Instead, I was annoyed.

I left Silver sleeping in the recovery room and headed toward my apartment. I needed to brush my teeth and take a bath. My leathers were caked in mud and blood and fuck knows what else. My hair was filthy. I was a mess. An alive mess, but a mess, nonetheless.

The sun was not quite over the horizon, making the sky burst into a palette of oranges and reds and yellows. As I walked the broken path of brick to my apartment, the beauty didn't help the dread that was creeping up my spine.

I was sad. Angry. Both? Drake had been my go-to for a good time for a couple of years. It was never anything serious, but we joked and had the occasional conversation. I considered him a friend of sorts. I hated that he was the spy. I hated that I lived in a world where he had to be one.

I got myself relatively clean and fed. Stewing in my apartment wasn't doing anyone any good. I was grateful when Jack knocked on my door.

"Ready?"

I wasn't sure I'd ever be ready for this. Taking down minions and other assholes was one thing, but going after Drake? This sucked. He had caused us unending grief, but no one wanted to be like Dagna here. We wouldn't be. But we still needed answers.

The sconces were low as we walked into the armory, casting more shadow than light in the large room. The forges had burned almost all the way down, which was unusual. I knew Drake liked to sleep in, but even he should be up by now. Where was he?

"Drake?"

Jack headed toward the back of the armory as I looked around the room. Drake wasn't on the couches or in the kitchen. He wasn't working at a table or by the forges. Had he gotten word that we were going to question him, and run? How could he have gotten past Jack's best lookouts?

"Blu! Over here!" Jack waved his palmbox flashlight at me from the armory's storage room. I ran back there. Drake was unconscious on the ground, bound and gagged.

"Styx! We need Sage. Drake's down."

Jack reached for Drake's pulse, then put his ear to his chest. "He's still alive."

I untied the gag, then sliced through the rope at his ankles and wrists.

"What the hell happened?"

Drake groaned and moved his lips. I couldn't hear him, so I bent down. He grabbed my shoulder and said one word before he passed out again.

"Iris."

FARA 70

I was determined to have a good day. It didn't matter that my abilities felt wonky, flickering in and out like some sort of short-circuiting lamp. It didn't matter that Ink was probably still in bed with the Victoria's Secret model. It didn't matter that I had killed multiple minions yesterday, or that Dagna and the Counselor saw me use my powers. I was going to go play with some awesome kids. I might even borrow a book from Blu. I was going to celebrate being alive.

I dropped off the basket that I'd borrowed at the greenhouse, then made my way around the side of the building. When I crested the hill, I stopped.

"Iris?"

Her always perfect appearance was in disarray; her hair was disheveled, and there was dirt on her face. Children cowered away from her, and then I saw why. Iris was holding a little girl by the hair, with a dagger at her throat. Their guardian was lying on the ground about ten feet behind her, dead.

"Iris, what are you doing?"

She still didn't move. The girl was trembling. I could hear the quiet sobs of the children. I motioned for them to get behind me.

"Why?" Her voice was flat, her eyes wild.

"Why what, Iris?"

She started to shake, like she was losing control.

"Why is it *you*?" What started as a whisper ended as a scream. "I grabbed these little fuckers to get Blu's attention! Why doesn't anything ever fucking go right for me?"

Gone was the sweet and clueless glamazon; in her place was someone who was as scary as Barrington Park. She was screaming so loudly that the little girl was trying desperately to get away. Iris tightened her grip. She definitely wasn't in her right mind. I had to tread carefully.

"Why do you need Blu?"

"Because I'm going to kill her!"

"Iris—"

"Drop your dagger. Right now!" I dropped my dagger. I hadn't even noticed that I had grabbed it. "Kick it to me."

"I'm not sure—"

"Shut up! Just shut your fucking mouth and kick it to me!"

I did. "Why are you doing this?"

She shook her head like she was trying to clear it. "My mother told me that I could come home once I did something *useful*. But telling her about the PITs wasn't enough. Of course it wasn't!" She threw her head back and laughed, the cackle vibrating through my bones. It didn't sound sane. At all.

She stopped laughing abruptly and leveled her gaze at me. "She told me to *kill Blu*. How am I supposed to do that? The bitch won't even give me the time of day. I can't get her alone. But maybe I could kill enough of these kids to get her attention. She's always had a soft spot for kids. But now, you show up and fuck it all up again!"

"Iris—"

She dug the dagger into the little girl's throat, causing a drop of blood to appear. "Shut your fucking mouth! You know what I think? I think I will kill you. Maybe my mother will consider that *useful*. Ever since you came along, you've fucked everything up, so I'd be glad to do it."

"Let go of the girl—"

"I said shut up! Yes, you need to die. I'm sure of it now. Then my mother will approve. And plus, I fucking hate you."

I needed to keep her talking while I figured out what to do. My powers were short-circuiting with no rhyme or reason. Had I used too many? Was there a limit to what I could do? I didn't have time to consider it. Anyway, my aim wasn't very good on a good day. I couldn't risk electricity or fire with the little girl in the way. I didn't have a comm and I wasn't sure how often people walked this way. So, I was left talking to a girl who not only hated me, but was a scary Froot Loop. I needed time to think.

"Why do you hate me?"

"Because, *Fara*,"—she said my name like it was a disease—"everyone *loves* you. You come along, and everyone falls all over themselves to make you part of the Team. It didn't matter that I had worked for years to get on the Team. Plotted and planned so that I could get more information, to be *useful* to my mother. Seduced Ink so he might recommend me. But no. They shunned me and took you. He ditched me for you. Stupid, ugly you. And now you'll die."

"No one has to die, Iris."

She snorted. "Naive, aren't you? Of course someone has to die. It's the only way."

"Only way for what?"

"For fuck's sake! Are you not listening or are you just that stupid? My mother has hated Blu ever since she burned down her summer cottage. And now it's up to me to kill her. She promised that this was the last thing I had to do. But she'll *definitely* take me back if I kill you too."

Holy shit. Dagna was Iris's mother.

How was that even possible? How did she end up here? I had so many questions, but none of them mattered right now. What mattered was getting these kids to safety.

"What do you want?"

"I want to kill you, slowly."

"Let go of the girl and I'll go with you willingly."

She raised a perfect eyebrow at me as she considered it.

"You'll die for these kids?"

"Yes."

"Then you really are stupid." She shoved the girl to the ground.

"Run." The girl blinked as I stared at her, willing her to understand what I was asking her to do. I saw the moment she understood. She ran to the other kids and whispered to them; then they all sprinted toward the Quad. Now what? My abilities were flickering in and out. I needed them to hold out just a bit longer. Until the kids got away.

Iris turned back to me, pointing her dagger in my face. "Where's Blu?"

I shot a tiny electric ball in her direction—it was all I could muster. Her eyes got wide as it missed her by less than an inch. I felt my powers wink out again.

Shit.

I dodged when she slashed at me with her dagger. I had no way to defend myself. I didn't have armor, or a sword, or a dagger. I just had me. I needed something to block— something like a shield program. My powers winked back on. I sent a little prayer into the universe that it would work.

And it did.

The tiny electric balls I had conjured arched over my head, then spread around me like a sphere. I was inside a lightning shield. Which would have been reason to celebrate, except that Iris was still trying very hard to kill me. It also was flickering in and out. To add to the chaos, the shield was draining my already depleted reserves, which was a problem. I would pass out soon.

"So that's why you're the chosen one here?"

"Iris, put down the dagger. This is only part of what I can do. I don't want to kill you."

"Even with your freak show abilities, I'm pretty sure I'm not the one that's going to die today."

With almost inhuman speed, she flipped her dagger and threw it. I screamed when it lodged into my side, my shield failing completely. I collapsed, trying to scramble backward. She sauntered over to me, a smirk on her face. My limbs like lead. What was happening to me? Why couldn't I move? I tugged at my abilities—portal, electric balls, anything—praying that they would work. But they were just gone. Their absence was like I was missing a limb. What was happening to my body? She yanked the dagger out of my side. I screamed again.

She was going to kill me. I was certain of it. My powers were gone. I couldn't run. I couldn't move. I could only watch as she straddled me, pinning my arms at my sides. Her smirk turned into a smile; she looked just like her mother.

She bent over to whisper in my ear, her dagger dragging across my chest, ripping open the fabric of my shirt, and my skin. "I'm going to enjoy watching you suffer. You'll know how I've felt my entire life. How it felt to be rejected by the Team. By Ink. By my mother. You'll hurt like I hurt. I'll make sure of it."

She pressed the tip of the dagger into my chest, carving something there.

I was helpless. No one was going to save me, and I couldn't save myself. I was going to die here. At least the kids had gotten away. At least the Team would know that Iris was the spy.

I wasn't sure how long Iris dug into my chest, chatting away like a madwoman as she did. I knew I was close to dying, though, because I was hallucinating; an angel had appeared behind her. His head was surrounded in light, but his face promised death. Iris was so intent on her carving that she didn't notice the angel reach for her arm. She screamed as he snapped her wrist and pulled her off me.

Ink.

"Fara!"

A tear slipped out of my eye. I was so grateful that I could see him one last time. But I couldn't get my voice to work. I didn't have long. My voice came out like a whisper, but he understood me anyway. He always had.

"You're my favorite."

My eyes closed, and there was nothing but darkness.

ACKNOWLEDGMENTS

So many people to thank! To be surrounded by such amazing humans is something for which I will be forever grateful. I am a really, really lucky girl!

So, in no particular order, a huge thank you to: my beta readers/friends/partners in crime, Tiffané and Andrea. Your insights, support, and reassurance had an immeasurable effect on this book, and on me. Jim, for being my beta reader extraordinaire, and coming up with one of my favorite character names of the series. My editor, Katherine Kirk, for truly understanding what I'm trying to do, getting the joke then making it funnier, and bringing out the best of my writing. I'm all out of emotional support kittens for the editing turmoil I put you through, but I'll try to see if I can find a suitable replacement. Matt, for being the person I ask when I have no idea where to even begin looking for the answer. Your wealth of knowledge makes my random "what if" questions extraordinarily more fun. Mom, for just being a general badass. Your support is everything. Love you. My kids, Alex and Charlie, for reminding me to follow my dreams and that jokes about balls are funny. I love you even more than 3000.

And to my readers. Thank you for sticking with me as I write this story. I know some of you are irritated (mad? About to riot?) because I left you with yet another cliff-hanger. I promise I'll finish the story. Truly! Just not in this book. One more to go. Love you guys!

Peach and Love, KOT

Made in United States
Orlando, FL
17 June 2024

47973277R00203